Puppet's Shadow

Emersyn Park

No portion of this book may be reproduced in any form without written permission from the publisher or author, except as permitted by U.S. copyright law.

This is a work of fiction. Names, characters, businesses, events and incidents are all the products of the author's imagination. Any resemblance to the actual persons, living or dead, or actual events is purely coincidental.

All rights reserved. No part of this book may be reproduced in any form or by any electronic or mechanical means, including information storage and retrieval systems, without written permission from the author, except for the use of brief quotations in a book review.

Any trademarks, service marks, product names or named features are assumed to be the property of the respective owners, and are used only for reference. Namely: *The Bachelor*, Mary Kay cosmetics, *Rocky*, *Pitch Perfect 2*, M&M's, *Anchorman*, *Dateline*, *Gone Girl*, Pura Vida, Jack Daniels, Captain Morgan, Jose Cuervo, Jim Beam, Johnny Walker, *Fire Starter*, NorthFace, *Footloose*, *The Parent Trap*, Lifetime, Diet Coke, YouTube, Titanic, Old Navy, COPS, Clairol, Vans, Wal-Mart, PopSugar, Victoria Secret, *Playboy*, Netflix, Nike, *What Would You Do*, *Candid Camera*, Ford, Buick, and *Breaking Dawn*.

Puppet's Shadow, 1st Edition

All rights reserved. Copyright ©2022 by Julie Frank

Cover design and image by Brandon W. H. Smith

Models: Caramie Malcolm and Crystal Smith

ISBN: 9798827556299

Library of Congress Control Number: 2022909320

Instagram: EmersynJulesPark

Facebook: EmersynPark

Website: www.EmersynPark.com

The idea that there's a highway to Hell and only a staircase to Heaven says a lot about anticipated traffic numbers.

Prologue

April 23, 2016

The sudden birth of the terror had formed just over my left shoulder. Hissing and crackles increased with each passing second. Amber and yellow flames shot out from under the door of the room next to the one that I exited less than a minute ago. The smell of burning wood, burning metal, burning plastic filled my nostrils. An aggressive, hungry fire beast chewed its way through anything that dared to cross its path while spitting out the contents of its destruction as ash. It crawled closer and closer to me as the floor beneath me warmed.

Smoke haunted the gaps around the door and sniffed its way ahead of the flames as if clearing a path for the pending destruction. Before I was able to assess my current situation, the killer smoke invaded my lungs. I started to choke as I collapsed onto the hard, wooden floor.

Out of the darkness, a figure - perhaps a guardian angel - appeared, grabbed me, and carried my obedient, limp body swiftly down the stairs and out the front door. The fresh air filled my lungs, forcing out the acrid fumes. The unknown male who saved my life dumped me on the freshly mowed grass and sprinted back into the mansion as I tried to collect my bearings.

Everything had happened so fast. My head was spinning, my lungs burning.

Through my one good eye that hadn't been sucker punched, I noticed that everyone from high school was standing or kneeling on the front lawn. The majority of the crowd was holding each other, tears rolling down their cheeks, screaming and crying. A small group was completely speechless while a few others used their cell phones to call for help. A couple responsible teenagers took control of the situation, ordering people around, asking if everyone escaped, making sure everyone was safe. And those of us that were close to the flames were still in a bit of shock. Our primary focus was on breathing.

While the buzz from my alcohol and weed consumption was quickly wearing off, my throat was raw from inhaling the smoke. My head pounded in regret. Even though I was unable to participate, I heard the other partygoers' chatter from under the safety of the big oak tree.

"The flames were everywhere."

"Anyone that was near the garage is toast."

"Literally, burnt toast."

"I bet it was lightning. A sharp, quick bolt of lightning. I think it struck the east wing of the house."

"I had no idea that the storm was right on top of us."

"Do you think anyone's dead?"

"Maverick's parents are, for sure, gonna find out about this epic party. He'll be dead come Monday."

"Shit, man! All of our parents are gonna find out. Mother Nature is one evil witch."

Someone was tapping me repeatedly on the shoulder. I recognized her from school. She had a short, stylish bob with diamond studs in her ears as well as a dainty one in her nose. Her kind face was familiar, but I was having a hard time concentrating. I couldn't understand what she was asking me. Her lips moved, but the meaning of her words couldn't be interpreted by my ears.

In the tree's shadow, I noticed another person lurking, intensely staring at me. She was dressed in dark clothing, and her hair was wet and clinging to her face. Under her long, soaked bangs, her eyes were questioning.

I returned my focus to the patient classmate kneeling in front of me. Pity and concern filled her eyes. "Honey, you're safe now." Her finger tapping my shoulder had turned into a gentle upper back pat once my bloodshot eyes searched hers. "Help is on its way.

Firetrucks and ambulances, all headed this way. Please tell me your name. Can you tell me your name?"

Like another bolt of lightning striking my head, my thoughts cleared, and I instantly remembered what had just happened moments before this disaster. The moments that led me into the hallway. The moments that included the punch to my right eye. I remembered her.

"Piper?"

Chapter 1

Maddy

We nicknamed it *the twin switcheroo*. In my highly valued opinion, it was the ultimate benefit of looking exactly like someone else. If I couldn't be an original, at least there are perks of having someone look exactly like me. That was the fact that I used numerous times to persuade Piper's involvement.

The ultimate California babes, we were blessed with long, thick blonde hair, big blue eyes, slightly turned-up noses, and flawless figures; however, we were born and raised in the multi-seasonal state of Minnesota, not California. Our tanned skin wasn't earned from the Californian rays but from tanning beds. Our striking beauty was like the first signs of spring - long-awaited sunshine warming skin, the happy chirping of birds filling the yard, neighbors greeting one another after a long, cold winter spent indoors. Smiles bursted with anticipation as the first signs of spring made its appearance. Though we emulated spring, one of us was anything but on the inside.

Inside her spring shell, Piper was as bright and welcoming as a spring day. Hair blowing in the gentle breeze. Rays of sunshine surrounded her, making her glow like an angel. Spring forecasts included early mornings, enjoying coffee on the back deck as the world awakened, sunny afternoons laying under the warm rays to absorb Vitamin D, endless happy memories of laughing with your family and friends around campfires. Spring was welcomed and anticipated.

Inside my beautiful spring-like shell lay a Midwest winter - cold, bitter and harsh. With my arms crossed tightly over my chest and my back stiff, I stood a half-inch taller than Piper at five feet seven inches. Like a spring day that appeared warmer than it was, a glance out the window portrayed the bright sun shining on the earth. A turquoise-blue sky beckoned. But after taking one step out the front door, the frigid wind slapped you across the face. That was me. I was Winter, and picture-perfect Piper was Spring.

Piper didn't enjoy the twin switcheroo nearly as much as I did. Most of the time, the switcheroos were my idea and involved my own personal advancement. Yet Piper - a massive people-pleaser - was always trying to make me happy. It was one of her fatal flaws. To add to her innocence and naivety, she attempted to talk sense into my stubborn head every time I invented a reason for a twin switcheroo.

"I don't think it's a good idea. What if we get caught?"

"We aren't going to get caught, Puppet." That was her family nickname because we all knew I could convince her to do what I wanted; she was my own personal pawn. "You gotta live a little, or you're gonna end up like Mom - on a high level of anxiety meds."

"Hey! It's not fair or nice to speak about Mom that way. She's trying."

I'd gone too far. Puppet Piper was a momma's girl. In fact, she was also a daddy's girl, the teacher's pet, and everyone's favorite twin. Pretty much everyone adored her. I loved *and* hated her for that quality. No matter what I did, she was the sweet, innocent, good-hearted twin. Of course, she earned those traits fair and square. Piper couldn't even kill a spider. Instead she would capture it and let it lose in the 'wild.'

"Spiders do more good than harm, Maddy. God created all creatures with a purpose."

I doubted her theory since I was more of a stomp on it before-it-disappeared-kinda-gal. "Puppet, there is no way that is true."

"It is. Spiders help control the insect population, so without them bugs would eat all of our crops. We would have no food." She was proving her point as she grabbed a ripe plum from our fruit bowl, taunting me with its juiciness and sweet scent. Her teeth pierced the skin.

"If God created spiders to decrease the number of insects, is He then admitting that the bugs He created *before* spiders were a mistake? Therefore without a purpose?"

As she rolled her eyes at my question, she replied, "Just let it go, Maddy."

I inherited my inquisitive, deep-thinking nature from Dad. He joked that before a baby was born, its soul was required to stand in different lines for the baby's personality traits. There are lines for shyness, patience, selfishness, knowledge-seeking, extroversion, and politeness. Every new soul stood in line, but some traits soaked deeper into their spirits to create a strong personality.

"Some souls return to the back of a line if they really liked that virtue and wanted to absorb another dose. For instance, a greedy person never stands in line for generosity. Instead, he meanders to the back of the greed line and receives a double, maybe a triple dose of greed. While some souls, like Piper's, for example, waited a long time in the sweetness line, maybe even returned a couple of times."

Even though Piper appreciated his explanation, I wasn't a fan of cheesy compliments. "Dad! That's so cringy!"

He ruffled her hair, and we all laughed. It was true - she was sweet and thoughtful, but it was corny when he talked about it.

"Now, Maddy, her soul devoured a double dose of drive and ambition when those lines were short. We all know that she wouldn't have waited in *any* line too long - she has no patience. Another line she didn't bother with - patience. However, Maddy, because you are strong-willed, you'll be able to accomplish anything you set your mind to." He reached his arm out to ruffle my hair too, but I anticipated his move and ducked in time for him to not mess up my perfectly-styled hair.

Some people might argue that Dad's comment about me wasn't as complimentary as Piper's, yet pride swelled in my chest knowing that my parents recognized that I was destined to achieve success. I agreed - I was driven and ambitious. I didn't back down easily.

However, Dad's theory didn't factor in that as twins, we might have started off as one soul. Science reports that identical twins begin with one egg being fertilized, but early within the first few days, it splits into two. We started as one soul and then divided in half soon after fertilization. According to Dad's calculation, Piper hogged all the patience when we split - which wasn't like her since she was also extremely generous. Maybe then she also seized all the goodness and thoughtfulness. The remaining personality traits - temper, impatience, and stubbornness - were assigned to me.

Her heart of gold and all her good intentions made me appear more evil, more scandalous, and more troublesome. Again, I didn't deny these facts. The steep bar just represented the fact that it was more difficult for me to get away with anything. Teachers, my parents, literally the whole tri-state area believed that my actions leaned on the side of morally-questionable. I'd long ago accepted my role as the 'evil' twin. However, it was still a thrill to pull a classic twin-switcheroo – I enjoyed playing the good girl role occasionally. Piper's portrayal as me had to be short and constructive because acting didn't come as naturally to her as it did to me.

Therefore, I usually requested or suggested these schemes when I knew she'd be more than likely to agree. She excelled at schoolwork, and it was easy for her. She enjoyed it. Switching for a quiz didn't bother her as much if I promised to study as well. Pulling a switcheroo on a family member or friend bothered her more than helping my GPA.

"Piper, it won't take long, plus you're so much better with words than I am. I'm all sass, and you're all charm." I was buttering her up, but she knew this. She knew that she could handle this serious, important conversation better than me. "Do this for me, please, sis. You know how badly I *need* this job. It'll keep me out of trouble. And I'd be *so* good at it. Please! Please!"

"Oh, all right. I'll do it. Don't beg. Desperation isn't an attractive attribute." A small, excited scream escaped my lip gloss-coated lips. She smiled. "You're so excessive, Maddy. If I'm pretending to be you for this hour-long critical job interview, then you need to be Fritz's chemistry study partner." She was using her I'm-older-than-you-by-two-minutes voice.

"Oh, please no. *Anything* but time with Fritz. Don't you have laundry or chores that I can do for you? I'll even pick up dog poop. Tell Fritz that you have massive menstrual cramps or something. Reschedule for later." I threw back my head and covered my face with my hands.

Fritz was her steady, boring, lack-of-a-personality boyfriend. He was as straight-laced as my sister but was outlined with a hard, muscular body. The kid was ripped, but in my honest, harsh opinion, *dumb jock* was stamped all over him. Sure, he was nice to look at, but that was it. And according to my loyal sister, he never laid a horny hand on her gorgeous teenage body. Only innocent make-out sessions. *Boring.*

"Sorry. Those are my uncompromising conditions." Piper eventually complied with schemes, and I usually let her think she won. "I'll woo Mrs. Yates so you can become her official, underpaid butt-kisser. But you, dear sister, must quiz Fritz before his Chem test. You need to be patient and kind to him. Or he'll see right through you."

"Puppet, I know next to nothing about chemistry. He is gonna be able to tell by *that* simple fact. Plus, *chemistry* is not something that sexy, husky Fritz and I have in common."

"I'll supply all the answers to the study guide. You ask him the provided set of questions and make sure that he answers them correctly. Easy peasy lemon squeezy. But if you can't agree to my conditions, then you can head to your fabulous job interview with Mrs. Judgy-McJudgerson."

She didn't like Mrs. Yates, Pine Hills professional party planner. Piper thought she was an uppity, rich country club brown-noser. And she was completely right, but Mrs. Yates was my idol - I wanted to frequent country clubs. I wanted everyone who was anyone to know my name. I wanted to wear only fancy designer labels and real, high-quality diamonds. I never wanted to worry about money or worry about hitting the bottom of my bank account. I wanted to be the next Mrs. Yates.

My heart might have been a tad bit hollow, but I had lofty goals for myself and my future. And this entry-level job was the first stepping stone to reaching my goal of success. If I didn't nail the job interview, I'd never have a chance. But I knew I'd fumble my words, say something unintelligible or embarrass myself completely. It was something I was known to do when I was nervous or felt intimidated - which wasn't often - but admittedly, Mrs. Yates intimidated me with her poise and confidence.

"Puppet, you drive a hard bargain, but this job interview is important to me, and I fear that the real me might say something stupid. You're better with the formalities. I guess if I must spend a long, excruciating hour with Fritz, I'll do it. We have a deal." I extended my manicured hand for her to shake and confirm our twin switcheroo.

Laying on her stomach on her bed, she shook her head at me, but a large smile emerged on her face. "How do you do that? You make it sound like you're doing *me* a favor and not the other way around. I hope someday you'll use your superpower of persuasion for good."

"You nail this job interview for me, and I'll use all my powers for good by learning everything there is to know about organizing important events for the high-class, uptight yuppies of the world." I leaped off the edge of her bed, and I saluted her like I was agreeing to a formal oath.

She giggled at my dramatic gesture. I could always make her laugh, and she always had my back - even when I didn't fully deserve it. We were a wonderful team.

"Now, Piper, please hop in the shower and scrub yourself squeaky clean so I can doll you up for *my* life-altering interview. I have the perfect killer outfit in mind." Dressing her up was fun. She was a blank canvas that I coated in makeup, jewelry, and fancy clothes. Then she became...me.

Another giggle escaped her lips even though she was fighting to stay serious. She sat up and readjusted her homework onto her lap. While she shook her head and rolled her eyes, she answered, "Okay, okay, but you'll need to wear what I'm currently wearing because I saw Fritz already this morning for coffee. So, wipe off your makeup and do your part."

I stuck out my tongue in utter disgust. Her style - if you called it style - consisted of baggy T-shirts or sweatshirts and straight-legged jeans. Nothing that fit her body or heaven forbid, showed her curves. Never any lace, straps, or sparkles. Plain Jane.

"Whatevs. I'll do my part even if it means wearing your ABC." I ended my sarcastic comment with an eyeroll.

"ABC?"

"You know, ABC gum – already-been-chewed. In this case, already-been-clothes, as in last century's fad. Out of style." I scratched my head before I came up with my phrase. "Poor plain Piper prepares to please people."

"Maddy, not everyone cares as much about appearances as you do. What's inside" - she tapped on her heart - "is more important than anything else."

"Puppet, you're such a sap. Which reminds me, what if Fritz wants to *actually* practice some *chemistry*? How will I fight him off? Or should I let him? Tell me dear, prude sister, what would you do if Fritz grabs one of my girls?" I cupped my left breast to show her what *girls* I was referring to.

She threw a pillow at me as I was opening her bedroom door. "It's a study date, nothing more. Leave your girls strapped in, Maddy."

As I started to exit her bedroom, which was directly across from mine, I stopped in the doorway with my hand resting on the knob. She had already returned to reading her novel. At the top of her head rested a haphazardly wound bun with several strands of hair laying loose and dangling around her flawless white skin. Her daily appearance was a low priority for her, yet she always managed to look naturally beautiful. While *my* look required hours to perfect, she was a genuine beauty of low maintenance. Even though I prided myself on my appearance and enjoyed the primp and priming, I was envious of her carefree attitude.

As I slowly pulled her door shut, my heart ached to be more like her - kinder, more easygoing, more generous. After she secured this job for me with her big words, ease, and charming personality, I vowed to be a better person. More like her.

Chapter 2

Piper

The twin switcheroo. I hated it. I didn't enjoy fooling an unsuspecting friend or family member. I never wanted to lie or trick anyone. My skin crawled whenever we pulled it off and another close friend didn't realize that Maddy was me. It was disappointing that my good friends couldn't notice the difference, and I didn't have the heart to tell them. Since I agreed to the masquerade, I felt largely at fault.

Maddy was a natural actress. When we were younger, playing pretend was her favorite activity. She relished being someone else, acting like she was rich and famous, pretending she was someone important.

"It's teatime, my ladies. Tea and crumpets to honor the queen." Her fake English accent was the icing on the pretend cake. With rows and rows of bracelets clanked on her slim wrists, she was dressed to the nines in glamor. Pearls, diamonds, and gold chains circled her neck. Every piece of Mom's jewelry paraded around the house on Maddy's body. Dressed in one of Mom's silky nightgowns, clogging around in a pair of high heels that were way too big for her, she dressed me up in whatever leftovers didn't fit on her wrists, neck, and fingers.

I complied with her request, which was exactly how I earned my nickname, Puppet. Plus, English history that Maddy was obsessed with, educated us that hundreds of years ago queens and kings hired their own private jester to entertain them and their guests in the castle. The jester performed at the royals' bidding. *Dance, twirl, jump, sit.* That was me, the jester - Maddy's entertainment - and Maddy was the queen.

Even though our lives were far from royalty, Maddy's creations often consisted of scenarios of royalty and the upper-class. We were a normal, middle-class family living in a suburb of the Twin Cities called Pine Hill. Our reality included four different seasons with a mainly flat landscape. Our split foyer home was built in the 1950s before the population spike, and Pine Hill was still a small town in Minnesota, separate from the hustle and bustle of the Twin Cities. Because of the timing of the build, our yard was spacious and edged with a large growth of trees. Our parents were a modest, Midwest-bred couple who held respectable nine-to-five jobs. So, Maddy's imagination was completely recreated from the books that we read and the TV shows that we were allowed to watch.

Even more than I hated dressing up and playing pretend, I loathed the switcheroo. In my opinion, it was a fancy name for a stressful game of dress-up *and* pretend.

About ten years ago, I recalled Maddy wanted to deceive our grandparents, who had been in town visiting for the weekend.

"Let's fool Grandma by pulling the twin switcheroo," Maddy suggested with a little twinkle in her eye.

"Nah. She confuses us all the time anyway."

"Oh, Piper, it's fun. I'm bored. Pretty please, Piper?"

I always caved - I was her little puppet.

Before I could change my mind, Maddy slipped her favorite glittery T-shirt that read *Grandma's Favorite* over my head - she was the sole receiver of Grandma's gift. I didn't own a matching shirt. The shirt that she gave me had a gray, dabbing cat on it.

Maddy dusted a bit of blush on my cheeks and lined my lip with clear lip gloss.

"That's enough. You know that she plans on caking layers of that stuff on my face anyway." I wasn't going to get all dolled up for a pair of grandparents that never acted like they even enjoyed spending time with children. The evening plans consisted of Grandma's makeover – because Grandma always planned it - a game of cards - Grandma's favorite game, Gin Rummy - and grilled burgers – Grandma's choice. If Grandma didn't win the card game, everyone turned in early.

Grandma's name was Mary Kay, and she always informed anyone she met that she was not *the* actual famous Mary Kay of the cosmetics world, even though she was a very successful Mary Kay cosmetic agent. And believe me, she sold and wore plenty of it. Under her layers and layers of primer, foundation, and powder - in that order - she proudly drove a pink Cadillac earned with her high sales. I wondered when she removed all her makeup, if her smile wiped off as well. She seemed as phony as her painted face and her over-bleached blonde hair.

Normally, Maddy hung on Grandma's every word while I preferred to scrub my face as soon as she excused me from the table littered with bottles and bottles of *liquid gold*. I needed to wipe off her makeup as well as her little hurtful insults that clung to me.

When she finished making us *gorgeous*, I glanced in the bathroom mirror and immediately was haunted by visions of JonBenét Ramsey - a gorgeous little girl who participated in numerous child beauty pageants. Her petite features were covered with a thick layer of expensive makeup, fake eyelashes, and crimson berry lipstick. Instead of a tangled hair style, JonBenét's hair resembled Reba McIntyre's style in the 80s – high, big and hair-sprayed. A petite child dressed as a showgirl. Imagining her ghost created goosebumps up and down my spine.

Whenever Grandma Mary Kay visited us from Chicago, she instructed us on how to apply makeup correctly and care for our youthful skin. "Girls, you need to know that you won't be this beautiful and ageless forever. You must maintain your beauty if you want to have everything your heart desires. I'd be an old spinster - perhaps even ugly - if I hadn't discovered how to properly accentuate my features."

At that moment, she adjusted her breasts to increase their exposure through the V-neck of her tight sweater. Her demeaning comments about physical appearances always filled my impressionable head with wonder.

"Grandma, are you saying that we'll only be successful and happy if we're beautiful on the outside?" I knew I was supposed to act easy-going as I pretended to Maddy, but I couldn't let her belittling comment go without being questioned.

"Maddy, you misinterpreted my comment. I'm simply pointing out the obvious - appearances are important. You don't see ugly people on the news or in the magazines. Ugly people are behind the cameras. Spotlights are for the gorgeous and glamorous."

"No one reads magazines anymore, Grandma. It's all on the internet," Maddy-as-me chimed in and gave me a little, supportive wink. Plus, she knew it would've been something that I'd say in response to Grandma's demeaning comment about women.

"The internet - what a joke. It takes away all the fun and adventure of discovery because you can find everything so easily. Right at your fingertips. And don't get me started on the Facebook. Complete waste of time." Grandma dramatically plopped down in a chair and dabbed off the imaginary sweat from her forehead with a monogrammed handkerchief that read *MK*.

But for the twin switcheroo, I needed to appear like I enjoyed every minute of the makeover and ate up Grandma Mary Kay's attention. So, I smiled, oohed and aahed at my painted reflection. As I pretended to be Maddy, I laid it on thick.

"Grandma, you're an absolute artist. If I may say so myself, I'm a complete bombshell!" I sunk my teeth into Maddy's little game. As I kissed my reflection in Grandma's handheld mirror and managed to leave a hot-pink lipstick kiss on my reflection, Maddy giggled at my exaggerated imitation of her.

Okay, making Maddy giggle was the only part of the switcheroo that I enjoyed.

Later, after Maddy politely excused herself to the bathroom to wipe off her makeup, Grandma Mary Kay and I were alone at the kitchen table cleaning up the aftermath of primping and priming. A lot of products were required to achieve this painted look. *What a waste of time and money.*

"Maddy, you're a gorgeous girl and full of sass. I love that about you. I know that you two girls are identical" - she put her freshly manicured nails to the side of her red lip-stained mouth and dropped the volume of her voice - "but you, Madison, are the knockout. Plus, you have the personality that demands people's attention. Those two qualities together are killer. Piper is plain. She blends in. All my magic makeup skills can't help her. Don't tell her that I said this, but you're my very favorite." She squeezed my arm as I stood frozen in place, and she returned to packing up her cherished supplies. She hadn't noticed that I was in a state of shock and hurt. Completely appalled at my own grandmother.

I'd witnessed Grandma's favoritism of Maddy before, and it hadn't bothered me in the least. It hadn't bothered me that this selfish, cold-hearted woman didn't like me - her conditional love wasn't important to me. But to hear those hurtful words coming from her lips was cruel.

She dismissed me with a slight wave and headed for the back patio where my parents were chatting with Grandpa. "Now, be a doll and run these toolkits out to my Cadillac so we can eat our probably over-grilled burgers at this tiny, scratched-up table."

Chapter 3

Eleanor

People-watching was my hobby, my main source of entertainment. Free, quiet, and no interaction was necessary. The people who walked in and out of my life were performing for my personal enjoyment. What they didn't know was that I was taking notes, thorough notes.

Everyone was guilty of people-watching - at the mall, in church or a at sporting event. We judged each innocent person that entered our line of view. Everyone did it - no one was exempt. The judgment could be simple and harmless: "she is short" or "he has lots of hair." Judgments could also become spiteful. "She is as wide as she is tall" or "he has so much hair that I bet his middle name is Sasquatch." It was human nature.

My notetaking of human behavior started out of boredom and loneliness. I had no friends or a family who loved me; therefore, my idea of social interaction was people-watching.

When my parents were still alive, I lived among pure dysfunction. Both of my parents drank too much and neglected their only child - me. When they were three sheets to the wind, their favorite hobby was to argue, cuss, and throw punches. My father was miserable; therefore, he subjected us to his endless cruelty every day.

"Go fix your hair, girl. It's hanging in your eyes. You look like Cousin It." Father would growl at me.

"Woman, I would've never married you if I had known the only thing you were good for were your skills in the bedroom." Even Mother was on the receiving end of his tongue lashing.

Mother was completely unaware how her own choices affected the outcome of her life. "How did I end up here? I was destined to be a star. Not stuck in this low-income housing, hole-in-the-wall apartment married to a shit-for-brains husband who won't get his lazy ass out of his recliner to maintain his goddamn minimum-wage job."

I'd quietly watch her from the entryway of my bedroom as she applied another coat of mascara to her already-caked eyelashes. As she was getting ready for her late-night waitressing job at a nearby bar, she talked to her reflection in the mirror. "Mr. Trey said I had real, God-given talent. My voice was like a fucking angel. But instead, I fell for a one-liner from Rocky-got-a-nice-right-hook-Cutter, got knocked up after one lousy roll in the hay and thought I was in love. And here, I am - living the fucking dream."

"You look pretty, Momma." I tried to drag her out of her pity party, but my words landed on deaf ears.

Because she stopped responding to anyone that wasn't waving a dollar bill in her face, she strutted past me as she headed out the front door of our tiny, dingy apartment. She slammed the door and didn't even turn in my direction to say goodnight or goodbye.

I slowly shuffled in my fuzzy unicorn slippers to the living room where my father had almost passed out. The scent of stale beer wafted up from the piles of Budweiser cans littering the floor around his worn-out recliner.

"Goodnight, Father. I'll put myself to bed." There was no reaction from the motionless body.

Hmmm... Both Mother and Father don't respond to me when I talk. Can they hear me? Maybe I'm invisible. That would be so cool.

I decided to test my theory. If he could hear me, I'd for sure gain a negative reaction. "Father? Rocky? I found a million dollars, and I'm giving it to that homeless man who you spit on yesterday."

Again, no movement from the snoring man in the recliner.

Yep, I must be invisible!

A child's imagination was a wonderful and powerful coping mechanism. My imagination helped me cope with the emotional abandonment from my parents. Physically, they were present in our small run-down apartment. But emotionally, I was alone.

That night when I crawled under the covers onto my lumpy twin bed, I imagined that I had in fact been born with a magical power - invisibility. I needed to learn how to use my gift to the best of my ability. In all the Marvel movies, the superhero needed to practice and learn how to perfect their power. Spider-Man didn't automatically know how to create webs and swing from tall buildings. He practiced. In the movies, sometimes he failed, but he jumped right back up and tried again.

With a flashlight under my blankets, I grabbed a school notebook from my backpack and started to jot down all the qualities that I should possess in order to become effectively invisible.

Quiet, make no noise.
Never seen or heard.
Float into a room like a feather in the wind.
No crashing waves.
Even breathing.

With my new self-proclaimed superpower, I learned the art of being completely silent. When you were mastering a skill, there were unforeseen consequences. By choosing to be very quiet, I suppressed my voice, necessary for becoming truly silent.

My light feet learned to barely touch the floor. I floated in and out of rooms. I controlled my breathing to an even, quiet level. All of my movements became soundless. I didn't clear my throat, cough, or sneeze.

Methodically, to eliminate unnecessary sounds, I never slammed a door or shut a drawer too quickly. If a door produced a constant squeak, I learned at the exact point of its rotation when the squeak occurred. I would either leave it open to that point and squeeze my way through or very slowly open it so that the squeaking sound would be weakened. If there was a loose floorboard, it was on my radar. My ninja skills were impressive. However, since I had no one that cared a lick about me, no one realized that I was invisible.

Chapter 4

Maddy

Being an identical twin sucked. I was always compared to Piper, and I'd never live up to the sky-high bar that she established. It was a pole-vaulting bar set at six feet, but I was given no freaking pole to vault with. From the start, I was set to fail. I couldn't even compete. Piper was the perfect one. The one with excellent grades, good manners, head on straight, and always said the right thing.

No matter how high I scored on an exam, Piper achieved a higher mark. Even if I managed to score one hundred percent, Piper would earn one hundred and five percent by supplying the correct answer to the bonus question. Completely irritating.

If and when something positive or thought-provoking escaped my mouth, people would question if I was pulling a switcheroo. "Piper? Is that you?"

I acted like the innocent comparisons or slight jabs didn't bother me, but deep down in my blackened, hollow heart, they did. They started to pile up. Even though I was an exceptional actress, pain, disappointment and hurt were natural human feelings - last I checked according to my two regular shags, Maverick or Daniel. I was human. And all my lady parts were working.

Around twelve years old, I started feeling as if I wasn't as first-rate as Piper. I noticed that my parents' expectations of my school grades weren't as high as Piper's. If Piper didn't achieve all As, Mom and Dad were asking her what happened. Worry filled their expressions. It never entered their mind that she was anything but deserving of a perfect score.

If my grades were mostly Bs filtrated with Cs, I was congratulated and patted on the back. They didn't expect me to earn As. They were accepting of my average status. For a C, no inquiries were made as to what had happened.

At first when I noticed the difference in expectations, I was relieved that I didn't need to be perfect, all-knowing, well-behaved, a downright goody-goody. What a relief. No pressure. I sat back and enjoyed not putting in the extra effort. I slacked off in my schoolwork, and my parents didn't seem to raise an eyebrow. I had it easy, and I liked it that way.

However after a few months, I started to question it. *Don't my parents think that I'm as smart as Piper? Don't they want me to achieve the same high goals? Have they given up on me? Do they love Piper more than me? Why don't they expect the same greatness from me?*

My mounting questions started to bother me. My self-confidence steadily declined. I doubted my abilities. I wondered if I was worthy.

If my parents don't think I can achieve great success, maybe I can't.

But after losing a few nights of sleep, anger formed deep roots in my heart. I was angry that Piper was so absolutely wonderful and perfect. Everyone adored her, even me. When she walked into a room, people smiled. When I entered a room, bodies stiffened and coiled in reaction. While Piper made everyone feel welcomed and at ease, my presence brought out tension and disappointment.

Then, under my newly-awakened sense of keen observation, I noted that my friend group was also of a lesser ranking in the expectations level. Piper's friends were all like her - perfect, intelligent, and brown-nosers. I flowed in the popular crowds, my name was listed on all the Snapchats involving a party, I never felt left out or bullied, but my friends weren't the high-achievers or athletes in society or in our school.

Dee, my best friend, had an IQ of one hundred and fifty, but she refused to apply herself to earn the grades she was capable of. When any exam was placed in front of her, it was as if she was completing an elementary level puzzle. Piece of cake. Another reason her grades didn't reflect her intelligence was because homework seemed like a waste of time to her.

"My parents don't care how I perform in high school. But if I can score genius-level on my ACT and earn a free ride to college, they'll be thrilled, but beyond that, they don't give two shits. My Pa already voiced loudly that he ain't paying a dime to help me after I'm eighteen. I've been riding for free long enough."

Dee's parents never even graduated high school, and her pa thought that they were doing just fine without the big fancy GED. "Schoolin' is a waste. Government just wants yer damn money. You can learn that shit in real life. Don't need to pay no institution for their big-ass ideas."

One positive thing that came from my realization was my ability to observe those around me. Before, I could honestly say that I didn't make much time or effort to be aware of anyone but myself. Selfish - yes, I had been. Still was, but at least I was aware that I tended to be self-centered. I also realized that I was wonderful at discovering the positives of a situation. Even if I wasn't going to win, I'd come out on top because I'd learn and never fail at that specific situation again. Strength and resilience. I was determined to prove everyone wrong. I'd be the more successful twin. I'd earn the highest income. I'd be the envy of everyone. Eventually, I would win.

Piper was everything that I wasn't, but I was everything she wasn't - see how I did that? While Piper wasted her time on greeting every human that she bumped into on the street, I strutted past the insignificant person. I had more important places to be.

But as I resolved to prove that my parents were wrong to underestimate me, my resentment towards Piper grew. Even though I knew deep, deep down in my cold, black heart that none of this was her fault, I still blamed her.

Chapter 5

Piper

Growing up as a twin sister definitely included many perks, especially because mine was Maddy. Creativity was one of her many positive attributes. As children, she'd decide that one afternoon we were having high tea with the Queen of England. We needed to get all gussied up - our best dresses, curled up-dos, a touch of makeup, and a pair of Mom's high heels.

The very next afternoon, she would claim our living room was a forest, and we'd build shelter before the massive storm rolled in. We gathered all the pillows and throw blankets in the house and barricaded ourselves behind the living room couch. She'd lay a white sheet over the top of our fort. In case we needed to stay safe under our shelter for hours, she grabbed a handful of fruit snacks and juice boxes for nutrition.

One of my favorite childhood memories was the time that Maddy coerced our parents into letting us spend the night under the moon and stars on the back deck. Dad agreed to Maddy's idea as long as he could participate in the fun. And Mom allowed this creative campout since she preferred it to last year's Christmas Eve notorious campout.

Wrapped in beautiful red wrapping paper, a large box was tagged, "For Madison and Piper, Love Dad." When it was our turn, we tore off that paper in a matter of seconds to reveal a four-person tent. He'd purchased it for the family to enjoy camping the following summer. Because Maddy wasn't thrilled with the contents of the biggest gift under the tree, she voiced her opinion.

"Why give us a gift that we can't even use for *six months*? What a joke! Piper, we got robbed." We were eight years old, and even though I agreed with her statement, I wasn't about to disrespect our parents.

"Madison!" Mom, the manner police.

"Madison, that's a rude *but* fair response to my gift." Dad was the logical one while Mom normally reacted with her heart. "That's why we aren't going to wait until summer to use it."

He gained everyone's full attention. We waited to hear what his solution was. Before Mom could stop him, he'd collected a hammer and a few nails from his garage workbench and nailed down the four-man tent in our living room right next to the Christmas tree and the fireplace where our stockings hung.

I fell asleep that Christmas Eve staring at the twinkling lights on our artificial tree. In between Maddy's heavy breathing and my dad's snoring, I heard the radio softly playing Christmas carols, and my heart felt peaceful and content. The next morning we discovered that Santa wasn't real because we caught Mom stuffing our stockings as we peeked our heads out of the tent. Mom was disappointed, but I felt relieved - no strange, bearded man was breaking into our house while we were sleeping.

Campout number two was destined to be more memorable than a living room campout. I benefited from Maddy's creativity and Dad's adventurous nature.

I could almost see Maddy's imagination spinning. Creating adventures was her cup of tea. "We'll build a real campfire, roast hot dogs for supper, and the only time we are allowed to go into the house is to pee." Maddy possessed the magical gift of making everything fun.

All around us, the noises of the summertime cicadas' mating season filled the air. The distinct smell of a fresh campfire lingered in my nostrils. Three s'mores later and with a bit of marshmallow crusted to my cheek, we finally settled down. Maddy, Dad, and I were lying in sleeping bags on the hard, wooden deck under the light of the summer moon and stars. The night sky was lit so bright, as if all the stars were shining especially for our backyard campout.

"Piper, do you see that really, really bright one right there?" I nodded as Maddy pointed towards the clear night sky. "That one star always reminds me of you - bright, shiny, and one-of-a-kind. It's always there, just like you."

As Dad sniffled, he wiped a pretend tear off his cheek. "Dang, Jellybean. I think that's the nicest thing that has ever come out of your mouth." Dad loved to tease, and he was right - Maddy didn't often provide compliments.

Maddy gasped at his teasing jab. Their father-daughter relationship included lots of hearty giggles and clever remarks.

"Don't mind him, Maddy." I squeezed her hand, and we returned our attention upward to the sky. "Thank you. I'll never forget about that star."

Maddy slapped her arm. "And that pesky, good-for-nothing mosquito, Minnesota's state bird, reminds me a lot of you, Dad." She was witty. Always quick with her tongue.

Dad's booming laughter escaped from his mouth. He rolled over in his sleeping bag and started tickling her. Then he reached over her and tickled my sides. Our giggles filled the warm summer night, almost as loud as the male cicada's mating calls to his future mistress.

That slumber party under the stars was magical. We always talked about recapturing that night and doing it again, but we never did. I cherished it as the night that my sister compared me to the North Star.

Being Maddy's sidekick meant that someone always had my back. And if you had to pick a side, you, for sure, wanted her on *your* side. She was a devoted, hard-core ally that would defend her person to the grave.

Another great example of her creativity was her invention of Shadow. Every child constructed a version of this game - Copycat, Follow-the-Leader, or Repeat. But we called our version of the game Shadow, because we were versions of each other's shadow. It wasn't too difficult a concept. Whatever I did, Maddy did the exact same thing. She mimicked whatever I was doing. Sometimes, I would copy Maddy as well, but Maddy preferred to pretend to be me. I was rarely the focal point, so I basked in the attention that Maddy was willing to give up for me as she played my shadow.

As a ballerina, I extended high on my tiptoes and gracefully danced around the living room. Being my shadow, Maddy would follow right behind me dressed in black, like a real shadow. My parents often requested a routine where we'd turn on music and dance in the living room. Maddy and I would dress in the same clothing, float in and out of the room with Maddy copying every one of my movements. Because of all our practicing, our mimicking skills became quite harmonious.

After one of our dance routines, Dad commented, "Mirror, Mirror on the wall. I can't tell the difference at all."

Chapter 6

Eleanor - 2006

My father Rocky earned his name just like Dennis Rader, the infamous BTK killer, earned his. Actions. BTK - bind, torture, kill. My grandfather named his only son after the famous Sylvester Stallone movie, *Rocky*, and my father lived up to his name. As his regular punching bags, Rocky enjoyed physically and emotionally abusing us. He was a master at verbal jabs. I was often referred to in third person, which convinced me even more that I was invisible.

From his nightly reclined position, Rocky's stomach growled. "This child of yours is worthless. Can't she at least make me some dinner?"

Mother was leaving for her night shift waitressing. "She's six, you idiot. You're a grown-ass man. Can't you make yourself a freakin' sandwich?"

I was actually eight years old at the time of this conversation. I couldn't decide if I was proud that my mother stood up for me or saddened that she didn't even know her only daughter's correct age.

That night after Father finally passed out and Mother was working, I mustered up the courage to stand next to him as he snored like a freight train. His mouth hung wide open, and his breath smelled like rotten mushrooms and hard-boiled eggs. His coarse whiskers were black and sprinkled with gray. He needed to shave, but he only shaved on Sunday nights. Using Mother's tweezers, I plucked one of his thick, black hairs - because the gray ones bothered him more - from his chin to test if he could easily be woken.

No response. He didn't even flinch. He was out cold.

I tiptoed to the kitchen and tied a white dish towel around my neck like a cape. Out of the cupboard, I pulled out a large glass measuring cup. I slowly filled it with warm water - like relaxing bath water. Being careful not to spill a drop, I slipped back into the living room carefully holding the measuring cup. After I positioned myself on the floor next to Father's recliner, I delicately picked up his left hand by the shirt sleeve and lifted it into the warm water.

According to an infamous story that some mischievous boys on the school bus shared, if the hand of the sleeping victim was placed in a cup of warm water, the sleeping person's body would automatically relax enough to relieve himself without even waking up. These boys practiced this prank at a slumber party over the previous weekend. The victim's newly earned nickname was Wet Walter. I decided to test their story.

I patiently waited, crouched next to the old, musty recliner. Five minutes later, I checked the water by dipping my index finger in it. The temperature was cooling, but that was when I noticed the stain on the front of Father's jeans and the slight smell of urine.

The science experiment was a success. My abusive father had peed in his favorite chair.

A sinister smile crept up on my young, not-so-innocent face.

Instead of his bloodshot, angry eyes staring back at me, I noticed the blue veins on the back of his eyelids. When he was sleeping and calm, he was an attractive man. He kept a five o'clock shadow on his face. Mother suggested to me that it wasn't because it was popular and he looked good with one, but to hide scars that his father had created with a belt and fork.

Papa Kent, my grandfather, was a malicious, angry man. Stories of Papa Kent's abuse are legendary in my family, and I felt blessed to never have met him. His frustrations were taken out on his wife, Grams, as well as his own children. Like father, like son. His fists would bleed long before he was finished punishing his family. The night he died, he'd been infuriated with Grams because she hadn't been able to scrub a dried bloodstain from one of his shirts. It was her blood - her fault. The stain had been created from a bloody nose that he had inflicted on her. Her punishment was a beating with a wooden spoon. He beat her fingers until they became bloody, swollen sausages.

When he was finished and Grams was screaming in pain, he plopped down in his chair with his beer. Moments later, he clenched his heart and called to her for help, but she didn't move. From the kitchen, she recognized what was happening, and she silently watched him suffer a fatal heart attack.

Rocky had come home from his after-school job to discover his father dead in his chair, and his mother sitting at the kitchen table staring into space. Her swollen hands were wrapped in wet, bloody dish towels. She claimed that she couldn't dial 911 because her fingers were too swollen from her beating. Grandpa Kent had died hours before the ambulance arrived, and Grams lost both of her pinkies.

As I flipped my cape over my shoulder, I crept back to our dingy kitchen, quietly dried the measuring cup, and placed it back in the cupboard. I was a bandit, sneaking around in the middle of the night - in reality, it was only eight o'clock - and punishing a bad man for his rude behavior. The Batman theme song played in my head. My invisibility could be used for good. I'd admit that *good* was used loosely.

As I crawled into my bed and pulled up my ratty comforter to my chin, I was still smiling.

Unfortunately, my triumph didn't last long. The next day at school, the school counselor visited our classrooms teaching us that no one should ever touch our privates or lay an angry hand on us. We needed to know the difference between appropriate and inappropriate touching.

"Good touches make us feel warm inside and bring a smile to our face, like when your grandma hugs you tight because she missed you or your friend squeezes your hand to show you support. A bad touch is something that you don't want to do, and it makes you feel sad. Maybe your tummy feels sick or the touch hurts you. No one should ever touch you in anger."

From the front row, my hand shot up.

"Yes, Eleanor, do you have a question?" Standing tall at the front of the class room in her coordinating blazer and skirt, Mrs. Malcolm was a first-year counselor who introduced this new program to our school. She was enthusiastic about helping and educating people about how you should be treated in relationships. My guess was that she had virgin ears. She hadn't met anyone like the Cutter family yet.

"Even our parents?" My mouth formed the question before my brain could stop it. I needed clarification on this discussion. I definitely was taught a different opinion at home.

"Even what, with your parents? Can you elaborate, Eleanor?" As she addressed me, she shot a couple of frowns towards my snickering classmates.

"Even our parents aren't allowed to use their fist or the back of their hand on you? Not even a dinner fork or a wooden spoon? That isn't allowed?"

Mrs. Malcolm's eyes clouded over in sadness. She gently placed a caring hand on my shoulder. "No, Eleanor. Why don't you and I talk about this later?"

As a diligent school employee, Mrs. Malcolm wanted to discuss the appointment with one of my parents. She was inexperienced and naive and wanted to make sure that she did her due diligence. She had no idea that her inquiry would lead me down a darker path.

When our home phone rang, I was sitting at our kitchen table working on my math homework. My mom answered it and was immediately defensive about receiving a phone call from the school.

"Eleanor made an inquiry about something that we were discussing in class, and I'd like to follow up with her privately to discuss." I heard Mrs. Malcolm's kind voice on the other end of the line because the volume on Mom's phone was on high.

"What the hell are you talking about? I'm sure that I - as her mother - can make sure she understands. Eleanor ain't dumb. Maybe just too curious sometimes. But no need for some fancy head doctor to confuse her more." Mom crossed her arms across her chest and watched me through the slits of her stern stare. Steam rolled out of her ears.

"Nothing like that, Mrs. Cutter. I'm aware that Eleanor is highly intelligent. She's performing quite well in all her classes. You should be very proud. I'd like to meet with her during her study hall period. She wouldn't need to miss any instruction time. I was calling as a courtesy to let you know my intentions."

"What about?"

"To be honest, Mrs. Cutter, we were discussing abuse."

"Abuse? What the hell for?"

"It's part of the third-grade curriculum in health class to educate our children that the school is a safe place. That no one deserves to be treated poorly."

I heard the silence that Mrs. Malcolm allowed from her end of the phone. I was sure that she was praying my mother would break down and admit that we needed a *safe* place to stay. Mrs. Malcolm had underestimated my stubborn, callous mother.

"How nice of you to be concerned for Eleanor's well-being. What did you say your name was again?"

"My name is Mrs. Malcolm. I'm the school counselor."

"Well, Malcolm, you can take your unwanted concerns and shove them where the sun doesn't shine. Leave my daughter alone and don't ever call again." She slammed the phone down and glared at me. "Look what you've started! Your father is gonna be so pissed! What the hell did you say to her, Eleanor?"

For my innocent, three-word question during health class, I earned a massive cigarette burn on my thigh and a hard kick to my ribs. All wounds that could not be seen by any responsible, caring adult. Mother had decided that Father didn't need to know - she'd take care of the punishment herself. She promised that it was nothing compared to what Rocky would have done if she informed him. I should count myself lucky - I still had all ten fingers.

Chapter 7

Maddy - 2006

Twin telepathy - it was real. It sounded witchy and fairy tale-ish. Technically, I wasn't a believer in all that fluff. There were no unicorns, and if you actually climbed to the end of the rainbow, there wouldn't be a real pot of gold. Fairy tales had never been my bag. Life was not a fairy tale - if you lost your shoe at midnight, you were drunk. True statement. Been there, done that. No prince had ever knocked on my front door the next day to return my bra - shoe.

But even as crazy as it sounded, twin telepathy was legit. I didn't care what scientific research suggested. Were any of those so-called scientists twins themselves? I didn't think so.

Piper and I often felt what the other twin was thinking or feeling. However, it wasn't like her sweet, patient voice was bouncing around in my head saying actual words to me. I *felt* her communicating with me. It was hard to explain. The most accurate thing that I could compare it to was sound waves. Sound waves weren't visible to the naked eye, but your sense of hearing captured what your eyes couldn't see. We had a shared frequency with one another.

The first time that I distinctly remembered it happening was when Piper and I were eight years old. Mom and I chose to stay home to watch *Pitch Perfect 2* while Piper and Dad went sledding. Under a soft, buffalo-checked flannel blanket and dressed in my favorite sweats, I snuggled up to Mom on the couch. Warm and cozy. Safe and dry. We each had our own bowl of buttery popcorn, sprinkled with peanut M&Ms, sitting on our laps. Large mugs of hot cocoa with melting marshmallows were steaming on the table next to us.

Out of nowhere, chills sprinted up and down my spine. Enormous goosebumps covered my arms while my teeth started to loudly chatter.

"Madison, what's wrong? Why are you shivering? Do you feel alright?" Mom instantly noticed the change.

From my cozy position under the blanket, it was hard to explain to her why I felt ice-cold. Her hand checked the temperature on my forehead.

"I dunno. I'm freezing and scared." I managed to spit out a quick response in between shivers. *Where is this strange feeling coming from?*

"Scared? What are you scared of, Madison?" Mom was rubbing my arm and shoulders as if her back and forth motion would scrub the goosebumps off.

Between the sharp chattering of my teeth, I tried to explain, "I don't know where Dad is."

"Dad? He went sledding with Piper." Mom paused the movie and turned her full attention to me. She wrapped her arms around me, trying desperately to warm me up. "Wow. Your body is very cold. Let's turn the fireplace on. You drink your hot cocoa and see if that warms you up."

When Piper and Dad returned about an hour later, they explained to us that Dad lost track of Piper in the pitch-black night. "There were so many kids flying down that big sledding hill. While she whizzed down the hill, I sneezed my standard three sneezes in a row, looked up, and she'd disappeared. When I finally found her, she was covered in a blanket of snow, shivering fiercely and crying. Poor Puppet." He ruffled her messy, stocking cap hair and headed to the kitchen to make two more cups of hot cocoa.

Mom and I both glanced at each other as an intense light bulb ignited in our brains. We realized what happened between Piper and me. While I was at home all snuggled on the couch with Mom, Piper had experienced intense feelings of fear, and somehow, those feelings invaded my brain as well.

"That's amazing. Madison, do you think that's why you were cold and scared? Piper was sharing her feelings with you?"

My eyes were wide with wonder and shock. I nodded. Piper joined us on the couch, curious to hear more of what Mom was talking about. "Girls, this is an unexplained twin gift. I have read many articles about this. I always wondered when you were babies if you had this ability. You can feel each other's deepest feelings. Has it ever happened before, that you're aware of?"

I remembered Piper and I looking at each other, and at the same time, we nodded our eight-year-old heads. She knew what story I was going to tell Mom because we were just as curious when it had happened months before.

"This summer when we were riding bikes, I was super far ahead of Piper. She crashed her bike, and her knee bled quite a bit and was all banged up. I didn't hear or see her fall, but all of a sudden my knee started to throb. I stopped my bike and turned around, saw her lying on the side of the road, holding her bloody knee."

We couldn't explain it or describe what happened back then. And of course, like any unexplained force of nature, it didn't happen every time one of us felt intense physical or emotional pain. It was random. But after that night, we started to understand that it *was* happening. Piper kept a diary with actual events and dates to see if there was a pattern, but we never recognized one. Sometimes, there were visceral feelings that neither of us could claim. It was as if they were coming from someone else - another connection.

As time went on and our bodies matured, so did our emotions. In addition to the typical elementary emotions - joy, sadness, fear, and anger - as teenagers, our hormones raged with jealousy, regret, romance, and even lust.

Trying to shield Piper from seeing my heart and soul became a tiring task in itself. It was an incredible gift to be able to summon her when I needed her most, but when I was trying to hide something, this *gift* became quite a burden.

Chapter 8

Piper - 2009

Being the other half of a twin was a blessing and a curse. When we were younger, I never felt alone, I always felt safer with Maddy around. All my life I'd had Maddy - or honestly, I should say that Maddy had always had me. I'd been her little sidekick as soon as we exited the womb. Mom liked to remind us that we were always happier together, whether it was sleeping in the same crib, same room, or playing with other kids. We wanted to be near each other.

I remembered being scared of the dark, and before I could even comprehend my own feelings or call out to my parents who were in the next room, Maddy joined me in my twin bed, hugged me, consoled me, and made sure that I was okay. It wasn't like she could hear my voice in her head, just a feeling that something wasn't right. It was a solid connection that Maddy and I had with each other's hearts and heads.

For example, when our faithful, snuggly Sheltie, Baxter, was hit by a car, Maddy hadn't been home. She was attending a cheerleading camp in Andover, a northern suburb of the Twin Cities. More than sixty miles away.

However, as soon as I discovered Baxter lying on the side of the road near our house, my heart ripped to pieces. Instant tears tumbled out of my eyes and onto his fluffy brown fur as I leaned over to cradle him in my arms and carry him home. Seven-year-old Baxter had been full of energy and raced everywhere. He was like a toddler who ran from room to room, never walking. Wheels on cars or anything that moved - a squirrel, a bunny, a fly, a leaf blowing in the wind - he barked at and chased. He was easily entertained. No matter what we tried, we couldn't break him of this natural instinct, so we adopted a family rule that we never let him loose in the front yard. Baxter had been sentenced to a life of mischief in our fenced-in backyard.

As I carried his limp body towards our house, my cell phone vibrated in my back pocket. There was no way that I was setting him down until I was in our backyard where he belonged. The caller would have to wait.

As I crossed our front lawn, I noticed that the gate to our backyard was slightly ajar. He must've recognized his chance to escape and never looked back. I bet he was running at full force into the busy street.

Oh, Baxter...

After the caller hit my voicemail, she hung up and dialed again. I knew it was Maddy. Not only because she was too impatient to wait for a return call, but because she knew something bad happened. She sensed the ache in my heart even though she was miles away.

On the fourth ring, I laid Baxter down on our freshly mowed lawn and sat cross-legged next to him, petting his soft fur. I pulled the phone out of my pocket. Before I could even say hello, I heard her frantic voice.

"Piper? Piper? What's going on?" While she felt my anguish, her worry and anxiety radiated towards me. She was crying before I told her what happened.

I loved Maddy with all my heart, but I didn't want her to know what was going on in my heart or head all the time. I possessed individual feelings that I wanted to keep to myself. That I wanted to figure out my way through on my own without Maddy's opinion or judgment.

When I was a child, I remember watching a turtle at the zoo. His shell was the only thing visible. He looked like a rock in the middle of his gated pen. Slowly and cautiously, he'd poke his little, wrinkly head out to search his surroundings verifying his safety. A sudden noise would scare him, and he'd revert into the comfort and security of his hard shell. No wonder he never wandered very far. He was so afraid of the happenings around him that it was simply safer to stay in his protective shell, where no one could see him.

That was what my true feelings felt like. I was too afraid to *feel* for fear of Maddy knowing. However, it rarely worked. The only way that I could imagine that anyone could hide their true emotions was with medication – drugs. I wasn't willing to try that.

Chapter 9

Eleanor - 2009

The phone call from my school counselor and my mother's punishment sparked my plan to right *my* universe. I wasn't going to be a victim like my mother, like my grandmother. I wanted to die with all ten of my fingers. No one would be able to push me around. To an outsider, it looked like silent acceptance as I said nothing to stop the abuse, and that was exactly how I wanted it to appear. I quietly accepted the emotional and physical abuse from both of my parents while silently plotting my revenge. My patience would be a valuable asset.

When my father's temper flared, he lashed out without a second thought. He didn't seem to receive any visible satisfaction after slapping my mother or me. It'd become an everyday occurrence. For me, it was the couple of hours afterwards that my best ideas were created.

With the knowledge that after my father consumed his nightly share of alcohol he'd sleep like a rock, I continued to play minor pranks on him for years for my own amusement. I also discovered that by the time he passed out, he had a foggy recollection of the couple of hours *before* he drank himself into a stupor.

In sixth grade, I staged the scene as if he fell asleep in the middle of enjoying a can of vegetable beef soup. In actuality, he'd finished the dinner hours before. Only for my science experiment, I had noted the different timeframes.

Eleanor's Home Science Experiment

Purpose: *to entertain and right my universe*

Materials:

- *Bowl of boiling-hot vegetable beef soup*
- *Small hand towel*
- *Spoon*

Hypothesis: *I believe when the subject slightly moves in his recliner, the cup of boiling hot vegetable soup will tip over, causing him to scream and curse.*

Procedure: *After carefully and quietly placing the hot bowl of soup onto his lap while the subject is unconscious, I will patiently retire to my bedroom to wait for the subject to awaken.*

Conclusion: *This experiment was a success. Within five minutes, the subject coughed during his slumber and knocked over the bowl of soup onto his lap. He screamed and cursed repeatedly. Eventually, he dialed 911 himself.*

When the normal signs of his drunken comatose stage started, I retrieved his empty bowl of soup that he had discarded onto the tray table next to his recliner. When I grabbed the bowl, the silver soup slipped onto the plastic tray table. My eyes widened. I quickly looked at my father's face for a sign that I woke him up. Nothing. Freight train snoring continued.

The boiling-hot soup experiment ended up causing first and second-degree burns. Because of the location and severity of the burns, Rocky stayed in the hospital for several days. Those few days were perhaps the happiest, most carefree days for Mother and me. Our home was peaceful.

The night before Rocky was scheduled to be released from the hospital, I sprawled out on the couch - no one wanted to sit in Rocky's stained recliner - watching an episode of *Dateline* after Mother left for her waitressing job.

I won't blame the TV show for my idea. New ideas to harm Rocky were already sprouting in my mind. However, this particular episode ignited a spark that couldn't be blown out. I sat on the edge of my seat taking in the facts. A monstrous idea was born.

The narrator explained that Mr. and Mrs. Tarrell were a lovely, prominent couple who were well-known and respected in their Driftwood, Texas community. Mr. Tarrell - Gene - started his oil business with a small savings, and he met the love of his life, Ava, when he hired her to be his administrative assistant. Their family verified that it was a quick, passionate courtship. They seemed blissfully happy and had been married for thirty years. No one suspected any marital trouble.

After celebrating their wedding anniversary with an Alaskan cruise, the couple returned home, and Mr. Tarrell immediately started to feel ill. He assumed that he'd caught a virus while on vacation. He hated doctors and thought he could overcome whatever ailment he had on his own. So, he stayed home from work while his attentive, loyal wife waited on him.

Breakfast, lunch, and dinner. Even cold washcloths for his violent headache - Ava was right by his side for whatever he needed. She mixed thallium into the rhubarb strawberry jam topped on his morning toast, stirred it into the mayo spread on his turkey sandwich, and added a teaspoon or two of it to his chicken noodle soup. She was on a mission, and having him home for three meals a day was bound to speed up her plan.

However, what initially threw her off the investigator's radar was that Ava had fallen ill as well. On the day of the funeral, Mrs. Tarrell had been admitted to the hospital. Her doctors told investigators that she was gravely ill and wouldn't release her to attend her husband's funeral. They were searching for someone who wanted to kill both Mr. and Mrs. Tarrell. Who would benefit from both of their murders?

The investigation only turned up dead ends until Gene's autopsy report came back with high traces of poison in his blood. Oddly enough, the hospital had also discovered small traces of thallium in Ava's blood. However, the levels were significantly different.

With this key piece of evidence, the investigators created a timeline to pinpoint the consumption of the poison. Because Gene was at home under the care of his wife, the finger was easily pointed at his caregiver - Ava. She prepared and served all of his meals. Mrs. Ava Tarrell was arrested for the murder of her husband.

During her interrogation, she eventually admitted to the poisoning. Ava claimed that she poisoned herself attempting to cover her tracks and establish herself an alibi. She served herself a very small dose of thallium in her morning coffee.

Most of the community couldn't fathom why. They had it all. Their friends believed that they were happy. They were both successful and well-respected. But for Ava, it was simple greed. She was done sharing and wanted her husband dead so she would be the lone benefactor of their wealth. Ava had been caught and sentenced to prison for the rest of her life plus sixty years.

Mrs. Tarrell's fatal flaws worked hand-in-hand with each other - greed and impatience. Smaller doses of thallium over a long period of time would've killed him, but she lost patience. She tried to speed up her plan. Of course, people would question and investigate his death. He was a popular, public figure in their community. He held an important job as a CEO of his own oil company.

If the murderous plan worked for me to kill my father, I would most definitely write to her in prison thanking her for the idea.

In my case, there would be no investigation because my father wasn't a well-known businessman but instead a well-known alcoholic who caused many public disturbances with his rude, obnoxious behavior. I'd bet my favorite pair of Black Hills gold earrings - which was my most valuable possession - that people would assume his liver finally gave out or he got alcohol poisoning. Honestly, I was banking on those two assumptions.

After methodically imagining for years about killing my father, it became more like a homework assignment - a science experiment. I tried to think of all the possible outcomes, tried to imagine how it could go wrong. I outlined the steps to complete the assignment, looked for faults in the timeline, considered it a draft until it was perfect - no room for error. *Will he be able to taste a half teaspoon? If he does taste it in his beer, will he throw it out? Probably not. How do I hand him a fresh one without making him suspicious of my kindness?*

I've always wanted my parents to play more active roles in my life.

Chapter 10

Maddy - 2016

My life escalated downhill after Piper failed to land that part-time, entry-level job with Mrs. Yates for me. Maybe I was being dramatic, but it was a life-altering event. It was a make-or-break situation for me. I was banking on that job to make me the top dog of my friend group, award me as the highest achieving teenager, propel me to the next income level. But instead of victory - like I was used to - I tasted the gravelly, gritty taste of complete defeat. I lost. I wasn't better than the rest. I was a failure. All things that I wasn't used to.

But in reality, I didn't lose - Piper did.

It was her fault that I made some choices that didn't line up with my moral upbringing. It was her fault that I couldn't seem to move past the failure.

In hindsight, I shouldn't have bragged about the job *before* landing it. I shouldn't have declared to everyone that I applied. Maybe I shouldn't have put the cart before the horse - a phrase Mom used that made absolutely no sense to me.

Why would a horse be in a supermarket in the first place? And why would you put a shopping cart anywhere near a horse? In my imagination, a two-thousand-pound Clydesdale horse pranced in his horseshoes down the skinny supermarket aisles. The *click-clack* of his heavy feet echoed on the hard linoleum floor as a reminder that I, in fact, did put the horse before the cart and was dealing with those repercussions.

Piper bombed the interview. In retrospect, I shouldn't have asked her to pull a twin switcheroo for something that held so much importance to me. When we traded places, it was for pure entertainment or my own selfish gain. The switcheroo never failed me. Piper was smarter, kinder, more thorough - all the qualities to make a great first impression. I knew I could perform the job as Mrs. Yates' personal party-planning assistant. I just doubted my interviewing skills.

During our Life Preparation class, we practiced interviewing, and all the answers that poured out of my mouth were off-point or lacked true feeling.

The teacher couldn't hide his disappointment. "Maddy, have you simply memorized answers from the interview questionnaire? Your answers to these questions should come from your heart. If you really want this" - he referred to my pretend interview guide - "event coordinator job, you need to think about how *you* feel, what *you* would do, what *you* would say. Memorizing answers from a website will not grant you your dream job. You need to answer the questions with your own genuine responses. I should feel how important this job is to you."

Needless to say, my grade for that assignment was a C-minus. A C-minus would never land me a job working for my idol, Mrs. Yates, the most fabulous, talented, successful party planner in the tri-state area. Nope, only an A would do. And who did I know that earned an A in that class? My very own identical twin sister.

Rebellion became my diversion from dealing with the disappointment. Cutting school led to some great new adventures. Instead of attending school, Dee and I hopped on a city bus heading for downtown Minneapolis. We explored the city, bought some weed, got high under a bridge, and even declined money in exchange for sex. We learned more in those seven hours than we would have if we attended school.

However, the last lesson I learned that afternoon was burned into my brain and affected me much more than the drugs did.

The city bus route dropped me off a block from home. As I strolled home reminiscing about the day's events, I opened the front door to discover a pair of discarded high heels in the entryway. Just a few inches from that, a black pencil skirt and a white silk blouse. I held my breath. The next item that came into view was a pair of black lace panties. I was home an hour before the school day even ended.

With my breath caught in my throat, I heard the couple in the upstairs hallway. I didn't think they even made it to the bedroom. They were panting, groaning, and moaning. *Who was it?* I didn't recognize the clothing.

I quietly retraced my steps out the front door and gently pulled the door shut.

Who is in our house having mind-blowing sex?

Automatically, my eyes moved to the garage, and through the side window, I identified my dad's Jeep parked in his stall. My mom was definitely not wearing a size two pencil skirt and sexy underwear.

Without the job that I had been banking on and with the knowledge that my dad was cheating on my mom, I decided to focus on a new hobby. I needed a distraction.

His name was Mr. Jarro, our new, young, attractive Spanish teacher. Last semester when he joined Pine Hill High School, he was my Study Hall teacher. We didn't have much interaction except when I asked to be excused to my locker...the bathroom...the counselor's office...the library.

As I'd casually approach his massive oak desk, his eyes focused on the book that he was reading. After I cleared my throat to earn his attention, his hazel eyes with golden specks would slowly travel up my midriff, my chest, my neck, my lips, and finally to my big blue eyes that returned his look of desire. Small beads of perspiration formed on his forehead. He shifted awkwardly in his desk chair as if something was prodding him and making sitting difficult. I could guess what was making him squirm.

I was aware that I had this effect on the male population. As any intelligent woman would, I used it to my advantage. My YouTube bingeing paid off - I wore two bras to help boost them a bit. One pushup bra and one plunge. The purpose of the different types of bras worked together to give my breasts the perfect lift and shape. Almost irresistible.

With my breasts perky, my slim waist was enhanced and showed off the curves of my seductive hips. Even my face held perfect curves. My cheeks weren't hollow like the models in my fashion magazines but plump. With a touch of blush, I would highlight the bottom of them like Grandma MaryKay taught me. My lips were heart-shaped, suggesting that I was always prepared for a deep, passionate kiss. Or perhaps something more scandalous...

When I finally decided that seducing Mr. Jarro was my next project, I felt better. I secured a goal, something to distract myself with. I did consider it a challenge even though

I knew that he was interested and attracted to me. Because he was an authority figure, a relationship with him would be taboo. If we got caught, he'd be fired and chastised by the community. Plus, I would've done something that no one else had done. I liked being whispered about as I walked down the hallways. I controlled those rumors. I heard the words my classmates voiced behind my back.

"She is a vixen."

"She literally chewed up the football team and spit them out in a matter of weeks."

"Did you hear she literally banged both the Thury brothers in one day? They didn't even know what hit them."

A few months before, Dee had offered me a dare that I couldn't resist. Ever since Dee and I had become friends in our preteen years, we had loved this game. She appreciated that I was always up for it. Even though we were clearly past that age, it was fun to reveal a truth or complete a dare to liven things up a bit.

"Truth or dare?"

"Dare." After I discovered how much fun dares were, I never picked truth anymore. Dee was well aware of this fact.

"My dear Maddy, for this ultimate dare, I'm even willing to pay you at its completion. I dare you to seduce eleven jocks in sixty days. Eleven football jocks. The gentlemen can be members of the offensive or defensive team. I don't care. For every day that it takes you, you lose ten dollars, so the faster you sweep them off their feet, the more moola for you and your weed habit." She was such a bitch. I loved her.

"What kind of proof do you need? And what is your definition of *seduce*?" I loved a good dare. I needed the rules laid out, because I didn't like to lose.

"Well, I don't really want my best friend to contract any sexual diseases during the course of this challenge, so seduction can be different depending on the victim."

We were sitting on the bleachers during halftime of the homecoming football game. The area around us was unoccupied for the moment because everyone had run to the concession stand for snacks.

"For example, Chad McGuire - he'd be an easy score. For him, I'd accept a heartfelt proclamation of his love. He's so easy that I bet you might even get a heartfelt text telling you that you're his dream girl. Don't wanna rob that preacher's kid of his virginity though. But for Jeremy Portner, I require a pair of his tighty whities. And I won't accept ones that are greased."

Honestly, I had enjoyed the dare - toying with the boys - but it turned out to be too easy. One by one, the targeted football players either fell in love with me or were quick to please me or just wanted an easy lay. Afterwards, the rumors and nicknames aimed in my direction were quite hilarious. My all-time favorite nickname that ended up spray-painted on the outside of my locker was *pig-skinned temptress*.

Therefore, I decided on a secret dare - Mr. Jarro's seduction - for my own knowledge and enjoyment. I would seduce Mr. Jarro, someone who was an authority figure, a consenting adult, someone who should know better.

Dare.

After I had my fun, I'd confess my secret to Dee. She already was impressed with my seduction skills. This self-proclaimed dare would blow her mind.

Chapter 11

Piper - 2016

Maddy had gotten out of control. Not that she could ever be controlled, but somehow, her disrespect for authority rose to a whole other level. She had become unreasonable. In the old days - which seemed like a very long time ago - I'd rationally discuss her questionable choices with her. Eventually, she saw reason. Unfortunately for me, I became my parent's crutch.

"Can you talk some sense into her, Piper? She doesn't hear a word your father and I are saying. I think she mutes our voices." Mom hated confrontation. She avoided them like a germaphobe avoided touching doorknobs or light switches.

During our childhood, the issues that I'd step in for were minor. For instance, Maddy would refuse to do the dinner dishes because she'd recently painted her nails. They were dry hours ago, but she argued that they might chip, and heaven forbid, she'd need to repaint them all.

"Do you know how long it takes to paint your nails to look like this?" She would dramatically hold up her freshly-painted, pale pink fingernails. "If only my tight-ass parents would pay for a manicure, I could have them done by a professional and dried within minutes. But since I need to do them myself, it takes a lot of time and patience."

I bended. I compromised. I always received the raw end of the deal as the peacemaker. That was my permanent role in our family. Maddy caused the spikes in temperature, and I cooled things down. She was the fire, and I was the ice.

I agreed to wash them if she dried and put them gently away.

"I better not dry in case my polish gets on the drying rag. Holler for me, Piper, when you're done drying them, and I'll race down and put them all away. Thanks, Puppet!" She dashed off to her room where I was sure she completed many tasks with her fingers without messing up her perfectly painted nails. It was just the beginning of her struggle to win power.

As the digits in our age increased, so did the problems that Maddy caused. Whatever was forbidden or morally questionable, Maddy was interested in. Alcohol, cutting class, sex, drugs, stealing. If my parents, myself, society, or any authority figure told her no, she questioned why. However, unlike a toddler, she didn't just question the reasoning – she made it her mission to discover why it was illegal or morally wrong. Rules were meant to be bent and questioned. Her favorite quote was *well-behaved women rarely make history*. Maddy *was* making history.

Maddy claimed that I was jealous of her, that I wished I was her.

She couldn't be more wrong. She was extremely popular and gorgeous, but she was also hollow and empty. She had no one special in her life, not a steady boyfriend or a loyal best friend. Because she was so self-centered, she couldn't see outside of the Maddy bubble. I knew she loved me, but just as I was sure of her love, I was also sure that because she was so self-involved, she'd shove me to the side if it benefited her in any way, shape, or form. She'd somehow make it my fault.

I loved my own life, my friends, my boyfriend. I wouldn't trade them for anything. I valued loyalty, friendship, and honesty - party invitations, a million Snapchats, and hollow compliments were not something that I desired.

She believed that I purposefully tanked the interview with Mrs. Yates. Honestly, I didn't. I'd never intentionally hurt Maddy or anyone I love. That wasn't how I operated. She should know that and know to never accuse me of that, but she hadn't been herself lately - too high strung and anxious. I thought by attending this interview for her, maybe I could relieve some of her stress. But since I didn't get the job for her, it just caused another huge boulder of stress, worry, and anxiety. If she was a balloon made of hot air, I could easily pop her with one little prick of a needle.

Mrs. Yates was the owner of a successful party-planning business called Plan to Party. Our little suburb, Pine Hill, was located on the southwest tip of the Twin Cities, where she earned a reputation for throwing epic celebrations. Planning Prince's fortieth birthday party in 1998 at his Minneapolis mansion awarded Mrs. Yates the reputation that she had strived for.

Of course, I felt terrible for messing up the interview. Actually, everything had been going extremely well until the conclusion of the interview when Mrs. Yates asked me if I had any questions for her.

"Well, yes, in fact I do, Mrs. Bates-"

"Yates. It is Yates, with a capital Y. I'm not Mrs. Bates of Psycho Hotel. I've heard the nicknames and have grown tired of the games." She started to pack up her laptop and slid Maddy's application into the top drawer of her desk. Then she proceeded to turn off the lamp that was sitting on her desk before I could even comprehend what had happened.

I remained in the stiff leather armchair across from her massive desk, legs crossed in my too-tight, borrowed mini-skirt, freshly manicured nails placed politely on my lap. Shoulders back, face forward, and eyes always on Mrs. Bates... Yates! I meant Yates. Shit.

"Oh, my goodness. I'm so sorry. That isn't at all what I meant, Mrs. Yates. I know your name and would never disrespect you."

"As far as I'm concerned, this interview is over, Miss Sterling. I haven't risen in the social scene by settling. I will not settle by hiring you after your weak apology. There are a million eager young ladies who could perform this job." She stood up from behind her desk, indicating I should do the same. Her irritation was reflected in her narrow, harsh stare and her stiff, upright posture.

I was too shocked to move. *Maddy is going to kill me.* How did this happen? I wasn't one to call people nicknames or make fun of them in any way. The only excuse was that I let my guard down. Got too comfortable and mispronounced her last name.

Reluctantly, I admitted defeat, and I stood up. I extended my hand in one small final polite gesture. She glanced down at my peace offering and totally dismissed me.

"You may show yourself out, Miss Sterling. I need to get back to work."

I slowly withdrew my arm - the olive branch. "Again, I'm so sorry. I never meant to call you by an incorrect name. I'll show myself out."

Maddy was never going to forgive me or understand how I could make such a mistake. But a small part of me questioned Mrs. Yates' response.

Seriously? A bit excessive, don't you think? Say your name, Mrs. Yates, ten times in a row, and see if you don't hear at least one that sounds like Bates.

However, no matter how ridiculous I thought it was, Maddy wasn't going to agree. If I determined that Mrs. Yates' reaction was over-the-top, I was one-hundred-percent confident Maddy's would match or even be slightly more extreme.

Chapter 12

Eleanor - 2014

There were two sides to every story, and I was aware that a stranger wouldn't necessarily believe me if I claimed that my life was fucked up. From the outside, I appeared like a normal young lady. Weighing in at one hundred and twenty pounds and five-feet-six inches tall, I had a healthy physique, thick, shoulder-length straight brown hair. I was well-behaved in school and received excellent grades. My clothes were clean, sometimes too small and never in-style, but other than that, I was a typical teenage girl, or at least that was what I convinced myself that other people thought. I tried to blend in.

Teenagers exaggerated all the time. However, unfortunately for me, I wasn't stretching the truth. The universe was lucky that I turned out as admirable as I did. The odds hadn't been stacked in my favor.

Following the hot soup science experiment that sent my father to the burn unit, Mother never asked me any questions. She didn't question the events of the evening described to her by the police.

Not even a simple *where were you, Eleanor? Rocky only knows how to run the TV remote. The microwave is too complicated for his dumb ass. Did you warm up the soup for him?* Or *why?*

The emergency personnel called her at the bar asking her to come home. I remembered hearing the paramedic talking to her on the phone. Initially, he simply requested that she come home because there had been an accident; however, I assume from the side of the conversation that I listened to, she wasn't handling the lack of information very well.

"Mrs. Cutter, your husband has had an accident… No, he is still alive… Well, we're here at your home because he called 911… He has severe burns on his…groin area…It looks like it was from soup, very hot soup."

When she arrived, Rocky had been sedated, so he wasn't screaming like he was when the first splash of boiling hot soup fell on his lap and burned straight through his worn-out sweatpants. From my corner of the room, I watched her as she answered questions.

"Where were you at 8:10 this evening?"

"Seriously? You're gonna ask me my freakin' alibi? You called me at work, remember? I was at work!" Mother didn't handle stress well. She was pacing back and forth in the kitchen as she looked around our apartment. With her head tilted to the side like a puppy did when it heard the word *treat*, she eyed me up and down when Rocky was taken away in the ambulance. I could see the wheels turning, but like a hamster on a wheel, she wasn't making any progress.

Years later, she still didn't question his sudden death, as Rocky wasn't exactly the vision of a healthy lifestyle. As a heavy drinker who smoked like a chimney, he didn't exercise, and unless Budweiser was made from vegetables, he didn't consume anything healthy. When Mother's friends stopped by to share their condolences in the weeks following his death, I heard her mumble that she was sure that it was his liver. However, out of the corner of her eye, she'd suspiciously glance in my direction to gauge my reaction.

After Rocky was eliminated from our lives, Mother and I adopted a new normal. We led separate lives, co-existed in the same apartment. In the mornings, I walked to school and returned home as she was getting ready to go to work.

A few things changed. There was no stale beer lingering in the air, and a fresh coat of white paint had lightened up our living space. We didn't tiptoe around anyone for fear of poking the bear. We opened the drapes, used plug-in air fresheners, and always kept the toilet seat down.

But some things never changed. She still didn't show me any affection, attention, or care. I was still left to raise, fend, and take care of myself. There were days that we didn't even speak to each other.

To pay our bills, Mother continued to waitress double shifts most days. Thankfully, her curvy figure, big smile, and flirtatious nature earned her generous tips. We were able to stay in our dingy apartment that I'd called home my whole life. Sometimes, you needed to be thankful for the little things.

As a neglected child, I grew up not focusing on possessions or gestures of affection. For example, she bought groceries and, as she reminded me, "I let you eat it, don't I?" She shared food and her income with me. Honestly, I didn't remember ever going to bed starved for food, just love. For this small token, I was grateful.

So, when it was my sixteenth birthday, I didn't expect a gift nor did I even think my mother would remember. Birthdays were simply another day. Forget Valentine's Day, the Fourth of July, Halloween, Thanksgiving. When Rocky was alive, the only thing he liked about the holidays was to pocket the time and a half-pay. Any holiday that had to do with religion was mocked. Christmas break was just a couple weeks out of school that meant I stayed in my room reading books - my only distraction from my rotten life. Celebrations were a normal activity.

However, after Rocky died, I wondered if some of our family traditions could change. When I inquired if we could purchase a Christmas tree, Mother and I ended up in a heated conversation.

"Eleanor, are you even aware that Christmas is a celebration of Jesus' birthday? Do you really think there's a God? And if there's a God, do you want to support one that blessed us with this wonderful life?"

Even though we were on the same page with our religious beliefs, I also enjoyed pushing her buttons. I had learned from the best.

"God didn't give you this wonderful life, Mother. This is the result of your life choices. No reason to blame a higher power for the rotten life that you earned fair and square. You need to take responsibility for your misery."

"You're a little bitch, you know that?"

"Learned from the best."

I didn't win that argument - we didn't buy an evergreen tree. I wasn't necessarily interested in celebrating Jesus' birthday. The pretty glow that the lights created in the corner of a room was the only reason that I wanted a Christmas tree.

The holiday that I chose to celebrate was my birthday. I'd saved up enough money with my dog-walking jobs to hop on a city bus, treat myself to a movie, and splurge on every bit of sugar from the concession stand. I was looking forward to watching *Gone Girl* at a local movie theater.

As I was getting dressed in a pair of clean clothes for my solo sweet sixteen adventure, my mother knocked on my door. She wasn't one for pleasantries or even a polite goodbye before heading off to work her dinner shift. Normally, the slam of the door would announce her departure. We didn't waste words.

I was a bit hesitant by her sudden, polite gesture - a knock - to enter my space.

"Come in?" It came out like a question because I was so shocked that I wasn't sure if I had heard a knock, or maybe she dropped something on the floor near my bedroom.

As she peeked her head in the door, the first thing that sprouted in my mind was that she looked old. On a normal day, we never stood close together, so I hadn't noticed. But close up, I could see the bags hanging under her glassy eyes while wrinkles surrounded their oval shape. Her skin, which used to be wrinkle-free and glowing, now appeared yellow and tired. Gray sprinkled her dark hair that was tied up in a high ponytail. The years since Rocky passed had been hard on her. She worked more than fifty hours a week on her feet. Additionally, her steady consumption of alcohol reached a new level. The moral of the story was that she didn't take care of herself. Never had, never would. A lot like Rocky.

"Happy Birthday, Ellie." She hadn't used my nickname since I was young and we were both happy. When she took two steps into my room, she glanced around like she'd never been in there before. Honestly, it had probably been a few years. Her eyes stopped on my drawings that I had taped up above my needed-a-paint-job desk. One drawing was of our neighbor's cat Willow as it perched itself up on their deck banister. It amazed me how it could continue to balance like that for so long when obvious laws of gravity were being fought. Willow wasn't a thin cat. She was lazy and an obvious over-eater. It had taken me hours to sketch her, and she sat there the whole time.

The second drawing was of Piper. I had sketched it when she was studying in the library one afternoon. From the opposite side of the table, I had sat mesmerized. We hadn't been friends yet, so I awkwardly admired her from afar. Her close physical presence was too distracting for me to study, so I sketched instead.

I memorized her details - her pouting lips that appeared stained from licking raspberries, her dainty nose that was slightly up-turned at the tip, and the copper-colored freckles that dusted her cheeks. Her hair was tied up on the top of her head in a messy bun, but a few stragglers fell down along her cheekbones. No excess makeup coated her face or eyelids. Her eyelashes were faintly brushed with a few strokes of mascara. Without sounding too prideful, my drawing was an amazing portrayal of Piper. However, no one outside my room would see it.

Her gaze was focused on her schoolwork. Out of habit, she was biting the bottom corner of her lip. Her right hand was jotting down notes from her textbook. On her left wrist, I drew a bracelet that I imagined giving her someday. It was a white Pura Vida bracelet with a delicate white daisy on it. I'd overheard her retelling one of her friends about the study date with Fritz when he brought her a dozen daisies, her favorite flower.

"Fritz is so observant. He noticed that I doodled little daisies in my notes. When he finally got the nerve to ask me out, he bought me real ones. Now, in his notes to me, he draws loops around a dot."

I thought it was pretty cheesy, but then again, I'd never been in love, so maybe if I was, it would change my perspective. The highest feeling I've ever had was infatuation.

My mother had never met Piper, so I was sure that she had no idea who I'd drawn a portrait of.

I cleared my throat so that I was able to choke out my gratitude. "Ummm...thanks."

"I got you a little gift."

If I thought I was shocked by her sudden appearance in my bedroom doorway, I was sure my facial expression revealed a higher level of astonishment. She handed me a pink gift bag stuffed with matching pink tissue paper. When I took it from her, I noticed that her gift was rather heavy. *Maybe a jar of spaghetti sauce?* I had no idea.

"It's a dildo. I wish someone would've given me one when I was your age. I humped any penis that smiled at me. This miraculous toy could've helped with my raging hormones and then maybe I wouldn't have ended up in this dump pregnant with you." Raising her arms, she pointed to our apartment.

I would've liked to remind her that Rocky had been dead for years, and yet we still remained living here. She was used to blaming him or God for everything bad in her life. She couldn't even stop after he was dead and buried.

Furthermore, I couldn't find the words. I was speechless because she remembered my birthday and took the time to buy me a gift. Of course, I realized it was an exceptionally inappropriate gift to give her sixteen-year-old daughter, let alone anyone but yourself.

"Plus, you don't seem to have any friends or potential, so condoms and birth control seemed like a waste of money. This little purple guy seemed more up your alley. You'll have to pick up some batteries, but give it a whirl. Life changing."

As she started to pull my bedroom door shut, she commented, "You could at least say thank you."

I picked up my jaw off the floor and managed to utter my appreciation for her unexpected, unsuitable thoughtfulness. I wished I had the power to rewind my life and enjoy the idea that my mother loved me and remembered my birthday, and then end the scene there. Erase the giant phallic gift and the cruel jab about me not having any friends. Then it would've been a memory I could have cherished; however, like normal, the moment was tarnished.

There were two sides to every story, but the facts remained the same - my mother gave me a dildo for my sweet sixteen. Sweet sixteen and never been kissed. But according to her recommendation, I should learn to sexually please myself with a big purple dildo operating on two C-batteries.

Messed up? Yeah, I thought so.

Chapter 13

Maddy - 2015

I knew that I was no angel. I was aware that I pushed people's buttons, pissed people off, took advantage of their weaknesses, and even participated in illegal activities. To feel alive, I wanted to feel, not drift through life. I knew that we were all different; Piper would rather live simply surrounded by only family and a few friends. If you drew her lifeline on a piece of paper, it would be straight. No sharp spikes, no risks, no fun. PG Piper.

My life resembled a heartbeat monitor - up and down with pages and pages of activity. I never planned on sliding into the things that I wanted. Hell no! I grabbed and yanked the things I craved. And I would never settle. I just wasn't made that way. Maybe Piper and I split that gene. She was patient and willing to wait for things to happen, while I was sprinting to the finish line to seize my wildest desires.

With that being said, hearing the word *no* wasn't a welcomed response. It ignited a flame of interest. I wanted what I was denied even more after hearing that two-letter word. There was no holding me back. As a child, if I asked for a scoop of ice cream and my request was denied, I couldn't leave the yearning alone. Even if I wasn't hungry for ice cream anymore or we had gotten a cookie instead, I would later sneak to the kitchen, dig into the freezer, and eat right out of the carton of rocky road. I'd gorge myself until my stomach hurt. My body would regret my compulsion, but my mind was victorious in winning the battle.

I must've been wired differently. As soon as I heard the word *no*, I wanted to know *why not*. During my childhood, my mom claimed that I had two favorite questions - *why* and *why not*.

As my responsible parent, she informed me of all the dangers and consequences of what happened to people who smoke. I heard everything that she explained, but the question that really interested me the most was if an intelligent person knew that they'd have a higher risk of getting lung cancer because of continued smoking, why did they keep doing it? In the years before this scientific discovery, I could understand the temptation - it looked cool, everyone was doing it, it relaxed you, it suppressed your appetite. But scientific studies had proved without a doubt that smoking led to lung cancer.

Most recently, the tobacco industry created an option to rid smokers of their biggest complaint - which surprisingly wasn't lung cancer - but smelling like smoke.

Introducing the vape pen! If you thought holding a smelly, flaming cigarette looked hot, check out this cool, high-tech vape pen.

Not only did the tobacco industry eliminate the awful smell, but they also made it taste better. The new fruit flavors appealed to the younger generation of smokers. Mango was my favorite flavor - it reminded me of the fruit snacks I used to consume.

After deciding to experiment, I understood why people still participated in dangerous activities when they knew the dangers - curiosity. In my situation, I believed that I was invincible. I was young and had my whole life to worry about dying and cancer.

My curiosity was to blame for a lot of my poor choices. Sometimes, I simply wanted to see what would happen. I was performing my own experiments - I learned something in school called *trial and error* - on my own body, at my own risk.

When vaping stopped being a thrill, I turned to alcohol, but not the typical teenage wine cooler. Hell no! For years, I'd heard the stories and the country songs about all the wonderful men of alcohol - Jack Daniels, Captain Morgan, Jose Cuervo, Jim Beam, and Johnny Walker. I wanted to meet them and create my own tall tales of our adventures.

Vomiting and dry heaving for four hours led me to conclude, "Maddy doesn't handle alcohol well." Half a bottle of Jim Beam and coke was too much for a girl of only one hundred pounds.

Maverick drank the other half, and he wasn't sick. He claimed that his only side effect was a headache. Thank goodness that my family assumed that it was the flu and nursed me back to health.

Marijuana entered the party scene as soon as alcohol was ejected. It was easily accessible since it was becoming medically legal in several states. The relaxing effects were fine for the nights that we hung out in Maverick's basement and turned on a comedy like *The Hangover* for a couple of hours. Every joke and punchline was beyond hilarious.

Mr. Jarro - Daniel Jarro - was another obvious *no*, but that, of course, added to the excitement of my personal dare. The chase wasn't much of a chase since I knew he was interested in exploring every nook and cranny of my body. His eyes gave away that much.

When he finally surrendered to his desires for me, my body experienced a thunder of desire as his mouth traveled all over my body. Thank goodness for a mature, skillful lover. Sex would never be the same. My flame of desire burned for him.

Speaking of fire... In elementary school, a fireman - a well-built man wearing a very solid uniform - visited our class to discuss the dangers of fire. What we should do in case of a fire emergency, what happened if our clothing caught on fire - *stop, drop, and roll* - what to do if we saw smoke - *get low; smoke likes to touch ceilings* - and what number to call – *911*. In the video that he showed the class, a house was completely engulfed in flames within ten minutes. The fireman explained that in one hour, the house was reduced to ash. My classmates' eyes were wide with wonder and fear. Mouths were shaped in the letter O. There was no side talking or inappropriate giggling.

But what I recall most of all was the overwhelming curiosity that filled me. Watching a fire take over a home in a matter of minutes. Engulfing everything in its path. Eating, chewing, and spitting out everything. I wasn't afraid. What I felt was *dazzled*.

When I arrived home from school that afternoon, I did exactly what the fireman told me *not* to do - I played with fire. I found a box of matches and some cardboard and hid in the backyard.

It wasn't long before I created a small fire. It was a caveman fascination, and I enjoyed watching the destruction. Everything that the beautiful yellow and amber flames touched turned to ash. A piece of paper sizzled in a matter of seconds. The stick that I found flamed right up and became too hot to hold.

I didn't become Drew Barrymore in the *Fire Starter*, but it was then that I realized adults had secret reasons for telling us no - they kept all the best things for themselves.

Chapter 14

Piper - 2014

When I met Fritz, I had been anything but impressed. The entire female student body thought that he was dreamy and the most eligible sophomore wandering around our over-crowded halls. Everyone knew Fritz. He was confident and involved. A Zac Efron-like boy living in Pine Hill. When his beautiful, full lips formed into a smile, a small dimple magically appeared on his left cheek. He casually ran his long fingers through his wavy, sandy brown hair. He waved at buddies with his bulging biceps as they passed between classes. Always surrounded by friends - laughing and having a good time.

But to me, his Sociology tutor, he had been simply another smelly, male hormone who probably didn't understand feminism, so he requested a female tutor. I hadn't been thrilled with this late-notice assignment. I had received an email from my tutoring instructor, Ms. Knutson, during the last period. I needed to follow up with her.

Fritz strolled in exactly six minutes late as I looked at my watch, then at him, and back at my watch. My stiff back pinched in anger as my nostrils flared. Before he was able to utter a weak, lame-ass apology, I informed him with my teeth tightly clenched, "My time is as valuable as yours. Just because it's a free tutoring session, it doesn't entitle you to be disrespectful."

With my foot, I shoved the hard, metal chair out from under the table, an obvious signal that he should sit down so we could get started. Ms. Knutson's email had informed me to review the chapter on the five basic sociological perspectives. As soon as he sat down, he fumbled with the zipper on his NorthFace backpack, quickly pulling out his notebook and sociology textbook. He was a bit rattled. Fritz probably thought his charm and good looks would excuse his poor manners. He was wrong.

"We'll start with functionalism. This concept explains that all sections of society are reliant on each other to maintain normalcy." Sociology spiked an interest with me so it was easy for me to get lost in the content.

He cleared his throat to get my attention because I was absorbed in sociology terms. "Sorry to interrupt, but do you have a pencil that I could borrow?"

If I was only slightly annoyed by his tardy arrival, I was fuming by his inability to be prepared. Steam rolled out of my ears. My cheeks burned with rage. I quickly retrieved a sharpened pencil from my backpack, tossing it in his direction as I continued to discuss the five basic sociological perspectives.

"Family, government, economy, education, and religion are the social institutions that functionalism affects. Without balance in government, for example, our economy suffers."

"I'm so sorry. Miss...? I didn't get your name."

I paused long enough to answer his question even though I wasn't interested in getting on a first-name basis with him. "Piper. Now, can we get back to the assignment, please? You've wasted over ten minutes of our time already."

"Yes, sorry. I didn't want to seem...rude." He said it as if referring to *my* behavior. "I appreciate the help, Piper, I really do. Functionalism..." He was frantically writing down the definition that I rattled off a few seconds ago.

"It's in our book. You don't need to write it down."

"It helps me to remember. It's okay. You do your part, and I'll do my best to keep up and absorb it all."

I could tell that he was really trying to be nice and polite. I took a deep breath and continued. My volunteer tutor job was to assist other students in getting caught up in their schoolwork, help them to better understand the material, and create a great reference on my resume - not to make friends. I was good at my job. Even though that afternoon's session started off rocky, I vowed to help this walking hormone understand sociological differences in cultures.

When our hour was up, my mouth was dry, and I was sure that his hand ached from all the pages of notes that he vigorously scribbled. He'd asked a few relevant questions regarding the material that made me question why I was tutoring him. He seemed to understand the basics but maybe was a poor test-taker. I wasn't sure, and I wasn't allowed to know – above my pay grade as a volunteer.

"Thanks, Piper. I sure appreciate the fifty-four minutes, and I promise to be on time next week. My name is Fritz, by the way." He flashed one of his famous grins that made all the girls melt - yep, now I got it. My knees felt a little weaker when the smile was pointed in my direction.

"You're welcome. And yes, I know who you are." I awkwardly started bagging my textbook and supplies. He left the small tutoring room as I kept my eyes down on my belongings.

I had not expected that flutter in my heart or weakening of my knees. That had never happened before.

"You're an idiot, Piper." Sometimes talking to myself helped me gain perspective so I wouldn't be tempted to tell Maddy. She was just as honest as my head and often as brutal. "Seriously, he's a big-time jock. Not going to be interested in a nerdy loner like you. Stop with the butterflies."

I tutored Fritz for a total of three more sessions, and each time, he asked insightful questions that made me wonder why he needed a tutor in the first place. But again, not my deal. But still...

At the beginning of the fourth and final tutoring session, Fritz peeked around the doorway. Only his head was visible to me. His knee-weakening grin spread across his boyish face. "I'm two minutes early. Can I come in?"

His punctuality had become a bit of a joke between us. He was always early after that first session and very appreciative of my time when the session was over. During our second tutoring session, he told me, "I've always been pretty casual about clocks" - and gave me a little wink - "but what you said that first day really resonated with me. I never thought about how my tardiness might make someone else feel. I just thought that being late didn't bother me, so it was okay. But you were so right. I should value other people's time as well. Coach Wagner really appreciates the new-and-improved punctual Fritz."

When he asked permission to enter the room because he was two minutes early, my smile crept onto my face without hesitation. His charm and wit were breaking down my wall.

"Yes, please come right in."

That was when I noticed *why* he was only peeking his head around the doorway. In his hands, he gripped an enormous bouquet of white daisies - which he knew was my favorite flower because he had asked me why all the doodles in my notebook were dots with loops around them.

"I know I'm no artist, but that's a daisy. Not a dot," I'd refuted.

"Oh, yes. I see it now. Cute."

And a couple of weeks later, there he was standing in the entryway of the tutoring lab holding at least two dozen yellow dots with white loops around them.

Wall broken.

He asked me out halfway through the tutoring session. We were discussing how an individual was shaped by the society in which they lived.

"Of course, I would be a completely different man-"

"Man?" Teasing him felt natural. Maddy would call it flirting, but I hadn't had much experience with flirting, so I didn't know.

"Yes, a man. I'd be a completely different *man* if I'd been raised in Alaska, for example. Instead of baseball, I would've played hockey and learned to fish rather than golf. Not sure what else I know how to do. I seem talentless at the moment."

I giggled at his analogy. I couldn't imagine it because previously he told me hated everything to do with fish and seafood - the smell, the scales, the taste. He thought that they were too squirmy.

Our eyes met briefly. We were sitting next to each other - he had pointed out at our last session that if he sat next to me, I wouldn't have to keep turning my laptop so he could see what I was referring to. When he had arrived at session number four with flowers, he settled in the chair next to me. Felt awkward initially, but he had a way of putting me at ease.

"I asked you out yesterday after lunch, and you just laughed in my face. Honestly, I'd be lying if I said it didn't break my heart a little."

"Huh? What? You didn-"

"But your sister kindly explained that she was your identical twin. I knew you had a sister, but you didn't mention that she was an exact replica of you." He was grinning from ear-to-ear as he shared the story of his recent public rejection.

"Sorry, the fact that I was a twin never came up in conversation. You must've talked to Maddy after lunch yesterday."

"Yep. It was Maddy whom I embarrassingly hit on and was harshly rejected by. Completely made a fool of myself in front of Maddy and her giggling posse."

I could only imagine the scene - Maddy surrounded by her heavily made-up, stylish, hair-teased friends. I pictured Dee, Tania, and Kat sizing up every inch of Fritz. Cataloging, judging, and absorbing everything about him from the approximate shoe size, the name brand of his jeans, shirt tucked in or out, shaving status, and every strand of his wavy hair. I was a bit surprised that Maddy turned down his invitation and didn't mention it to me last night.

"In between her loud cackle and her friends' giggles, she managed to tell me, 'You must be Piper's new tutee that she claims is super hot and munchy.'"

My cheeks flushed to a flaming red color. Oh, Maddy, how easily she could embarrass me with her blunt honesty. A couple of nights ago when we were sharing stories about our days at school, I did mention Fritz. I said those exact words - *hot* and *munchy*.

How was it that she could remember my exact words, but she couldn't pass a memorization test to save her life?

"Hey, don't worry. It's all good. Except that now that I *know* that you think I'm hot, I think you'll accept my invitation to a movie this weekend." He winked at me, flashed his award-winning smile, and nudged me with his shoulder.

He was right. I said yes and silently thanked Maddy for using her big mouth. It helped to break the ice.

Chapter 15

Eleanor - 2016

After losing both of my shitty parents, I earned the title *orphan*. Most people were saddened by that word. The word *orphan* suggested loneliness, abandonment, and lack of love. The famous Orphan Annie from the movies only wanted someone to call family. She yearned to be loved and cherished. Her naivety led her to believe that *family* was a magical word that would lead to security and acceptance.

If I could've had a conversation with red-haired, sweet Annie, I'd persuade her that being part of a family didn't guarantee love and fulfillment. I'd show her the physical scars - the cigarette burn on my thigh, the one-inch scar above my eyebrow from a flying plate because Rocky's dinner tasted like shit - and detail the mental ones - too many to list. Sometimes, like in my life, family brought out the worst in each other.

My mother always pushed Rocky's buttons. She knew every one of his limits and was well-versed in where his patience stopped and where his rage started. Making him snap was a game to her. It provided her more fuel to not love him and provided her someone to blame for how miserable her life was.

For my father, the word *family* granted him his own private punching bags. Behind closed doors, within our four walls, he released his rage without any witnesses, without any disorderly conduct violations. We received - but didn't accept - his physical and emotional abuse because we were his family. I was taught and believed that this was the purpose of a family.

For me, the word *family* meant being trapped. These two adults who were supposed to unconditionally love me and keep me safe were the two people who caused me the most heartache. Because of them, my heart felt hollow. For fear of punishment, my emotions were kept to a minimum. As a child, if I became excited about a discarded set of broken crayons, Rocky would snap them into tiny, unusable pieces. If I cried because I didn't want Mother to leave me alone with Rocky while she went to work, I would be slapped for my excessive emotion. Friendships were almost impossible for me to maintain due to my lack of self-worth. It was easier to stay hidden in the shadows where I avoided all contact with people.

At seven in the morning, there was a knock at our apartment door. I was getting ready for school. I hadn't even noticed that Mother didn't come home the night before. I didn't shed a single tear when the officer informed me about the accident.

My mother drove her car straight into oncoming traffic after too many cocktails following a night shift. I was an official orphan. I felt free. I had no one to tell me what a waste of space I was, no one to scream profanity at me, no one to claim that I was the reason for their misery.

The young male officer dressed in his freshly pressed blues inquired if I had someone I could live with. My facial expression must have revealed a look of utter confusion.

"You're only seventeen, right? Until you're eighteen; you legally need a guardian to live with. It's the law."

"I'll be eighteen next month. I'll call my grandma. My dad's mom. I'm sure that we can work something out until I'm eighteen."

"Your landlord informed me that your mom was behind on the rent. They'll want you out by the end of the week. I'm sorry, Miss Cutter. If you need help moving your things, please let me know." He held out a wrinkled business card.

"No worries. I don't have much. Thanks for stopping by."

Did I really just thank the officer for stopping by to tell me that my mother is dead? I must've sounded like a complete idiot.

As I closed the paper-thin front door, I looked around the shabby apartment. Everything in this shithole was all mine. They were both gone. A smile formed on my face. I couldn't help it. I didn't think that I'd ever been this happy or relieved in my whole seventeen years. Even though I didn't know where my next meal was coming from, my heart was at peace.

Grams and I had always tolerated and somewhat enjoyed each other's company. We were both survivors of abuse. We were a lot alike in other ways too. Besides the space between our front teeth and our lack of tact, neither of us said much. We were both observers and didn't like to waste words. It was a coping mechanism.

When I called her to inform her that my mother had died, she abruptly responded, "Definitely landed in Hell on her big fat ass."

Grams' comment brought another smile to my lips. I'd smiled more in the last couple of hours than I had for months. It felt foreign. It was no surprise that Grams wasn't saddened by my mother's death - there was no love lost between the two of them. They both equally detested the other.

"Grams, can I stay with you for a while? I guess Mother didn't pay last month's rent, so they're kicking me out at the end of the week. And since I'm not eighteen, I can't live on my own."

"Sure, honey. I ain't got much, but I can share what I do. I can't even climb the damn stairs anymore, so the penthouse is all yours. Will be nice to have someone around." That was the nicest thing someone had said to me in a long time. Grams had been through a lot, and I appreciated anything that she was willing to share.

"Thanks, Grams. I look forward to staying with you. I'll help with whatever you need. And I promise not to be a bother."

After our little pleasantries were done, we briefly discussed funeral arrangements.

"Ain't gonna waste my money on her soul. She was the Devil's child. No funeral." Grams had no money to spare. When my father died, we didn't have a funeral either. Too expensive and honestly, we knew that he traveled straight to Hell, so why bother with formalities that wouldn't make a difference anyhow. "Loved my boy, but he turned out as rotten as his daddy. Can't save souls that have already made a pact with the Devil."

Moving in with Grams had seemed like a step up for my life. I was thrilled with our arrangement. There were two bedrooms and a bathroom on the top floor of her small, old home. I used one bedroom for myself and to store my wardrobe. In the second room, I moved the couch Mother and I purchased after we sold everything that reminded us of

Rocky. We threw out his beloved, old recliner - good riddance, because neither one of us wanted to keep things around that reminded us of him.

Grams physically needed help with chores around the house - from yard work and fixing a step on her front deck to everyday cleaning. Her knees were shot after too many years of extra weight and not getting to the doctor soon enough to do anything to repair the damage. She didn't even attempt the stairs to the second floor and claimed that she hadn't set a foot up there in years. It was completely disgusting - dusty, moldy, packed with boxes, but it was all mine.

The bathroom reeked to the high heavens - after a short week of living with her, I was already adopting her sayings. A plumber needed to fix the toilet and make sure there were no leaks before I planned on using it. But this felt like a home, like a family. Grams wanted me and needed me.

As I was unpacking boxes that I'd thrown together from the old apartment - figuring I'd sort them out later - I discovered a large manila envelope labeled, *Important*. Of course, I was curious to see what my mother would consider important. I tore it open.

There were two bank statements. One was under my mom's married name, Mary Jane Cutter, and the other statement was listed in her maiden name, Mary Jane Lacey. The Cutter bank statement was familiar to me because I used it recently to pay the overdue utilities and water bills before I moved out of our apartment. There had just been enough in that account.

However, the Lacey one claimed a balance of ten thousand dollars with a steady deposit made every month. The description line read, *CHILD SUPPORT for E. Cutter*.

Reading those four words made me tip over as I was squatting over the cardboard box. I landed on my ass with my mouth wide open. My brain couldn't comprehend what I was reading. My mother had been receiving child support...for me?

Rocky wasn't my biological father? Thank the Lord! But did he know? Why was the account listed in my mother's maiden name? My hunch was that she was hiding the money from Rocky, but why didn't she use the money to pay our bills?

I searched the statement for the date. January 13, 2002. That was fourteen years ago. I wondered if the account still existed and what the current balance was.

When I dialed the number listed on the bank statement, the receptionist wouldn't give me any helpful information. "You aren't listed on the account. Even though your mother is deceased, I'll need a copy of her death certificate before I can discuss her account or relinquish the assets to you. I'm sorry, Miss Cutter, but my hands are tied. It's the law."

The law sure wasn't very helpful - I couldn't live alone because it was the law. I couldn't get my hands on the money because it was the law. Were these laws supposed to help me?

I patiently waited and checked the mailbox every day for my mother's death certificate. In this age of technology, relying on snail mail for essential, vital information seemed idiotic. According to the state of Minnesota, it could take up to thirty days to rule her death as official. And then I'd have the power to find out who was making the monthly child support payments into my mother's unused account.

It might have been quicker to dig up her body and drag it to the bank myself.

Part of me wondered if she was blackmailing some lonely old man. Tricked him into believing that I was his daughter. Maybe he was married and needed to keep the affair and me a secret, so he paid her to shut her up.

The other part of me dreamed that Orphan Annie was right. My Daddy Warbucks was out there and couldn't wait to meet me. He'd adopt me and bring me home to live in his warm, inviting mansion where he'd spoil me rotten. His servants would wait on me, and I'd have no cares in the world. And Orphan Annie and I would be best friends.

I giggled at my unrealistic fantasies. Unfortunately, my mother blackmailing someone was the most likely scenario.

Chapter 16

Maddy - 2015

In order for Piper to complete a switcheroo for me, I promised several things that I didn't intend on following through with. This was not unusual. My poker face was ready.

"Another US history quiz? Seriously, Maddy, you can study for this, and I could help you. History is very interesting. Think of history like one of your reality TV shows - scandals, sex, murder, and mystery. It's all there in history." She used her fingers to count her points. "Watergate - scandal. Bill Clinton - sex. John F. Kennedy - murder. Alcatraz - the mysterious escape in 1962." She glanced down at my incomplete study guide.

I was no dummy. I enrolled in classes *after* the semester she'd completed them. That way she could always sub in for me if I needed her to. Or I purposely chose a desk behind a brainiac so I could borrow some of their answers.

Work smarter, not harder.

"Your quiz is on the US presidents. I can study with you, Maddy. I even have a fun way to remember all their names: Wilma And John Made Merry And Just Vanished."

I looked up at her with my crazy eyes darting back and forth.

She giggled. "The first letter of each word in that sentence is the last name of each of the US presidents in the order that they served our country. Washington, Adams, Jefferson, Madison, Monroe, Adams, Jackson, Van Buren. We could make up new sentences that would amuse you more, if that would help."

I shook my head. "Not interested. I have no need or interest to retain this information, Piper. My only interest is earning a passing grade so that I don't have to retake this boring-ass class, and I can graduate from this lame-ass high school to move onto bigger and better things. As a party planner, I'll never need to recite the US presidents in order to land a job."

"What if the party is *for* a US president?" She raised her eyebrows at me, trying to pique my interest. "Maddy, it isn't right. I can't keep doing this for you. You need to be responsible for your own grades and future. This is the last one. I'm finished. This was a childhood game that I should've discontinued a long time ago."

I'd agree to whatever terms that she set as long as this quiz was behind me. I had no interest in learning a bunch of stuffy, wrinkly old men's names.

While Piper was in my history class, I attended her science class. Unfortunately for me, Eleanor, my sister's leech and charity project, was her lab partner. Piper had drawn me a little map of where she sat in the room. Third row on the right-hand side of the room at the lab table next to Eleanor.

"Eleanor is always the first to arrive and takes her seat on my right. Let her lead the assignment and the discussion. Science excites her, so she'll be chatty." Piper explained to me.

"Eleanor Cutter?"

"Yes, Maddy. She's quite nice if you'd give her a chance."

"Don't have time for a chance. Just need you to ace my test. Thanks for this, Puppet!"

"Then, after the Yates' interview, no more switcheroos, right? We're retiring this game?"

"Piper, you get so uptight. Pull that cob out of your butt. Loosen up and have fun with it. When you play me, you need to be more carefree and flirtatious." I flashed her a little wink. We had been lying on her double bed discussing our plans for the next day of school. We needed to wear the same style jeans so we wouldn't need to switch those and the same gray T-shirt under whatever jacket - me - and sweatshirt - Piper - was wearing. One loose ponytail - me - and one messy bun - Piper. We'd wear similar shoes since we had different size feet.

"Flirtatious? That's the adjective you're going to use to describe your ridiculous behavior that you radiate toward the entire male student body? It's almost too sweet to describe you." I knew I could get her to loosen up a bit. She was teasing me. "How about *seductive* or *provocative* or even *scandalous*?"

"Well, I'll have to look up what those big words mean, but if they mean super friendly, then yep! That's me."

She tossed one of her throw pillows at me. "Oh, Maddy, there's never a dull moment with you around."

Eleanor nudged me with her sharp, boney elbow. "Hello, earth to Piper. Did you get my text?"

After I finished my boredom-yawn, I shook my head at her question. Piper was right - Eleanor was a talker. All I had to do was nod every now and then to let her know that I was still paying attention.

"Piper, there's something I need to tell you." Eleanor's voice had dropped almost to a whisper. Her eyes darted back and forth to make sure no one was eavesdropping on our conversation. *Don't worry, no one cares what you say, nerd.* "Are you free after school?"

I had no idea what Piper's response would be, if she was busy after school or not, and there was no way I'd continue this charade a moment longer than I needed to. I informed her that I was busy.

"Well, honestly, I can hardly wait any longer to tell you. It's gonna be life-changing, Piper. I guess there's no time like the present." She firmly plopped down in the chair and arranged herself so she was perched on the edge of her seat. Her big bug eyes honed in on me as if I should know what was happening. It was hard to play along when I was utterly uninterested in what she was about to say. "You might want to lean in a bit. I don't think that you'll want other people to overhear what I'm about to say."

"I don't understand." This sounded juicy. Maybe I *was* interested. I sat up a little bit straighter and tentatively leaned a smidge closer to Eleanor, who smelled of moth balls and Lysol spray. If this big nerd proclaimed that she was in love with Piper, I wouldn't be surprised at all. It was obvious how she yearned for my twin's attention.

My eyes were locked on the space between her teeth.

"Remember that banking statement that I mentioned a few weeks ago? The one with all the money in it?" She paused, waiting for a response. I nodded so she would continue. In order to relay this conversation to Piper, I'd have to pay attention. I didn't want Eleanor to realize we'd pulled a twin switcheroo. "Well, before school this morning, I stopped by the bank with my mother's death certificate so they would give me the account information. And I *got* the info." Her one eyebrow rose.

Wish I could do that. Neat party trick. I vaguely remembered that someone else could raise their left eyebrow, but I couldn't remember at the moment who... From Eleanor's tone of voice, I could tell that Piper was supposed to know what she was talking about.

Use your top-notch acting skills, Maddy. I widened my big blue eyes and leaned a bit closer. Even though I needed to breathe through my mouth in order to sit that close to her, I managed to ask, "And?"

"Piper, you aren't going to believe me when I tell you this, but it's the absolute truth. And never in my wildest dreams had I thought that this would be the answer. The monthly deposits into that untouched account were made by your father, Ryan Sterling."

No acting skills needed - I was shocked. *What the hell is she talking about? Dad made monthly deposits into a bank account? Why?* Eleanor's mom died - that was part of the puzzle. But I was missing too many pieces. My head swarmed with questions.

She reached out and put her warm, pale hand on my arm. I looked down at her gesture. I didn't understand.

"Piper, as weird as this sounds, it's true - we *are* half-sisters."

Chapter 17

Piper - 2016

Once a month, I entered the school before anyone else. As I strolled down the deserted hallway, the echo of my footsteps bounced off the walls. The smell of bleach lingered in the air after the overnight cleaning crew had finished their job of sanitizing every surface. Everything was still and peaceful. Lectures and the latest gossip hadn't yet poisoned the peace and quiet in the solid, sturdy building. It was hours before the chaos of the school day began. My feet led me to my favorite room in the building: the library.

Because I'd volunteered in the library since my freshman year, the librarian had gifted me a master key at the beginning of my senior year. "This is completely unheard of, Piper. I know that I don't need to say these words out loud, but I'm going to because it'll be my hide that is skinned if anything happens. You must *not* lose this key or even disclose to anyone that you possess it."

It was an enormous responsibility that I had been granted. I felt complete gratitude and pride at having the school's trust. I hadn't taken my duty lightly. The only people that knew I opened up the library once a month was my family. Fritz didn't even know.

I loved to sit there as the sun rose and pressed bright, warm rays through the thick east-facing windows. Small dust particles danced in the air. I walked through them, causing them to float around my shape. They reminded me of that scene in *Footloose* when individual dancing broke out. The dancers - dust particles - separated to allow the solo performance but continued to dance themselves.

Not only did I love the sunshine awakening the room, but I also loved the smell of the books. Old, dry, musty pages of entertainment. Sometimes in the quiet of the morning, I closed my eyes and pretended to listen to the characters of my favorite books speaking to me.

Beth March would tell me, "Every day I lose a little, and feel more sure that I shall never gain it back. It's like the tide, Jo, when it turns; it goes slowly, but it can't be stopped." And Kristin Hannah would whisper that "she knew this pain would fade again; like a sunburn, it would heal itself and leave her slightly more protected from the glare."

Harper Lee would advise, "You never really understand a person until you consider things from his point of view...until you climb inside of his skin and walk around in it."

As one of the stipulations of my library access, the librarian Mrs. McIntyre asked that I reshelve returned books. She was a new mother of twins, and after coming back from her maternity leave, she begged Principal Klawonn for an assistant.

Solution - free student assistance. Requirement - student with a key to the high school. Win-win.

After reshelving twelve books and dusting the fiction and mystery sections, I stuck in my earbuds, cranked up the volume to my favorite song, "Backroad Song" by Granger Smith, pulled out my advanced biology assignment, and plopped down on my stomach to get comfortable on the donated, lumpy couch.

Before I knew what was happening, someone aggressively covered my mouth with his hand, slid a blindfold over my eyes, and effortlessly flipped me onto my back and tied up my hands over my head. Because I was taken by complete surprise, this entire ambush happened in a matter of about twenty seconds.

I'd never been so scared in my whole life. My heart pounded in my chest as my heart beat overtime. My nostrils flared open as far as they could to steal air that my lungs desperately needed. Instant tears poured out of my eyes. I tried to bite the hand that was covering my mouth, but it was cupped firmly.

A rag replaced the rough, strong hand. I was completely vulnerable. Alone in the school at least an hour before the staff would arrive, two hours before students would filter in. Twenty minutes earlier, I'd said goodbye to the night janitor.

But who was my attacker? Who else had access to the school? Or did he break in?

While my logical thoughts tried to make sense of what was happening, my assailant tugged down my jeans to my ankles and cut off my underwear with something sharp - most likely a pair of scissors. I tried to spit out the rag so I could cry out, but my efforts were fruitless.

I wiggled and thrashed around on the couch to only receive a soft slap across the cheek. Odd. Why such a gentle slap when I was obviously about to be raped? Then I felt his hot breath and a tickle of whiskers on my neck as he sniffed my neck. *Is he smelling me?*

Because the volume on my earbuds was set at eight, I couldn't hear anything. I wasn't sure if he was panting or humming to himself. I could only hear my playlist. I never heard him enter the room or sneak up on me, but I heard his deep, raspy voice in my ear when there was a break in the music. He whispered, "Geez, taking this fantasy to a whole other level. Even a different perfume."

He pulled my arms over my head and yanked my sweatshirt above my head. After he pushed my bra off my breast, he suckled them aggressively. With his body pressed to mine, I could feel his desire pushing through his pants.

When his mouth stopped sucking on my nipples, his wet lips pressed on my neck. His teeth penetrated my skin. I turned my head back and forth trying to headbutt him. All my attempts were failing. His heavy breathing was an obvious sign that fighting him off turned him on more.

I decided to do the opposite - play dead. *Isn't that what possums do to make their mate less interested?*

It didn't work. He wasn't a pointless marsupial.

Seconds later, he entered me forcefully. With each penetration, he grew harder, and my fight for survival had died. I yelped in pain as I was ripped apart. I tried to concentrate on my breathing. If I could just breathe, maybe I would live.

There was nothing that I could do to stop him. The top of my head hit the back of the couch as he pounded into me. My hands were bound above my head with my shirt. My jeans circled my ankles. Laying helpless below him as he finished inside of me, I realized that it was over as quick as it had begun.

Oh my god...what if he kills me now?

But he didn't. Instead, he removed the stuffed rag from my mouth and passionately kissed me - at least, if you didn't consider the circumstances. It was a one-sided passionate kiss. His soft hands gently caressed my face, and his hostile tongue searched for mine. He was out of breath.

My response was shock and fear. He was obviously very turned on by what had just happened, and with his deep kiss, he thought that I'd feel the same way. I literally couldn't move. Tears continued to roll out of my eyes and pool inside the blindfold.

When he removed his mouth from my face, he chuckled in my ear. I could only hear a portion of what he whispered because the next song on my playlist was picking up the pace.

"Sorry about cutting off your panties. Need to go commando today. Total turn-on, by the way." He pulled my jeans up around my waist and yanked my sweatshirt down over my exposed breasts.

He whispered in my ear again, but I could barely make out his words because Little Big Town was belting out the chorus of "Tornado."

"I'm gonna -"

Lift this house.

"Now -"

Spin it all around.

"-d. Thank -"

Toss it in the air.

"- later -"

Put it in the ground.

He kissed the top of my head as he removed the blindfold and the binds that were holding my wrists together.

In hindsight, I knew that I should've screamed bloody murder. I should've opened my eyes and cataloged a list of details about him so I could report this violation to the police, but mentally I couldn't. I pressed my eyes shut as tight as I could and willed myself to go back in time - ten minutes before I was raped.

Erase this emotional wound. Dealing or thinking about what happened was too much to bear. Since my senses of touch, hearing, smell, and taste would forever be scarred by this man, I didn't feel the need to involve my vision in this trauma.

I'm a tornado, and I'm coming after you.

Chapter 18

Maddy - 2016

I lost that feeling of contentment - when you were happy or at peace with your life. I didn't know when that feeling stopped being a possibility. I just knew that it wasn't there. In the mornings, I didn't wake up refreshed and with a sense of endless possibilities. The feeling that filled my shell was more like dread. The majority of the time, emptiness inhabited my body.

Oddly, sadness didn't consume my heart when Mr. Jarro - Daniel - rejected me. I showed up at his apartment like I had done every Monday night for the past eight weeks to entertain and satisfy my sexual desires. Instead of him opening the door to welcome me inside, he blocked the doorway and informed me in a not very gentle way that our *thing* was over. He no longer wanted to explore my body, to whisper his desires in my ear, to nibble my earlobe, to hold me just minutes after climaxing. Our give-and-take was over.

"Excuse me. Who do you think you are? Why do you get to end things when it's convenient for you?" I'd seen him eyeing the new perky secretary in the office. She was more his age, but I wasn't used to being on this side of a breakup.

"Madison, I told you that our arrangement was only temporary. This" - he pointed at my chest and then at his - "wasn't a real thing. You fulfilled some of my fantasies, and I helped you get what you needed in my class. *Dar y recibir*. Sorry if you assumed something different."

I hated when he threw Spanish words into our conversations. He did it to make me feel inferior, make me feel beneath him.

"Oh, hell no! I knew what this" - I indicated more forcefully between our chests - "was from the start. How perverted of you to act out your sexual fantasies with a student struggling in your Spanish class. You won't get away unscarred, Daniel." My eye began to twitch, which it did when I was upset.

"Oh, yes, I will, Madison. Unless, of course, you don't mind not graduating in a month and retaking Spanish *este verano*." He looked directly at my twitching eye.

Damn it!

"After I expose how you seduced me, no one will force me to retake your class." Even though it had started as a personal dare to see if I could seduce him, I had to admit that I had enjoyed our encounters. What we might have lacked in common interests, we made up for between the sheets. He was an amazing teacher - not of Spanish. Hell no! I hadn't learned a word beyond *adios, hola*, and my favorite phrase, *vamos a follar*. The only lessons I had learned from him were sexual.

He was dressed in the same clothing he wore on the first night of our affair - in a plain white T-shirt and worn-out jeans. The T-shirt was wrinkled and gave the impression he'd just gotten out of bed. His jeans were faded with rips in the knees. His appearance screamed sexy. Everything about him filled my heart with desire. His lips were plump and full. His wavy hair - that I loved to run my fingers through - was a beautiful shade of chestnut, but his five o'clock shadow contained an auburn tint. I loved the color of his red-tinted beard. When the morning sun pierced the broken blinds in his bedroom, they sparkled to a golden hue.

On one of those quiet mornings when the sunshine tickled his whiskers, I'd secretly taken a picture with my phone. We were still tangled in the sheets from our activity the night before. He had peeked, noticing that I was awake and still lying naked next to him.

"Even before I opened my eyes, I knew you were still here because I could smell your sweet perfume. Tell me again where your parents think you are." He always wanted to make sure he knew the 'story.' He often reminded me, "You can't tell anyone, Madison. I'll lose my job, my reputation. We'd never see each other again."

"They think that I stayed overnight at Dee's. It's cool. Her parents are so preoccupied with their own lives that they'll never know or care if I was there."

"And Dee? What does she know?"

I hadn't revealed anything to Dee and that was what I told him. The story that I confessed to Dee was that I was seeing an older man. Since I was only seventeen, he'd be arrested, so we had to be very careful until I was a legal adult. Dee didn't bat an eye.

"You go get some, Mad! And give me detes on the mind-blowing sex. That's a fair trade for my silence." I held up my end of the bargain and recounted tales of our bedroom rodeos.

After Daniel brushed the hair from my eyes, he asked me, "*Otra pregunta* before you need to bugger off - did I hear you roll your Rs yesterday in the hallway when you said hello? Have you been practicing?"

Daniel Jarro with a fancy rolling R - I couldn't properly pronounce his last name and as a Spanish teacher and my lover, that bothered him. He wanted me to practice, but I had better things to do.

"Umm...no. You must've run into Piper in the hallway. She has rolling Rs mastered."

As I looked him up and down as he tried to break up with me, his attire had a different vibe. Plain white T-shirt and worn-out jeans screamed that he was trying to hold onto his youth, trying to appear relaxed and unfazed. This scene was foreign to me. I was unfamiliar with someone breaking up with *me*. Normally, I was the one to call it quits.

"Unfortunately, Madison, that's where you're incorrect. You think that you pursued me and that I acted on impulse, but *princesa*, I did not. I know that you can't get your official diploma without your Spanish credit. I have access to your records, Madison. You needed me as much, if not, more than I needed you."

His eyes traveled up and down my body as he purred that last sentence. I thought that he was going to change his mind and invite me into his apartment for one last buck. We'd recently role-played that I was his ranch hand. However, this stubborn cowboy's resolve was stronger than I thought.

"Madison, I know you. You don't care a lick about me. The only reason that you're hurt right now is because you don't accept rejection well. *Eres jovén*. You'll see this as a mistake soon and be thankful that it ended when it did." The left side of his lips lifted as if in a half smirk saying, "That sums it up. You are dismissed." He slowly closed his apartment door and left me standing in the hallway.

Damn it!

He was right. Honestly, I found his personality and interests - other than me - rather dull. When we weren't tangled in his bedsheets, the conversation didn't stimulate any interest. He wanted to discuss politics and current events.

Blah...blah...blah.

However, under the covers, he always owned my full attention. Obviously, I hadn't been a virgin when I began sleeping with him, but high school boys had *a lot* to learn. I'd miss those sweaty, orgasmic moments with him the most. He would trace the outline of my body with his index finger. It would brush the contours of my face, down my neck, over my shoulder, down my arm, and to my wrist. I remember when he had noticed my small, red, cloud-shaped birthmark on my wrist for the first time.

"Do you have any more of these on your body that I need to discover?" he had purred in my ear. His pillow voice always sent shivers up and down my spine.

Damn it!

He scheduled a test in his Spanish class the following week. Part of me wanted to turn around, pound on his door, and beg him to reconsider.

Keep me around until the end of the school year so I can breeze through graduation.

But like he said, he knew me.

Hopefully, my current grade in Spanish was high enough to suffer a failed test score. Since Piper was unwilling to perform another switcheroo, I would need to be creative with my test-taking ability - or lack thereof. I had no idea how I was gonna pass it.

I possessed a morsel of damaging information that Daniel wasn't aware of. More than a picture. More than a document. I didn't feel that this was the time to use it. I decided to hold onto my valuable knowledge until I needed to cash it in.

But when I did use it, Daniel would realize that it hadn't been me who fulfilled his last sick sexual fantasy, but someone who looked just like me.

Chapter 19

Piper - April 17, 2016

Telling Fritz I was pregnant over the phone after he lost a baseball game where he struck out two out of the three times that he batted wasn't the best timing. When was a good time to tell your naive high school boyfriend that he was going to be a dad at eighteen years old? I would speculate that the answer was *never*.

"What? What did you say, Piper? Did you just compare my loss of a game to you being pregnant?" He was as shocked at my poor delivery as I was. Those two little words - I'm pregnant - came spilling out when he started to whine about his deflated ego.

Unfortunately, my response was loud sobbing from my end of the cell phone. I pictured Fritz on a noisy, crowded school bus filled with sweaty jocks, who I was sure were all pouting about the big loss. He wasn't alone and wasn't able to properly hear what I was announcing to him. I prayed that no one overheard him. We didn't need this shameful news to spread on social media before we were even able to process the life-altering news ourselves.

"Shit. Are you sure?"

"Yes, I'm sure." That came out a bit sarcastic.

"How many tests did you take? The accuracy for home pregnancy tests is only like fifty percent, right?" Fritz had lowered his shaky voice so that no one could hear his sensitive questions. I imagined his eyes shifting to the nearby seats to make sure his closest teammates weren't eavesdropping on our conversation. Thank goodness for noise-canceling headphones.

"Fritz, I'm pregnant. I took three tests. I haven't had my period for two months and am utterly exhausted all the time. My breasts are tender, and obviously, I'm moody as hell. All the classic signs." I felt the need to spell it out for him, which rather annoyed me - another symptom of pregnancy, irritability. I should've been more patient with him. This wasn't the easiest news for either of us to digest.

The knowledge had only been mine for a total of two hours. Fritz had been competing in a baseball game in a neighboring town when I peed on the first stick. Before the two pink lines appeared, I had a sinking feeling that the results weren't going to progress in my favor. Normally, I passed every test, so why should I worry about this one with a fifty-fifty chance? I should've waited for him and done it together. This news wasn't something that I was prepared to deal with, especially alone.

The first emotion that had reared its head was dread. All my life I earned an easy, smooth path by working hard and following the rules, at least until recently. One rule was broken: *don't have sex until you're married* - who did that anymore? And my punishment was a life sentence.

Parenthood.

That was my initial, harsh reaction. Not proud of my first thought, but it was real.

Next, there was despair for this innocent baby who was growing inside me - unwanted and unplanned. He deserved a more positive response to the news of his creation. Babies were miracles and deserved to be cherished and anticipated.

Then self-pity completely engulfed my entire being. *Why me?* I was a good kid. I was a rule-follower. I didn't sleep around - not including the rape. I could count the number of times Fritz and I went all the way. In the belief book of *who deserves to be tested*, I didn't qualify.

I dropped right to the bathroom floor and cried until my eyes were puffy and red, until my nose hurt from the constant wiping with my shirt sleeve, and until my throat was raw from the anguish, desperate cries to God begging Him for a false positive.

Of course, I realized in my head that Fritz might not be the father, but in my heart, I could *only* believe that he was the father. I hadn't told anyone about the rape. I blocked it from my memory. It was the most painful thing I had ever experienced. I didn't have the tools to handle the pain of the memory or the fear of my assailant, and furthermore, I did not *want* to handle it. My solution was to deny it ever happened. Pretend that those awful, agonizing ten minutes had not taken place. Denial was the only solution. It was only ten minutes of my life, so why did it deserve so much attention and heartache?

False positive. That was right. I'd read about that, so I had opened another package and dangled the stick under my stream of pee.

Two pink lines.

Damn it.

The shock, sadness, and self-pity continued to consume me. Another emotion entered the picture - fear. Fear of the unknown. Fear of disappointing my parents, Fritz's family, my friends, my teachers. Fear of the peer judgment that I claimed I never cared about. Fear for my future and how much my dreams for the future would change. Fear for my relationship with Fritz. Would we be able to survive? Fear for the tiny peanut growing in me. Physically, my body was ready for childbearing; however, even more importantly, mentally I didn't think I possessed the ability to parent a child. I was still a child myself.

Fear that this innocent baby could be the offspring of a rapist.

I peed on the third test. Not sure where all this liquid was coming from.

Two pink lines.

Shit.

At school the next day, my classes rolled together in a blur. I plopped down in the right desks, managed to respond appropriately, and functioned merely by moving one foot in front of the other until I saw Fritz on the other side of the hallway acting as if he didn't have a care in the world. Laughing and joking around with his baseball buddies.

I ducked into the nearest girl's bathroom and completely lost it. Tears sprang out of my eyes, my heart cracked a little because of the secret that I was keeping, and my weeping made my body shake.

After my five-minute tantrum in the bathroom stall, I splashed some cold water on my face and took a deep breath. Advanced biology was my last class of the day.

You can do this, Piper.

When I entered the classroom after the teacher had begun her lecture on the function of blood, specifically homeostasis, Mrs. Fode must have taken one good look at me and decided not to question or punish my tardiness. Plus, I had a reputation for being very respectful towards the faculty. This was not my norm.

From our lab table, Eleanor's face expressed a look of concern. Our friendship was a new development due to our partnership in this class.

Eleanor had straight dark brown hair that shone under the big iridescent overhead lights in the classroom. Her bangs were kept long, over her eyebrows so that she could hide her eyes when she angled her head downwards. During an assigned lab experiment, I'd commented on her silky hair, and she confessed that a hairstylist had never touched it. That made sense; sometimes her bangs had a jagged appearance.

Her mother was Korean, so she inherited her hair from her. Eleanor explained, "And I'm afraid to calculate what I've inherited from my father, Rocky. He's a pile of shit."

I peered around the nearby tables to make sure no one had overheard her cuss. "I'm sure he's not all bad, Ellie. Your mother had to have fallen in love with him for a reason."

"That's where you're wrong. She doesn't love him, and he bears not one positive quality."

My friendship with Eleanor was complicated. At first, it was a forced partnership since we were assigned as lab partners. But over time, I began to enjoy her sense of humor and eagerness. Additionally, she was smart as a whip and always said exactly what was on her mind. It was rather refreshing. No games.

I didn't know anything about her home life except for what she claimed. But whatever information that she chose to share broke my heart. Her parents paid her no attention, and she was left literally to raise herself.

Because my heart broke for her, I did everything in my power to make the one-hour lab enjoyable for her. Science was her jam. Everything about it excited her. I allowed her to lead the experiments, discussions, and finalize our assignments.

I tried to include her into my friend group - Carrie and Mya - but she stuck out like a sore thumb. She didn't even try to participate in the conversations that we discussed at our lunch table or sometimes after school out on the lawn. Boys, hair, makeup, and more boys. These topics didn't interest her.

Our friendship was an unusual one. We rarely socialized outside of school, usually only to study. I wasn't sure if she even knew how to be a friend. However, I discovered that afternoon when I tripped my way into advanced biology that Eleanor was the one friend I could lean on. Maybe it was because she had no one else to tell - my secret was safe. Maybe it was simply because she was there - literally sitting next to me in class. Or maybe it was because I valued her and her strong personality.

Whatever the reason, Eleanor was the second person who told that I was carrying Fritz's baby.

Chapter 20

Eleanor - April 20, 2016

The community of Pine Hill was composed of families who lived on a PGA tour-approved golf course and ran with the elite crowds of the Twin Cities, and also of families who lived in the old neighborhood of the original developers of Pine Hill. Our school district was proud of its diversity and wanted to show its support of the lower class. Obviously, the school board primarily consisted of the higher-class families. The working-class families didn't have extra time to serve on boards or volunteer committees, and the people who lived in my neighborhood were too worried about where their next meal was coming from, how they were going to pay rent, and how drunk they could get without a hangover.

Maybe that was just my family.

With the generous donations of the elite families, our school district was able to recruit and hire some of the best educators. Pine Hill High School was known for their high-achieving students and even pushier parents - or, the politically correct term would be *strongly supportive* parents.

Daniel Jarro was one of the newest members of the faculty. Fresh from Harvard with a graduate degree, he appeared refined, poised, and unapproachable. I wasn't going to convince Mr. Jarro that Madison was cheating - he was enamored by her and her bewitching charms - so I decided I would jump over his head, straight to the big guns: Principal Klawonn. I hadn't had many dealings with her, obviously, but I heard she was a reasonable woman who didn't play favorites. Before her reign over Pine Hill High School, she taught English Language Arts at a school for troubled boys. She had earned great respect from the teachers as well as the student body that feared her.

"Good morning, Eleanor. I was informed that you needed to speak with me and that it's an urgent matter. Please have a seat and tell me how I can help." She was seated behind her massive oak desk. Even though her head was bent looking at the paperwork laid out in front of her, her words were clear and confident.

I was a straight shooter and wasn't interested in a bunch of fluff. Since brown-nosing wasn't in my nature, I advanced right to the point of my early morning visit.

"Madison Sterling has been cheating off me all year."

As she looked up from her desk and leaned back in her chair, Mrs Klawonn eyed me suspiciously. "That's a huge accusation, Miss Cutter. Do you have any proof?"

I recounted the little experiment that I performed for my own verification at midterm. I'd called in sick to school on the day of our midterm exams in Spanish and world geography, both classes where Madison happened to be sitting behind me and over my shoulder. Without being able to look over my shoulder, Madison earned an F on her Spanish exam. In world geography, I didn't have any idea, but Principal Klawonn could investigate for herself.

"Ask her to translate anything in Spanish, and I'd bet my left arm that she wouldn't be able to say anything beyond hello and a few curse words." Informing Mrs. Klawonn about Madison's shady character was lifting a huge weight off my shoulders. "You can verify that grade on her Campus Portal. The whole class knew that she failed because her name was listed on Mr. Jarro's dry-erase board as someone who could take the make-up exam after school."

When I returned to school the following day after calling in sick and read her name in the messy cursive handwriting, I felt validated. Being right never felt so good. Madison Sterling would finally get what she deserved. However, nothing happened. Day after day, she giggled her way through class and acted like she didn't have a care in the world. Somehow, Madison had won again.

It was why I set up the meeting with the principal - I was tired of her getting away with her deceptions. "It might be weak proof to you. But I have a plan."

"I don't like the sound of that. This school doesn't tolerate shenanigans, Miss Cutter. I will not partake in any hidden cameras or microphones."

I sat up straight and verbalized my proposal. "Nothing like that, Mrs. Klawonn. Please hear me out. Tomorrow morning, if you'd allow it, I'll complete the final Spanish test and ace it. I'll take it again during third period with Madison Sterling. I'll incorrectly answer a couple obvious questions, where I'm sure she'll be copying everything that I write down.

"If I'm wrong - which I'm one-hundred-percent sure that I won't be - I'll take the grade of the test that I'm purposely bombing. I'm a straight-A student with an impeccable record. I've never been in trouble. I'm willing to bet my perfect record on this, Mrs. Klawonn. I'm tired of her getting away with it. If you look at our high school records for the past four years, you'll notice that we've been in one or two classes per semester together. Each of those classes is her highest overall grade because she has managed to sit near me. I've tried to talk to her about it. When I got nowhere with her, I tried to discuss it with the corresponding teachers. I'm at my wit's end with graduation around the corner. She needs to learn that she can't cheat to get ahead."

As I was talking, Mrs. Klawonn was looking up information on her computer. I was sure she was verifying my claims. I knew from the research that I completed on Principal Klawonn's career history that she did not tolerate dishonesty. She had a strict policy: trust and respect were earned.

Initially, she opposed my plan. She didn't like trickery or deceit, but she eventually didn't see the harm in proving my point. And honestly, I thought that she was curious as well. I convinced her that I had nothing against Madison personally. Just that morally, I couldn't allow her dishonesty to continue.

That was partially true.

Personally, I hated Madison. Everything that I deserved, the universe awarded her. *I should've been Piper's twin sister. My soul should've floated to the split embryo and been born as one of the twins. Piper and I should be together.* Instead, just over twenty-four hours after their mother gave birth to them, my mother ended up in labor with me. It wasn't fair. Even before I was born, the universe hated me. I should've been Madison. It should've been me playing hide and seek with Piper as a child and sitting next to her at family dinners.

Madison's defiance was more appropriate for a daughter of two parents like mine. Madison should've grown up in a dingy apartment with two parents who didn't give a shit about who she had sex with or how late she stayed out at night. Her rebellious personality would've fit in perfectly. I could only imagine the sass that she would've given Rocky, and his response would've been one of his famous punches, landing square on her jaw.

Currently, Piper was too tied up in her own drama with Fritz. We hadn't even managed to discuss my revelation since she confessed her pregnancy. I understood and was sympathetic to her needs. We had all the time in the world to be sisters, best friends, and constant companions. In the meantime, I'd secure my place in her life by destroying the one sister who took everyone and everything for granted. The one who stole the life that I rightfully deserved.

Chapter 21

Maddy - April 22, 2016

My eighteenth birthday turned out to be the most catastrophic day of my - Madison Mae Sterling - entire life. I wasn't being dramatic. I was speaking the truth. No cap. I'd been known to exaggerate in the past, but I wasn't exaggerating this time. Turning eighteen was supposed to be filled with happiness, excitement and pure F.U.N. In my book, F.U.N. stood for *Fancy Unbridled Non-stop FUN!* Not *Freaking Unstoppable Nightmare*.

Unfortunately, turning eighteen for me was proving to be a real, hard bitch slap in the face. A harsh kick in the ass into adulthood. My actions lately might have warranted it, but it was still not welcome.

I briefly shut my eyes, took a deep breath, and told myself to pay attention to what was actually happening in front of me and not floating around in my head. *Stop dreaming about the past and be present.* Mom was rambling on and on, and it wasn't good. As soon as I opened my eyes, fresh tears ran down her cheeks.

"...seriously, Madison, I'd like to understand what you were thinking. Or if you were thinking at all. It's your senior year. You can't pull stuff like this and think it'll go unpunished and not tarnish your already polluted record. You keep digging yourself deeper and deeper into a hole. It's as if you don't care. Do you have no self-respect?"

With each word, her tone escalated, her voice becoming high and pitchy. My stone-cold silence added fuel to that fire of anger and disappointment. I glanced at my dad, who was seated in his usual spot on the living room couch. He hadn't managed to speak a word yet, but I recognized the look of frustration on his face. I'd already shattered his trust earlier that year when he came home from work and found me in the kitchen drinking the last drop of a bottle of vodka. I'd been completely wasted and couldn't carry on a conversation. Not my proudest moment.

But why is he home in the middle of the day anyway? Bringing home another little tart to shag while my mom is at work?

In my defense, I'd lost respect for him and was disappointed in him. I just couldn't form the correct words to have that conversation. And who *wanted* to have that conversation with a parent?

Hey, Dad, when I skipped school a couple of months ago, I walked in on you bonking some lady from your office. Sorry about that. I hope I didn't ruin the moment.

In my mind, a little battlefield formed in our living room. Dressed in camo from head to toe stood the soldier. Mom held the front line, firing and firing at my shield. Oblivious to the torment behind the front line, she fought - like a foot soldier - with all her courage and strength only to be stabbed in the back by her own comrade.

"Madison, what's going on? Please talk to us. We want to understand and help you, and we can't help if you don't open up."

I had nothing to say. No words could explain why I was making the choices that I was. Maybe she was right - I had no self-respect. It seemed whatever I did, it just wasn't good enough for them. Plus, I wasn't smart enough or nice enough. It was hard to explain the emptiness inside. Furthermore, I was too tired to try. Better to take the tongue-lashing so we could move on.

"Ryan, can you please talk to her?" Mom was stepping aside to let the tank through. Bringing in the big guns. Dad was the cavalry swooping in after the foot soldiers began and fought the hard fight. He was like the spy behind enemy lines.

Mom slumped down on the couch with a tissue box on her lap. She aggressively yanked out a tissue and quietly blew her nose. The white tissue symbolized her white flag of surrender.

Dad's facial expression spoke volumes. He was a man of few but important words. When he spoke, people listened, unlike Mom, who expressed herself a lot and who I was able to tune out. Dad's deep, commanding voice scared the neighbor's German Shepherd. Mad Dad, as Piper and I called him when we were little, was not someone you messed with. His left eyebrow was always raised whenever he was lecturing or speaking sternly. For the next five minutes, he'd demand my full attention, but when I glared at him, all I could think about was that Eleanor claimed that he was her biological father. I didn't see the resemblance, but then again, I didn't believe her. The broad was a wackjob.

Eleanor's allegation that she was our half-sister was still processing in my brain. I hadn't informed Piper yet mainly because I wasn't sure if I believed Eleanor. Plus, Piper kept this knowledge from me? Why didn't she tell me Eleanor's suspicions? I felt like I had the solution, and no one shared the initial problem with me. I could play their game.

But in light of my discovery of his infidelity, there might be a morsel of truth to her crazy allegations.

"Madison, your mother and I are at the end of our rope. In the past three months, you've stolen our liquor, skipped school, had sex with boys in our house, and crashed your car. We've been more than patient with you and your escalating misbehavior. Unfortunately, this time your large error in judgment may have cost you your future. Cheating on an exam isn't something that we can simply punish you for by taking away your phone or your car, and that would be enough. You're eighteen, as of today, and considered an adult. The school will choose the punishment. It's beyond our control. And with your school record, I wouldn't be surprised if they choose to suspend you. You'll be forced into taking summer classes in order to graduate and receive a diploma. And even your college may choose not to accept your enrollment.

"You screwed up, Madison. You screwed up big time. Your mother and I are beyond disappointed. We know that you're better than the choices you're continuously making. This weekend, you will stay home and reflect on what you have done. You'll be allowed twenty-four hours of quiet time to reflect before you *will* respond to our questions. You'll come up with concrete goals to correct this situation. I will not tolerate any more disrespect from you. You'll abide by our rules from now on, Madison, or you'll pack your bags."

A small, high-pitched sob escaped my mom's throat.

I heard both of my parents' speeches. Their stern and angry words bounced into the opening of my outer ear. Each word slid into the middle of my ear until finally reaching my cochlea, which was a fancy word that I learned in anatomy, for *inner ear*. I heard their voices. Sounds were exploding from their mouths.

But I didn't listen. There was a difference - which I'd mastered - between hearing and listening. To hear a person, one simply needed to have perceived the noise. When a person listened, that person was giving attention and consideration to the words.

My mom was right - I didn't care. I didn't have any self-respect. Nothing seemed to matter anymore.

I welcomed the imprisonment in my quiet bedroom. I was finished *hearing* them repeat every mistake that I'd made. I'd heard the drill. I just didn't care.

Chapter 22

Piper - April 22, 2016

My eighteenth birthday turned out to be the second-worst day of my - Piper Jean Sterling - life. The rape being the worst day. I knew that if I blew out all the candles on my cake, my wish still wouldn't come true. Going back into time wasn't realistic. I wasn't expecting colorful balloons, pointy party hats, and a tall chocolate layered cake. Maybe a small gathering with my friends, perhaps a small glass of sparkling champagne to toast my entrance into adulthood, and maybe a change of heart from my boyfriend. I didn't think that I was wishing for anything too extravagant.

Instead, when I woke up, my eyes were crusty from the late-night tears that I'd shed, plus they burned from the dryness created by the constant weeping. My nasal passage was moist and filled with liquid goo. Blowing my nose with cheap tissues, my nose was raw and red. Before I peeked in the mirror, I knew the skin around my eyes was puffy and swollen. I was a hot mess.

I stared up at the white ceiling in my room and recalled several memories of previous birthday mornings, how different each one had been. As a young child, I would spring out of bed and race downstairs in anticipation of what special breakfast Mom was surprising us with. It was usually a sugary treat iced with more sugar - heart-shaped pancakes with syrup, homemade waffles with whipped cream and colorful sprinkles, or chocolate donuts with pink frosting.

When I was ten years old, the morning of my special day, my eyes sprang open with excitement to attend the newly released movie, *The Parent Trap*. Maddy loudly vocalized that she was owed financial credit for the brilliant storyline - twins switching lives. Furthermore, she was also worried that our immediate circle would catch onto our shenanigans after seeing it.

As a preteen, I looked forward to wearing new clothes to school. On my twelfth birthday, a leopard-print shirt and a new pair of skinny jeans were the items that Mom and I took a special shopping trip to find. My new attire made me feel mature.

In the last couple of months, I'd grown up and experienced some very harsh adult realities - nothing that my charmed life had prepared me for. This new level of maturity had been forced upon me. I didn't yearn for adulthood like I did when I was an innocent preteen.

Turning eighteen wasn't at all what I'd imagined. My whole life, I imagined eighteen as a magical number. Once I turned eighteen, I'd feel that invisible direction towards the fulfillment of my adult life. The worries about my future would somehow magically be erased. Confidence would fill my soul. I'd no longer feel awkward, insecure, or lost. I'd become an adult.

However, on the morning of my first day of so-called adulthood, I felt no different than I had the day before - on the last morning of my youth. The only difference was that my sadness had increased due to my disappointment that nothing had magically changed. Instead, becoming an adult was harsh and heartbreaking. My imagination and false sense of security truly had led me astray.

Fritz and I had a big fight the night before, causing me to leave him abruptly. It was amazing how stress brought out the worst in people. Things had been tense between the two of us ever since I revealed that I was pregnant. It was like we both blamed each other. Of course, that was unreasonable, but it didn't stop us from snapping at each other. We were both irritable and afraid. Afraid to tell anyone else. As soon as it was said out loud, the words became our reality.

During the past couple of weeks, I wouldn't say that I'd become happy about our situation, but I'd admit that I'd become more accepting of it. It wasn't the end of the world. Teenagers in worse situations than us survived and grew to lead normal lives. Plus, Fritz was my support beam – without him and his love, I would collapse.

Last night, I tried to explain to him how I felt. "Believe me, Fritz. I wish this hadn't happened either, but it did. But not talking about it won't make it go away. We need to talk."

After having dinner with his parents, we retreated to Fritz's room to watch some mind-numbing TV. Their house rules didn't include no girls in his basement bedroom. Fritz was an only child. Maybe we wouldn't be in this situation if we didn't decide to play house one weekend while his parents were in Vegas.

When Fritz was agitated, he bit the side of lip like he was doing during our conversation. With the click of a remote, he shut off the TV and turned towards me. "Okay, okay. I know that we do, but I think we need to consider *all* options. You need to consider abortion, Piper. This is going to affect both of our futures."

"Fritz, I simply can't. This baby is a piece of you and me, created in love." I'd never accept that it was the rapist's child. I couldn't. Fritz was the father. In my heart, I knew Fritz and I could do this together, but I couldn't question the paternity. In order for me to survive this hurdle, I'd never look back, never think about that morning. Obviously, that was easier said than done. "Just because the timing isn't convenient doesn't mean the baby should be eliminated."

"When you call it a baby, you make me sound like a murderer. Right now, I can't even conceive that this pregnancy is anything more than a sperm-like object."

"Fritz, did you fail biology?" I was wrong to bring up his academic skills, but I'd been beyond irritated and heartbroken by that conversation. My jab was a low blow. "Sorry. That was uncalled for. My hormones are all over the place, and I lashed out. Fritz, let's move past that option for now. I don't think that we'll agree."

My jab caused a painful silence to surround us. Fritz tried hard at school. He wanted to do better, but his dyslexia caused him to seek tutoring, and many extra hours were spent on his homework.

"By the time the baby is born, we'll have both graduated high school. We could take turns with our continuing education. We could rent a small apartment in town to be near our families for their support. It'll be hard, but we can figure it out...together."

"You make it sound so simple and romantic, Piper. This isn't one of your Lifetime movies. It won't be like that." Fritz got up from his bed and started to pace his room. "How will I play baseball? I can't do that part-time. Baseball will pay for my college education. Plus, we'll be exhausted staying up all night with a newborn. One of us will need to land a full-time job. How would we pay for everything that a baby needs? Piper, you don't have to always be so good and perfect. We aren't ready to be parents. Everyone, even God, knows that. This was a mistake." He threw up his hands.

"A mistake? One that you and I made *together*. It isn't a wrong answer on a test that you can just erase, Fritz. We had sex knowing that this was a possibility. A risk. We should've been ready for the outcome if we were going to have sex." As I watched him pace back and forth over his bedroom floor, my blood pressure increased. As my chest ceased tightly, tears steadily poured out of my eyes. I knew Fritz was in pain too. On the outside, he was fighting to appear calm, but on the inside, his heart was aching just like mine.

"Everyone has sex. We did it only four times. This isn't fair, Piper. We shouldn't have to pay for the rest of our lives."

"Wow...Fritz, I've never known you to not take responsibility for your actions. I agree - we aren't ready, but it's too late for that. We're having a baby, and we need to figure out what to do. Life isn't always fair."

"Can you at least *consider* an abortion, Piper?" He stopped pacing, and his eyes bore into mine. He looked like he was holding his breath.

"Absolutely not. I can't terminate a life just because it isn't convenient timing for us, just because we aren't financially, mentally stable. It isn't the baby's fault."

As his questions and concerns poured out of him, his voice grew louder, higher-pitched, and his face grew red, and he dropped down into his desk chair in defeat. When I saw his eyes, once full of laughter and innocence but now desperate, tears rolled down my cheeks. He had valid points. I couldn't argue with that, but I wanted to see the positive side of this situation. I had to see the good.

"What about adoption? Would you be able to hand over our baby up to another family to raise with the possibility we would never see him again?" I needed to hear his answers to these hard questions.

It was obvious what each of us wanted to do. He wanted to erase this *mistake*. Go back to his life before I was pregnant. I understood. I would've loved that as well; however, I didn't have a magic wand to wave and erase the baby.

"If abortion is an absolute *no*, then yes, I think adoption would be better than raising it ourselves. We can't be who this baby needs us to be. We just aren't ready. I love you, Piper, but I know I'm not ready to be a father. I want to play college baseball. I want to move away and live with Maverick. I want to make some mistakes that won't completely change the course of my life. I want to *live*."

Fritz got up from his desk chair and dusted off a baseball trophy that was on his shelf. "I'm sorry, Piper, if that isn't what you want to hear from me. It's true. I'm not ready."

"It's okay, Fritz. We need to be honest with each other. Honesty is all that I ask." It was nine-thirty on a school night, so I needed to head home. Furthermore, I was exhausted all the time and yearned for sleep. We could continue this conversation another time.

I rose from my comfy spot on his bed. "I should head home."

Fritz made his way over and wrapped his arms tightly around me. I relaxed in his warm embrace. He made me feel safe. His arms felt right; my head fit perfectly under his chin. Neither of us wanted to let go. We wanted to stay frozen in this moment. Tears dropped from my eyes, soaking his T-shirt.

He kissed the top of my head and softly added, "And who knows what will happen in the next couple of months? There's a chance that you could have a miscarriage too."

My tears stopped. I held my breath while I tried to comprehend what he just said. I pulled away from the security of his chest. "You hope I have a miscarriage?"

He recognized the alarm in my voice. "I never said *hope*.' I simply said there was a possibility of a miscarriage. All pregnancies have a small percentage." He was backpedaling.

"If I had a miscarriage, you'd get your way. The *problem*" - I used air quotes - "would be gone."

"True. But I never used the word *hope*. I was simply listing all the possibilities. I thought that was what we were doing."

He was right - he wasn't ready to be a father. He wasn't mature enough to handle the responsibilities. My heart broke thinking about how wrong my romantic dream of our own little family was.

I picked up my jacket and headed for the door. Struggling to keep my voice even, I told him, "There is also the possibility that we won't be together in nine months."

Chapter 23

Piper - April 22, 2016

Even on a day when my mood was so sour that I didn't think it could be turned around, my best friends, Carrie and Mya, greeted me at my locker before the bell announced the beginning of our school day. Carrie was taping a *happy birthday* sign to the outside of my locker. Mya was holding the tape dispenser - she was the lookout. I smiled when I caught my friends trying to be sweet and sneaky. I'd bet money that the decorating was Carrie's idea and Mya went along with it - she was usually the naive accomplice.

My friends were golden. We'd been best friends since grade school. I met Mya at a church youth group event. She had a thick, brown bob that landed below her chin. Her big, pearly white smile was always on display - I swear she smiled in her sleep. When we were paired for an activity, I asked her how she got such a beautiful, perfect smile.

"My dad's a dentist. I swear his hobby is cleaning my teeth." Even then she smiled at her little joke. The two of us became inseparable. We discovered that we both had a fondness for being organized, working hard in school, and reading books. Mya introduced me to Carrie.

Carrie was born with a silver spoon in her mouth - one of Mom's famous sayings.

"How can a baby enter the world with a spoon in her mouth?" Maddy questioned the absurdity of Mom's phrase. "That makes absolutely no sense, Mom. Do you make these sayings up?"

Thank goodness for Maddy always questioning everything. I didn't even need to say a word. She was the first of the two of us to start talking when we were toddlers, and I didn't utter a word for another six months. My dad claimed that my first word was *Maddy*.

"Not literally, Madison. It just means that she hasn't had to ask for much. Everything was handed to her."

"Duh! Babies can't reach things so, of course, people handed her things. They have short little arms." Maddy dismissed the conversation.

Thanks to their discussion, I understood what Mom was referring to, and it was true - Carrie was spoiled. Even Carrie admitted it, but she wasn't going to complain about it. She grew up in a large estate on the southern tip of our town with an in-ground pool, a family cabin in northern Minnesota, someone that cleaned their house each week, and even took care of her if both of her parents were working. Her life was cush.

"Oh! Happy birthday, Piper." Mya's big brown eyes popped open as she spied me coming down the crowded hallway. She said it loud enough for Carrie to hear that they'd been discovered. Everyone needed to have two friends like mine.

"Happy eighteenth birthday, Piper," Carrie sang to me. She had the voice of an angel.

"You two sure know how to make a girl feel special." I grabbed each one into a half hug. We fondly referred to our friendship as the Cinderella Sisters - Carrie was Cinderella for obvious reasons, and Mya and I were the ugly stepsisters.

"You've been quiet and seemed a bit down lately. We wanted to cheer you up. Plus, you only turn eighteen once." Mya was the thoughtful, innocent one and always called it like it was. I was sure Carrie hadn't intended to give away the true reason for their thoughtfulness.

"Yes, and we want to take you to the new ice cream shop after school today. I heard they even make your favorite - peanut butter and chocolate." Carrie knew the way to my heart. "I'm buying."

"Sounds fabulous, girls. And sorry I've been a bit MIA lately. I'm getting out of my funk, I promise." Even saying those words brought a lump to my throat. They had no idea that I was pregnant and had been recently raped. I hadn't shared my pregnancy news with anyone but Fritz...and Eleanor. I wasn't sure why I confided in her. We were new friends, but she was a great listener and always seemed to be there when I'd reached a breaking point. And no one but me and my attacker knew about the rape. I figured if I didn't say anything to anyone it would go away.

Chapter 24

Eleanor

Jealousy formed in all shapes and sizes. No one was above it. It liked to spread in a person's core. Jealousy reared its ugly head even when least expected. Excuses were created and evil feelings were blamed. But jealousy knew better.

Jealousy had levels. Level one was the normal, expected level that happened because you simply wished you could be that person you'd been replaced with. For example, after a breakup, the rejected person would feel jealous of the stranger who was the replacement, his new flame. He firmly held her hand as they crossed the room – that used to be you. He threw back his head at something funny she said - he used to laugh at your jokes. Jealousy.

This level of jealousy was normal, acceptable, and almost expected. If only...

After the acceptable amount of grief from losing a relationship had passed, level two was reached. The desire to be with him, to hold him, to make memories with him consumed you. Your pillow became soaked with the tears you cried. You wore his old, worn-out T-shirt to bed. You dialed his number to hear his voice on his voicemail. Every pitiful act became routine as you suffered alone and in silence.

Level three was the stalker level. Not only did you reread all of his past texts and photos of him, but you started following him to work, to his favorite coffee shop, to his dentist appointment that you knew about because you accessed his Outlook calendar. Healthy boundaries had flown out the window.

Jealousy became an obsession. Everyday life didn't exist without him and knowing where he was at all times, who he was with, what he was eating, and how long he slept. Your own life took a backseat to following him, watching him, thinking of him.

Level four. You wouldn't idly sit back and watch him continue his life without you. You were compelled to interfere by helping him find his love for you again, and guiding him back into your arms. You left a note on the windshield of his car. Flowers were delivered to him at work without a card. Bumped into his mother outside their church - made some small talk. Asked about him. Broke into his apartment - technically, it wasn't breaking in if you knew where his hidden key was - and sprayed a bit of your signature perfume on his pillow and couch cushions. You left little reminders of yourself in plain sight - your old toothbrush on the side of the sink, a wine glass stained with lipstick on the rim. For an extra punch, you removed your current panties and tucked them under his pillow. You actively involved yourself in his life, without his acceptance or knowledge.

Level five was the peak, when your obsessive stage of jealousy took on a life of its own. You made excuses for the vindictive acts that you did to cripple him. Your feelings were no longer kept inside but had surfaced to an act of vengeance. Not only were you jealous of the life that this person was leading without you, but you performed acts which emotionally and physically caused him harm.

Level five was the phase when stalkers become instigators. No longer able to simply observe from a respectful distance, an instigator must punish her ex for the rejection and hurt. This level brought forth the acceptance that the relationship was over. Everything that was done for him had gone unnoticed and unappreciated. It was time that he paid for his rejection. No more playing nice. It was time that he paid for all the time and effort you'd put forth without an ounce of appreciation.

If level five stopped, it was most likely due to jail time. A person sucked into level five could not understand the gravity of their actions. It was either you or him – someone must go.

I used a male-female breakup as an example. Obviously, jealousy occurred with two females or two males as well. It occured with friends or enemies. It happened at work. It happened at home. Jealousy was everywhere and nowhere.

You didn't see her, but you felt her invading your soul and taking control over every thought and feeling. Her presence burned your skin and made the hair on your arms stand. Pulsing through your veins, she demanded total control.

I was Jealousy. And Jealousy wanted Madison gone.

Chapter 25

Maddy - April 22, 2016

My lack of reaction to the principal's and my parents' harsh yet honest words had worn me out. Even maintaining a poker face for a few hours was a lot of work. Plus, I'd snuck out last night for a few hours, so I welcomed a little nap. Being sentenced to solitary confinement would prove beneficial.

When I woke up two hours later, Piper was sitting next to me on my bed with a very worried expression on her face. She was brushing the hair away from my eyes. At first when I woke up and recognized her concern, I'd forgotten everything that had happened recently. A weak, sleepy smile formed. My eyelids were heavy, and her soft petting was calming.

"Maddy, what's going on?" She was worried about me too, but not in the yelling, screaming, angry way. "Rumor has it that you were called into Principal Klawonn's office this afternoon. I got home and Mom looked like she'd been crying, and Dad was already on his second gin and tonic. Tell me what happened, Maddy?"

Her words brought back the current stage of my reality. I remembered - I was the shitty one. The daughter who continued to choose poorly and didn't care about repercussions. Yep, I knew my place. My sleepy smile faded and was replaced with my signature glare.

My mood swings didn't phase Piper. She was often on the receiving end, but she tolerated it with a grain of salt. She never held a grudge or acknowledged the change. She was so much better than me.

"Maddy, please tell me. I'm worried about you."

I swatted her hand away. She knew that I didn't like to be touched.

As I sat up in bed, I calmly responded, "Are you truly worried about me, Puppet? Is that why you narked on me to Dad? Told him that you found weed in our bathroom? I'm sure you clearly explained to him that the joint wasn't yours because *you* would never do anything illegal or against house rules. Are you worried that if I straighten up, you'll have competition for being the good twin?"

"Maddy! I love you. I'm only looking out for you. Everyone is worried about you and your string of bad choices." Reading my mood, Piper stood up from my bed and casually looked around my room.

My walls had been painted a pale-yellow years ago when this was the guest room. That was before I requested my own space. We had shared a bedroom for sixteen years. It had been time. I didn't want to live in her shadow anymore.

I simply told her, "I'm fine. Quite happy actually. Happy eighteenth birthday, Puppet. Now, would you kindly exit my personal living area?"

Her puppy-dog eyes poured into me as if searching for answers, answers for the reason why I'd been acting like such a bitch lately. I shot a cold, blank stare in her direction.

"Happy birthday, Maddy. I bought you a little something." She reached into her sweatshirt pocket and pulled out a beautifully wrapped square box. The wrapping paper was gray and white stripes topped with a delicate pink bow. Not sure how she managed to not smash it in her hoodie pocket. She gently set the gift on the corner of my bed.

After holding down my stare for five seconds to see if I'd cave and divulge all my deep, dark secrets to her, she turned around and left my room, softly pulling the door closed. I was relieved. She was relentless sometimes with her caring, probing questions. Just because we were twins didn't mean *this* twin wanted to share everything with her. I was tired. I was tired of being compared to her. I was the wild one, and she was the rule-follower. I liked to party, and she preferred staying home. I drove too fast; she allowed everyone into the crosswalk even before they reached the edge of the sidewalk. Our differences were endless. And they all ended with Piper on top, and me laying flat on the bottom.

As I slid back down onto my pillow, I heard voices in the hallway. Our house had paper-thin walls. Quietly, I crept to my door and pressed my ear against the wood.

The voices were muffled, but I heard my mom say to Piper, "You tried, honey. I'm sorry, but she must work on whatever is eating her at her own pace. Maybe it's depression. Dad and I'll talk about getting her some professional help again." Then I imagined Mom embracing her favorite child and thanking God for the blessing that was her.

That's it! I had to get out of this house. I felt suffocated. Plus, it was my birthday, and Maverick, a guy I shagged occasionally, was hosting a little bash since his parents were out of town. Everyone who was anyone was invited. His parents were loaded. His parties were always epic. Fully stocked liquor cabinet, a warm hot tub, a sparkling swimming pool, excellent surround sound. Yes, that was where I needed to be. I had two hours to kill before I could escape. I decided to numb my brain with some time-wasting social media surfing.

Chapter 26

Piper - April 22, 2016

Carrie had been right - the peanut butter and chocolate ice cream at IC by Tyler was delicious. Two generous scoops of ice cream later, and I was sprawled out on my bed working on my history assignment.

There was a soft knock on my bedroom door. It was Fritz. After baseball practice, he occasionally stopped by. We either worked on homework together, or he joined us for a family meal.

But tonight, he hadn't pre-texted his arrival. After our fight last night, we hadn't talked or texted. We were cooling off.

When he let himself into my room, I could see the apprehension in his eyes and demeanor. We'd had our share of arguments, but nothing that included such strong emotions. We didn't need to always agree on everything, but I found it difficult to believe that a couple could survive a shared heartache when each person felt very strongly on either end of the spectrum.

"Happy birthday, Piper. Believe it or not, your parents waved me up here. They were a little sidetracked and having a heated discussion with Madison. They barely raised an eyebrow - just one of your dad's when he's mad." His voice was hushed and tentative. He was trying to be funny. "I feel so terrible about everything. Nothing came out of my mouth right last night. I'm not ready for that step…"

His voice trailed off. He wanted me to say it was okay, to let him off the hook. But I couldn't. I didn't want to. Maybe it was because I'd felt the same - I would be relieved to not have to make this decision. And for my punishment, I needed to keep him at arm's length. Punish myself by not allowing the man I loved back into my heart...just yet.

"Thanks for coming by, Fritz." My voice was flat - void of any real feeling. I stayed laying on my bedroom rather than jumping up to embrace him like I normally would. "But honestly, I don't feel up for company right now. I'm emotionally and physically exhausted. It's been a couple of long, hard days - weeks actually." My eyes returned to my homework.

"I understand. But even though you think I'm a real a-hole right now, please know that I do love you and wish I could do and say the right thing all the time. You deserve better."

Fritz had a heart of gold, I knew that. He'd always been so good to me. Perfect gentleman and a very good friend. I knew that with all my heart. But I was hurting too. I deserved and needed a little space to grieve our youth and innocence.

Plus, when he was so wonderful, I felt guilty for trapping him into this life when my rapist could be the father. As soon as that thought entered my brain, I shoved it out. No one was going to know that was even a possibility. Ten minutes of my life that had been erased.

"I know, Fritz..." I didn't give him the acceptance of his apology that he wanted. That was all I was capable of.

"I'll leave now if that's what you want." He paused, hoping for an invitation to stay as he was still standing near my bedroom door. His hands were jammed into his jeans pockets. I nodded. "But if you change your mind and want to celebrate your birthday, Maverick is having a rager at his house tonight to celebrate the baseball team's win over the Cardinals. I'd love it if you came."

Again, I nodded in acknowledgement of his words. Fritz knew that I wasn't into the party scene. Honestly, he wasn't either unless it had something to do with baseball or his best friend, Maverick.

Gently, Fritz pulled my bedroom door shut after he deposited a small, gift-wrapped box on my desk. It was wrapped with bright yellow wrapping paper, and instead of a bow, there was a white daisy on top - he'd been shopping at LaurieBelle's - it was their signature wrapping paper.

Fritz was notorious for being a terrible gift giver. On our first Valentine's Day, he'd purchased an oversized, white T-shirt that had the saying, *You are my favorite thing* written in red across the chest. In tiny, black letters under that, it said, *to do*. I'd laughed so hard when I opened it. He hadn't seen or read the small print.

"You said LaurieBelle's was your favorite shop, and it was the only Valentine's shirt they had." At the time we hadn't had sex yet, but Fritz had been ready whenever I was.

I didn't want to purposely hurt Fritz, but I felt empty. I had nothing to give. Keeping two enormous secrets was ripping me apart.

After a quick nap, I was awakened to Maddy's bedroom door being slammed shut. Nothing out of the ordinary except that I'd heard she was called down to Principal Klawonn's office before lunch. Rumors had been running rapidly through the halls of what was going on. Must've been some nasty heat that she got herself into.

I never crossed paths with Maddy the entire day at school until I arrived home after my ice cream date with Carrie and Mya. Team Mom and Dad had been seated together on the couch. Mom looked like she'd been crying, and Dad's deep worry line creased on his forehead. They seemed to have aged in the last twenty-four hours. Sitting in the armchair opposite my frustrated parents was my twin sister, Maddy. In contrast to our parents, her facial features showed no sign of emotion. No look of shock, worry, remorse, or satisfaction registered on her face. This was a familiar scene: my parents pressing and stressed and directing their focus on Maddy, who appeared like an ice queen. Cold, unemotional, and expressionless.

After taking in the scene, I awkwardly asked, "Everyone okay?" The answer was obvious.

My mom, who was always the first to pipe up, said, "Piper, would you mind giving us a few minutes alone with Madison?"

I knew the drill. I leave the room, they yell, and Madison sits silently without remorse or acknowledgement. My parents' blood pressure rose while Maddy somehow managed to become perfectly motionless.

"Of course." As the rule-follower, I kicked off my shoes and placed them in their designated spot.

I caught Maddy's eye as I exited the living room. I read hatred and disgust in the quick second glance. Another thing I was used to - Maddy had a gift for deflecting. Nothing was ever her fault. So, why her eyes showed disgust and anger towards me was beyond my knowledge. And it didn't bother me.

Whatever trouble Maddy created wasn't my fault - I knew this fact, but somehow, she resolved that I was to blame.

Chapter 27

Maddy - April 22, 2016

After being checked on by both of my parents before they turned in for the night, I carefully dressed in my favorite skin-tight faded denim jeans and the new white crop top that I lifted from Aeropostale earlier in the week. It fit perfectly, but I knew it would since I had the exact one in black as well. I actually paid thirty-five dollars for the black one. I was creating my own personal sale: Buy One, Get One FREE!

The rounded neck of the shirt showed off my collarbone that Mr. Jarro had described as *super sexy*. I fastened my big golden hoop earrings on my ears and remembered the gift Piper had given me. When I heard Mom and Piper talking outside my room, I must've buried it under my comforter as I snuck out of bed.

I found it in my covers and slowly unwrapped the box. Last year for my birthday, Piper had given me the hoop earrings I was wearing; they were my favorite. She knew my taste as well as I did. I was curious to see what she found this year.

As the last of the wrapping paper was removed, I pulled off the little lid on the box to reveal a bracelet. The wooden beads were brown and circled a golden bar that was engraved with *Queen*. I threw the bracelet on. Not allowing any build-up of emotion. It was the perfect gift again, and I didn't deserve it.

I stuffed a couple of pillows under my sheets, turned off the overhead light so only my childhood unicorn night light shone a small rainbow in the corner of my room. I laced up my boots and threw on a zip-up, heather-gray hooded sweatshirt of Piper's. When zipped up, the words across the chest read, *Good Vibes*. I stole it from the laundry the day after she ratted me out to Dad about my hidden joint. She had been searching the house, our school, her car, and her boyfriend's house for this sweatshirt ever since. Pathetic. It was just an ugly sweatshirt, but I knew that it was her favorite.

My phone read ten minutes after ten, and the weather app told me it was sixty degrees with an evening storm forecasted. Typical spring weather in Minnesota. Gonna be a chilly walk the seven blocks to the party. Glad I had this *nice* sweatshirt to keep me warm.

With a little muscle, I pushed up my bedroom window enough to maneuver my body through the opening. I had done this many times before, the night before, in fact. I quickly placed a small rock under the window pane and pulled it down so there was only a crack for an opening. Enough room to squeeze my fingers through to open it back up when I was done celebrating my birthday. That wasn't my first rodeo.

By the time I reached Maverick's house, the party was in full swing. Drinks were flowing, the smell of weed filled the air, music pulsed through the walls, teenagers filled every square inch. As I strolled through the door, I tied Piper's sweatshirt around my waist. Not my normal look, but I wanted to appear casual, blank. Everyone had heard about my possible suspension - it was all over social media. I wanted to appear unaffected.

Dee, my best friend, found me. "What's up, B? Happy freakin' birthday! You've had a helluva day, girl." She passed me her lit joint. "You can have that one. Don't say that I never gave you anything." Dee retrieved a fresh one from her back pocket. Dee and I had already exchanged a few snaps discussing my latest insubordination. I briefed her on the low-down on my crime and punishment.

Dee's need for adventure and blunt personality was what sealed her fate as my friend. Years before, she invited me to the Mall of America with her to do some shopping. During our day of fighting crowds and eating our way through the first floor, Dee - short for Deonne - taught me the art of shoplifting.

"First of all, Maddy, I selected you because you're white and don't look anything like a thief. Salespeople always watch the black girls as soon as we stroll into any store. They judge us before we even open our mouths or know how much money we have in our wallets. So, I figure while they're judging and watching me, you - my new white, hot friend - will be free to five-finger discount a loot."

The bus had just closed its doors and pulled away from the sidewalk as she blurted out her plan. I had no escape, and if I was honest, I was intrigued. That MOA trip sealed our loyalty and friendship, plus she was completely correct - our partnership worked. Salespeople suspiciously watched Dee while I was free to roam around the store pocketing anything without a security code on it. It didn't matter what we five-fingered - it was the thrill of the ride.

Years later and still joined at the hip, we finished our reefers and headed to the home bar for a cocktail. Standing tall and proud at the heilm of his party, Maverick was serving drinks.

"Good evening, fine-looking birds. Tonight's cocktail is a mixed concoction that I named Show Me Your Boobs for a Free Glass." I threw back my head and laughed at Maverick, who was one giant hormone. We obliged his request and showed him our goods. "Best sets that I've had the pleasure of viewing this evening. Thank you for coming, and happy birthday, perky bird."

In the house, by the pool and around the yard, a hundred teenagers mingled and illegally drank alcohol and smoked marijuana. Everyone was blowing off steam from a stressful week of testing. School would be finished for the summer soon - everyone seemed ready.

Several stiff cocktails later, Dee and I were standing next to the Olympic-sized pool flirting with a couple of randos, David and Jared. Conversation was flowing - we were enjoying ourselves. I laughed at something David said when I lost my balance. Even though the alcohol slowed his reflexes, Jared tried to grab me but only managed to grab a hold of the arm of my sweatshirt that untied from around my waist. Seconds later and fully clothed - except for Piper's sweatshirt - I fell into the gorgeous, crystal blue pool.

For a moment while I was underwater, I felt relaxed and calm. Just floating beneath the surface, I could see wavy figures of people along the pool looking over the edge to see who was under the water. I didn't move.

Another splash erupted in the water, and I noticed Jared swimming towards me. He grabbed me around the waist and pulled me up above the water. Automatically, I gulped for air. People were clapping, some were laughing, and a few decided to jump in and join us. As I pulled my body out of the water onto the side of the pool, Dee raced over to me.

"Maddy, are you okay? What the hell, girl?"

"Never been better. Feel wonderful actually." It was a weird sensation being underwater and not having the will to push yourself up for air. Felt a bit suicidal. Maybe that was what I had intended since I didn't struggle. I wasn't sure.

Dee handed me a towel and giggled at my drunken state of calm. Jared - my savior - patted my head and handed me the dry sweatshirt that he managed to save from my fall into the pool. After a few concerned friends checked on my stability, I pushed my way into the house to use the restroom. I needed to see what I could salvage of my appearance.

Luckily, I knew my way around Maverick's house. I headed downstairs to find an non-occupied bathroom. I happened to be in luck. Thank goodness for the invention of waterproof makeup. My eyeliner and mascara were intact. My perfectly constructed eyeshadow - thanks to many makeup instruction YouTube videos - had washed off as well as my lipstick.

Unfortunately, my new white crop top hadn't held up very well in the chlorine pool - it withered and wrinkled. The great neckline widened and was lopsided. So much for getting a good deal on my Buy One, Get One FREE sale. Regrettably, I removed my top and tossed it in the trash. After I toweled off my body a bit more, I slipped on Piper's sweatshirt, zipped it up to just above my midriff so my bra and cleavage were displayed.

Not bad.

I glanced around the bathroom for options on what I could do with my now tangled, wet hair. The bathroom must've been Maverick's because in the top drawer was several men's hair and shaving products. In the second drawer, I discovered a box of condoms and a baseball hat. *Jackpot.* Maverick was losing his Pine Hill High School baseball hat. Seeing the hat tugged on one heart string - probably the only one I had left.

Piper owned the same hat. Her steady boyfriend, Fritz, also played baseball on the high school team, and he had gifted her a hat for Christmas. As I secured it on my head and pulled my hair through the back hole, I looked at myself in the mirror, and my sister looked back at me. I was wearing her sweatshirt, her hat, and with my makeup half removed, I could easily be mistaken for her. A chill ran up my spine while an idea sprouted in my chemically hazed brain. I zipped up the sweatshirt.

When I left the bathroom, I painted on a smile that would even fool the biggest Piper fans. This was a party thrown by a baseball player, and everyone knew Piper dated a baseball player, so no one would be surprised if Piper made an appearance. According to me, she just arrived. This would be fun.

Chapter 28

Eleanor - April 22, 2016

Standing alone in the corner of the living room, I attended a famous Maverick house party, sipping a fruit concoction from a red solo cup. That was my first high-school party. I was a senior, and during Study Hall Maverick had accidentally invited his entire homeroom class to the party when the teacher had stepped out into the hallway.

"May I have everyone's attention? Fellow dogs and birds, I'm hosting a dope party at my digs Friday night, and you're all invited." Maverick had recently been awarded the title class clown by the school newspaper so as his newly awarded title would suggest, he dramatically climbed on top of his desk chair to make his announcement.

A few dogs awarded Maverick's invitation with a victorious howl, and the birds whistled their approval. But only awkward me managed to intelligibly vocalize a human response: "Even me?"

Why did I choose to finally utter words *then* after four years of high school managing to stay hidden in the background? Watching, observing, and taking notes was my skill. My silence was broken by two pitiful words that brought all twenty sets of eyes on me. My face instantly ignited to a flaming red.

Maverick - party boy and everyone's friend - glanced down in my direction to acknowledge me. He shrugged. "Sure, why not?"

Well, that was as close to an invitation as I was ever going to receive. I wasn't going to miss my first high-school party thrown by the most popular boy in our class.

I came alone, slithered into the kitchen, paid my ten dollars for a party cup, and found my way into a back corner so I could watch the characters of my own reality show let loose. The music was so loud that the base in the songs vibrated the house. The lights were turned down low, and a makeshift dance floor occupied the center of the dining room. The table and chairs had been pushed back towards the wall.

From my corner of the living room, I had a clear view of the kitchen and the open dining room, the back patio, the pool, and the staircase. Perfect position for my people-watching.

My classmates were scattered in different groups, chatting, drinking, and smoking. The females were wearing shirts that only covered half of their torso and tight, *tight* athletic pants with high heels. Odd combination.

Most of the males were dressed in T-shirts and shorts or jeans. Their attire was more my style. Casual and comfortable - not out to impress anyone.

Nervous Nancy, who parked her fat ass in front of me in Spanish, was not nervous after a few cocktails. She was floating from group to group with a pitcher of beer, filling up people's cups. "Cerveza?"

Bitchy Becca threw back her head, shut her eyes, and was dancing alone in the center of the living room. When she rocked back and forth to the beat of the music, her drink spilled and was absorbed by the already soiled rug.

Swapping spit on the opposite side of the room, Ashley and Hunter drew lots of attention because they had recently broken up. Huge, public fight at school - very dramatic. They must've worked things out or were in the process. His hands roamed all over her body. Their bodies were so close that from the shadows of the room, they looked like an alien with two kissing heads. *Get a room!*

As I emptied my cup, my anxiety and stress slowly eased from my body. I rolled my eyes at my stupidity. I felt lighter and didn't care that I was friendless in a crowded room.

Why haven't I done this before?

The alcohol tasted foreign but felt amazing as it invaded my blood stream. But if this was how I felt after just one drink, I wondered why Rocky hadn't been a happier drunk. I couldn't stop smiling. I decided that a second drink was appropriate for my first party, but that would be enough. I was well-aware of what happened after too many cups of liquid gold - Rocky got mean, and my mother got dead.

One more cup, and I'd be finished. Before I took two steps towards the bar, I recognized Piper walking straight to the kitchen. Maybe not completely *straight*, more like zig-zagged.

What is she doing here? She wasn't a partygoer or a drinker; we had that in common. Although I was pretty sure she was invited often, I was not.

She hadn't noticed me in the living room. She headed directly into the adjoining kitchen to Fritz's side. As soon as she was within arm's reach, he embraced her. When he kissed the top of her head that was covered with a baseball hat, he blinked a little too long. I noticed he was using the kitchen counter to support himself. Fritz was drunk.

I stood frozen a few steps out of my corner in the living room. I wanted to watch her for a bit before I talked to her.

Chapter 29

Maddy - April 22, 2016

As soon as I reached the top of the stairs, my eyes searched for him through the mob of noisy teenagers. This wasn't his scene, but I knew he'd make an appearance for his teammate and good friend. And I was proved correct again. He was standing with a group of baseball players in the kitchen next to the sink.

Even though Fritz wasn't my type - too studious, too nice, too goody-goody - I could admit that he was easy on the eyes. Standing six feet and one inch tall, his head was topped with a wavy mess of sandy-brown hair. It was obvious that he used a little product to keep it out of his eyes, but his effort appeared casual. His jawline was a defined square that his big smile filled. Piper claimed his smile was her favorite feature because when he smiled, his green eyes lit up.

But what turned heads in the hallways was his physique. Due to the daily visits to the weightlifting room and constant baseball workouts, Fritz had earned a great pair of biceps, six-pack abs, and overall lean muscle tone. If he had any clue how attractive he was, it would ruin the package. Fritz was oblivious to his good looks, or maybe he didn't care. His focus was on graduating high school at the top of our class, making it to the state baseball championship, and hanging out with my sister.

Honestly, Piper and Fritz were perfect for each other. Driven, intelligent, genuine, and good-hearted. They made me want to puke.

When I noticed him in the kitchen, I was surprised to see him holding a red solo party cup. If he got caught drinking, his state baseball dream would come to an abrupt halt. But then again, this was Fritz who I was talking about. His indiscretions would probably not receive any attention. He was the baseball team's golden boy.

As I started to make my way towards him, his sparkling smile spread across his face as he caught my eye. I noticed right away that his eyes appeared a bit glazed over. I was right - he'd been drinking. Fritz was full of surprises. And I loved being right.

"Piper!" he slurred. As he said her name, I noticed that he blinked a bit too slowly to be sober. "Oh, babe, you came."

This shenanigan was going to be much easier than I thought since he was sloshed. So far, I hadn't uttered a word to encourage the ruse that I was Piper. He effortlessly pulled me to his side without saying a word. Piper wouldn't be pleased that he was hammered, but I knew she wouldn't say anything to embarrass him. She would've waited until he sobered up, and they were alone. Pretending to be Piper, I kept my mouth shut and smiled.

"I was just telling the boys here about how River Falls didn't offer me a scholarship. They can suck it if they don't want me. I'll show them." He let out a loud belch that made his group of friends laugh, and it drowned out my response.

"You didn't get accepted to River Falls?" Now, it made sense why he was indulging in the bottle. Fritz had received a rejection. Probably not used to being told no.

In my ear, he whispered, "I told you, babe. But it's okay. We'll come up with a new plan. A better" - *hiccup* - "plan."

Honestly, I wasn't sure why I decided to pull a switcheroo alone or to this extreme. Maybe I intended to push her away. I wanted to hurt her for all the hurt that I felt when people compared me to her. I felt empty inside. Hollow. Alcohol, drugs, mindless sex, random shoplifting, and sneaking out of the house at all hours helped to numb the emptiness. But it never lasted long. They all seemed to delay the inevitable - the fact that I was depressed, miserable, and unhappy.

I wasn't sure how far I'd initially intended the night's switcheroo to go, but it was entertaining. I had nothing better to do. I was wet, dressed like her, and drunk.

Fritz still had one arm draped around my shoulders, and the other one was holding, and sometimes spilling, the contents of his party cup. He looked down lovingly at me.

"Babe, it's our song." Because of my enormous buzz, it took a second or two to focus on the music that was playing. Piped through the house's surround sound, I heard OMI's "Cheerleader." That was a very fitting song for Fritz and Piper. Motivating him as her cheerleader. Always on his side. All things she used to do for me when we were close.

Fritz pulled me tightly to his chest, wrapped both of his muscular arms around me in a tight embrace, and started to sing - off-key - the lyrics to the song in my ear. Underneath his embrace and terrible singing, I heard one of his buddies yell, "Get a room!"

Which, in Fritz's competitive nature, seemed to push him to a new limit of PDA. Instead of being embarrassed, he held up my chin towards his face and pressed his Angelina Jolie, puffy lips on mine.

Surprisingly, Fritz was an above-average kisser. I hadn't pegged him for that. I assumed his kisses would be aggressive and sloppy. I was pleased; therefore, I eagerly leaned into it and even placed my two hands on the sides of his face. We were really going at it. People started to ignore us, and we obviously didn't care that we were sucking face in the middle of a crowded party.

Chapter 30

Eleanor - April 22, 2016

Some people didn't deserve to be treated with simple respect or kindness. I didn't care if Grams repeatedly told me, "If you don't have anything nice to say, don't say it." Sometimes, I wanted to scream at people who deserved to know how rotten they were. I had feelings too.

Of course, I noticed the fuzzy-haired, grocery cashier roll her eyes when I was a nickel short in paying my bill. I recognized the irritated look, the judging eyes of the people standing in line behind me. I knew that they ridiculed and threw daggers at me. I wanted to scream the words in my head.

Nasty-haired bitch, don't you realize this is all I have?

But I didn't. My hurt feelings from the judgment of perfect strangers were shoved deep down with the rest of the pain. Stuffed deep down below the light of day. The lid was sealed tight.

I knew how to bottle up feelings. I was an expert at it. For my entire life, I'd been taught to keep my trap shut. "No one wants to hear you whining and crying again, Eleanor." My mother had no patience for me. I wasn't allowed to voice my opinion - good or bad. No one heard me. "Opinions are like orgasms, Eleanor. Mine are more important, and I really don't care if someone else has one."

Down, down, down my feelings went, like hairs in a bathroom drain. One slid down - no biggie - another and another - until months of long, dark brown hair tangled together in the drain, causing it to back up. A drop of tap water couldn't even squeeze down the drain through all the clogged-up hair. The only way to fix the blockage was to remove all the tangled hair with a harsh chemical. Weed through the mess. Find the root of the problem. Clean it out and start all over again.

However, my bottled-up feelings didn't get remedied with a bottle of Drano and a long sink snake - although the Drano did eliminate the neighbor's yelping dog, who barked and barked, day and night. Drano did permanently resolve *that* situation. Drano worked on sinks and neighbor's dogs. My clogged-up feelings had a different way of untangling.

For the aggressive, female driver who stole my parking spot in the packed grocery store lot, I slowly dragged my car key along the side of her cherry-red car door. Maybe she should've parked near the back of the parking lot to avoid these types of mishaps.

For the greedy, young man who daily cut in line to order his morning caffeine, I slashed his bike tire with a little pocketknife while he flirted with the barista. Guess he'd have to ask his new coffee-smelling fling for a ride home.

For the affectionate couple who purposefully discarded their weekly picnic trash next to my favorite oak tree at the city park where I enjoyed reading, I sprinkled sugar all around the trunk of the tree to attract an army of ants. Find another tree to shadow your love story.

Perhaps my actions were a bit harsh and over-the-top, but I begged to differ. I was righting the universe. It was as if I was karma's bitch and helping her punish a few minor league players in her game of life.

I wasn't a mastermind criminal. I simply recognized an obligation to help people discover the error of their ways. And like some criminals after an action of consequence was finished, my bottled-up feelings didn't overflow as easily. It was as if a little had spilled out, and I was able to carry on with my daily business without totally losing it.

But the whole situation with Piper and Madison put me over the edge of sanity. Madison was a self-centered bitch who chewed up and spat Piper out without a second thought. As one of Piper's confidantes, she confessed to me how rotten her sister treated her, how horrible Madison talked to her, and how broken-hearted Piper felt. I couldn't stand to watch this story play out. I couldn't stand aside without fighting back even though Piper was content with being Madison's scapegoat.

However, a very distinct line had been crossed. No longer was I able to sit back and let Piper handle it her way.

Typing swiftly, I sent her a text and attached an image that I snapped from the far side of the living room.

SOS.

Chapter 31

Piper - April 22, 2016

I'd been curled up in bed with my favorite author, Dianne Chamberlain, when my phone vibrated on my nightstand. I was ninety-nine percent sure that the text was from Fritz, begging me to come to Maverick's party. Parties weren't either of our scenes, but Fritz and Maverick had been best friends since grade school. Fritz would do anything to please Maverick, like attending one of his parties where most of our classmates ended up naked in his pool, puking in the bushes, or passing out all over the house.

It was my eighteenth birthday, and I wasn't in the mood for the teenage shenanigans that I was sure I'd end up babysitting and cleaning up after. No thanks, my warm bed and a good book was where I wanted to be. I needed to forget my own troubles for a few hours and be distracted by drama that simply existed on paper.

I licked my finger and turned to the next page. I'd been waiting for this book to be released for months, and I found it hidden under my pillow when I arrived home from school. Behind the front cover in her messy handwriting, Maddy had written, *Happy Birthday, Puppet! I hope the fantasy Dianne created satisfies your anticipation for her newest book. Love, the Queen.*

Yes, my sister was a pain in the ass. Yes, she was a real numbskull, but she wasn't heartless. She knew and listened to me, possibly with only one of her ears, but she heard me. Even though she rarely acted like it, I also knew she loved me. We'd get through this phase and one day be closer than ever.

Out of nowhere, my heart filled with anxiety just as my phone vibrated. I hated when a premonition occurred. Often, the feelings were warranted, but they came on with no warning. My fingers absentmindedly played with the necklace that Fritz had given me for my birthday. As soon as he left, I'd opened the box and put it around my neck.

My phone vibrated, indicating another incoming text. Past experiences indicated that Fritz would text me until I responded to his request or until I shut my phone off to silence the begging. Reluctantly, I grabbed my phone to read what the latest hustle entailed.

I was wrong. The two texts were not from Fritz - they were from Eleanor. The first one read, *You might want to come to Maverick's party.* The next text was an attachment. When I clicked on it, the image displayed two partygoers making out and causing a scene in the middle of the crowded kitchen. The couple resembled me and Fritz, but I couldn't recall when this party took place. I used my fingers to zoom in on the photo. The tall male was definitely Fritz, but only the back of my head was visible in his baseball hat. I zoomed back out and noticed that the picture was time stamped: *April 22, 2016 at 11:55 pm.*

It was midnight. This picture had been taken five minutes ago, and Fritz wasn't making out with me, but with someone who looked just like me.

Damn it, Maddy. How could you?

I shoved the covers off and climbed out of my warm bed. Earlier, I'd asked myself how my birthday could get any worse. I had my answer.

I threw on the jeans that I'd worn to school earlier and tucked my bedhead into a baseball hat. While I looked everywhere for my favorite sweatshirt, I received a third text from Eleanor.

SOS.

Chapter 32

Maddy - April 23, 2016

After five minutes of quality tonsil hockey, I heard some gasps - sharp intakes of breath - around us. Since Piper and Fritz weren't known for PDA, we were causing quite a stir. We must be really impressing them. I grabbed onto Fritz's shirt collar and pulled him closer. A few seconds later, Fritz's teammate Willy forcefully tapped him on his shoulder.

As he leaned close to Fritz, Willy cleared his throat and whispered, "Dude, ummm...you need to stop *that* and see this." From Willy's tone of voice, it sounded like an axe murderer had just walked into the party.

When we did halt our lip-smacking and wiped away the excess that pooled around the outside of our mouths, we followed Willy's line of vision to the doorway of the kitchen. Both Fritz and I were still trying to adjust our eyes to the light.

Since I was a seasoned alcoholic and drug-user, my eyes adjusted quicker to the image in the doorway. It was me...I mean, it was Piper. Red blotchy spots scattered across her face as heavy tears pooled in her eyes. Because her teeth were clenched, her jawline was stiff. Her hair was a disaster and her clothes wrinkled. I couldn't tell if she was more hurt or angry.

Fritz wasn't used to the delayed effects that alcohol had on his brain. Seconds passed before he was able to register what he was seeing. His eyes stared at her and then back at me.

I'd gotten used to recognizing the look of disappointment on people's faces - my parents, teachers, coaches, and employers. It was nothing new for me. Witnessing it on her face was a thousand times harsher. Yet it also felt refreshing, gratifying to witness her pain. I'd hurt my sister's feelings many times throughout our childhood, called her vile names, thrown blunt objects at her and even purposefully stolen her prized possessions - like her favorite sweatshirt that I was wearing.

But seeing the look on her face after she saw me making out with her boyfriend of two years even caused a small pinch in my blackened heart. Regret wasn't an everyday occurrence for me as of late, yet that was the feeling that crept out of the deepest, darkest corners of my soul. Seemed like fun at the time and rather dangerous. After being caught by the only human who would be destroyed by it, it just felt selfish and pointless.

Tears rolled down her cheeks. Her bottom lip quivered. Her neck and cheeks were bight red caused by the lack of oxygen supply between her sobs.

As I was taking in every aspect of her, I noticed we had pulled off the twin thing without even trying - we were dressed very similarly. The baseball cap from Fritz topped her head - just like the one I'd stolen from Maverick's bathroom - along with a different but similar zip-up sweatshirt. Since I had her favorite one, she had to dig a little deeper in her closet to find another.

In a Maddy-like move, Piper confidently stomped toward us. Her hurt and heartache were stuffed down, and only anger and hatred seeped to the surface. Everyone around us faded away along with the blaring music and the noise of the crowd.

Fritz's confusion radiated from his whole body. He looked at me, then back at Piper. When she finally reached the two of us, I heard Fritz slur, "Babe, I totally thought she was you..."

She believed him, and fortunately for him, he wasn't lying. Poor bastard. Caught with his pants down and drool on his face.

She simply put her hand up, palm side facing Fritz. She threw him a pitiful look before her hate-filled eyes glared at me. Using the same hand, she pointed her index finger at me. "You. Follow. Me. Now."

Chapter 33

Maddy - April 23, 2016

We had drawn a lot of attention by the time we walked out of the large kitchen and towards the staircase. I think someone turned down the music in order to hear our conversation better. All eyes followed Piper as she walked away from Fritz and me and headed for the staircase. She was leading me upstairs for some privacy.

Obediently, I followed her. I'd been waiting for this crusty old zit to pop, been picking at it for months. I tried to push her buttons. Yes, she was always the better person. Always making excuses for me. Always forgiving and forgetting so effortlessly.

I welcomed this altercation. Of course, I was beyond curious as to what she'd have to say. I'd crossed a major line. No denying that. But like some murder trials, there had been no premeditation. The opportunity had presented itself, and I took advantage of the situation...and him.

As we ascended the massive staircase, I looked back at the partygoers and their eyes following us. I wondered what they were thinking, seeing, and saying.

Which one is which?

Could he not tell he was kissing Maddy?

What is Piper doing here at a party anyway?

I wonder which twin is the better kisser.

Should we ask Fritz?

Which one fell into the pool earlier?

What the hell just happened?

Do you think Maddy has done this before?

With each step, I imagined that we were playing the shadow game. Piper was the real person, and I was her obedient shadow, following closely behind. That was how I felt. An empty gray shadow. Her left foot stepped; my left foot took a mirrored step. Her right hand grazed the wooden staircase. My right hand grazed the staircase.

When we reached the top of the stairs, Piper yanked on the first door that came into view. She pulled and pushed, and finally it obeyed. As she opened the door, she held her hand on the knob and allowed me to enter the room first. She dramatically slammed the door shut and turned on the flashlight on her phone to find a light or lamp to turn on. We discovered it to be a bedroom, perhaps a guest room. There were no personal effects, no clothing hanging in the closet.

After six steps into the room, I turned around, and I crossed my arms over my chest and stood as the accused waiting for the executioner to slay me with her sharp and mighty sword. I was ready for her tongue lashing, prepared for a physical attack if she decided to resort to violence. I was prepared for both types of punishments and was aware that I wouldn't come out victorious in either battle. But I didn't care.

Guilty of all charges.

Unfortunately for me, I hadn't anticipated her change in emotion. Minutes earlier and downstairs, her death stare had shot daggers at me. They were laced with poison. Fritz and I had a small chance of survival. Hatred was the emotion that I was ready for and expected to receive.

After the click of the lamp and a deep breath, Piper turned around with enormous tears in her eyes. As her lower lip quivered and her eyes searched mine for answers, her shoulders sagged. Her anger was replaced by pure hurt. The determined, angry Piper who had stomped up the stairs was replaced by a weak, heartbroken version.

"Maddy, how could you? What are you doing? How could you hate me so much? You know how much Fritz means to me. What have I ever done to you that would make you do this? Why? I don't understand. What's happened to you? What has happened to us?"

I knew her, my twin - she was devastated, and I had purposefully caused it.

Why am I not feeling awful? What am I feeling? Satisfaction? Why can't I feel anything? Not even a small itch of remorse?

"Maddy, please talk to me. We aren't leaving this room until you talk. You haven't been yourself lately. I love you, but this has to stop. Your poor choices are destructive. It's as if you don't care. Is that it, Maddy?" Like I knew her inside and outside, she knew me too. But this new self-destructive, prideful Maddy wouldn't let her know that she was right. Pride and resentment firmly stood in the way.

"Do you really want to know?" With my blood-shot eyes, I shot daggers at her. My senses may have been dulled by the alcohol and drugs, but my hatred for her boiled high. "Piper, I hate you. Being your twin sister isn't all it's cracked up to be. I'm so *sick* of everything being about you. Even if *I'm* making poor choices for myself, why do you assume it's about *you*?"

"That's not what I said. You're twisting my words. And why do you hate me? I've done nothing but love you. You continue to be downright cruel to me, and I forgive you, every time. What have I done to deserve this treatment, Maddy? Please enlighten me." She wiped her tears with the sleeve of her sweatshirt and slipped her hands into the pockets of her sweatshirt. She truly wanted to hear what I had to say.

As I sized her up and down with a bitter stare, the words pouring out of my mouth were laced with poison. "You *breathe*, dear Piper. By simply *existing*, you cause my life to be a living hell. I'm so *sick* of being compared to you - the perfect daughter, the perfect student, the perfect friend - no one can measure up. You win. You're wonderful, and I suck." My words got louder and louder as my rage consumed me. My anger seemed to be in sync with the spring storm that was building outside the window. "Do you have any idea what it's like to never measure up, to never feel good enough?" My arms were tightly crossed over my chest as I glared at her waiting for a response.

A sharp flash of lightning illuminated Piper's face giving her a haunted appearance.

My words stung. From the dim lighting in the room, I could see the pain in her expression. She shook her head. "This makes no sense, Maddy. No one compares us but you." She paused long enough to take a deep swallow. "You're the only one who thinks that there is a winner and a loser between us. We look alike - *duh*, we're identical twins - but we're completely different people inside. We have different preferences and tendencies. I like Diet Coke, you prefer Coke. You look gorgeous in pink; me, not so much. I couldn't do a high kick to save my life, and you couldn't cook a meal to save yours. These differences are what makes us so wonderful and unique. We are two different people. Heck, we even have different size feet - I wear seven, and you wear eight!"

She tentatively walked towards me as I was still standing with my arms crossed over my chest. I recognized her move - she planned on reaching out to touch me. I didn't move, except for a distinctive eye twitch that happened when I was upset. She noticed it and stopped walking.

Damn it.

"Maddy, I know something is going on with you. You've been marginally crazy the last few months. We need to figure it out, work through it. You have my full attention. You didn't need to seduce my boyfriend. I'm here. I'm listening." Her hands hadn't left the pockets, but I knew my sister well. It was killing her not to touch me, bring me back down off of the ledge.

The part of me that loved her identified that she was right - I did need to talk and get help. Obviously, I wasn't getting better on my own. But the other part that contained every ounce of my stubbornness had control over my tongue, and it would not budge. I was in a self-destructive pattern. It started with the failure to land the part-time job with Mrs. Yates, then the breakup with Daniel. Losing my self-confidence sent me down a hurricane of trouble. It was too much. I couldn't handle all the disappointments and failures. I felt broken and unrepairable; therefore, numbing the pain helped my survival.

We stared at each other - two mirrored images. Sizing each other up. She was waiting for me to confess what was eating me alive. She waited for me to break the silence. She was the patient one.

In our continued silence, we heard the muffled noises of the party as well as the booming thunderstorm that was brewing outside. The storm sounded aggressive. The thunder cracks shook the large house. And even through the closed curtains, the strokes of lightning penetrated the room, again giving our angry faces a sinister glow.

Every word that I spat out was laced with deep resentment. "Earlier tonight, you inquired about my day, why I was in Principal Klawonn's office. *You* are the reason I spent my birthday being yelled at. *You* didn't show up for our switcheroo, Piper, so I resorted to good old-fashioned cheating. If I failed another Spanish exam, I wouldn't graduate high school."

"That's not fair, Maddy, and you know it. I *never* agreed to another switcheroo. The interview with Mrs. Yates was the last one. I clearly recall telling you that you needed to legitimately study. I was no longer switching with you for major or minor life events. We both need to earn our own accomplishments and failures."

"Like your failure to land me that job with Mrs. Yates?" I snapped.

"Is that what this is all about? I've apologized and apologized. There isn't much more I can say. I'm sorry, Maddy, but isn't that even more proof that our switcheroo days are over? Fooling our teachers and friends was entertaining when we were younger and nothing essential was at stake."

"Yes, a fabulous idea to stop switching as soon as it blows up in *my* face. *My* life is ruined. *My* future plans halted. *You* ruined my chances with her. You, Piper. *You*."

"So, to get back at me, you planned on ruining my relationship with Fritz because you're pissed that I failed to impress a potential boss when *you* should've attended the interview *yourself* in the first place? You're an expert at turning things around, Maddy. Like how these last couple months of *your* misbehaving is *my* fault. Typical Maddy - placing the blame onto everyone but herself."

The claws were out. Rage rolled off both of our bodies. Steam puffed out our ears. Like in Spain, I was the matador waving the red cape, muleta, to irritate the bull - Piper - into a bullfight. *Wave the red cape to earn the attention of the bull. Rage blinds the bull. The bull can only focus on its rage. Charge! The matador wins.*

"And you, Perfect Piper, failed a task as soon as it was something you didn't give two shits about. You brush your teeth with one hundred percent concentration, yet the *one* favor that I begged for, you completely tanked. Coincidence? I think not. You don't want me to succeed. You don't want me to be better than you."

Her eyes narrowed into two small slits. "You know what, Maddy? I'm so sick of pussyfooting around your feelings. I'm sick of catering to how anything and everything will affect you. Everyone treats you like glass - afraid you might shatter. Afraid you'll snap. You're a royal bitch, Maddy. None of this is my fault. I will *not* accept the blame for your miserable life."

I clapped my hands. "Wow. Of course not. If you accept blame for it then you would have failed and would be less than perfect. And Perfect Piper never fails. She's perfect."

She hated the nickname Perfect Piper maybe because it made her feel less than perfect, focused on the fact that no one was perfect. I used that nickname - that I awarded her - to push her buttons, rip apart her patience - like the bull who hated the cape waved in his face. In one evening, I managed to press many of her buttons.

This final one shattered her common sense and ignited her rage by shoving me so hard that threw my body into the hard wall behind me.

The sheer force of impact knocked the wind out of me. I struggled to catch my breath. *She shoved me.* I had *not* seen that coming. I wanted her to react. I had known the rage was building in her but hadn't seen the attack coming.

Again, I clapped my hands a couple of times and flashed her a sinister smile.

"Perfect Piper pounds her pretty, popular princess of a sister. Nice one."

"Enough, Maddy. I've had enough of your mouth. There is a limit to how much I can forgive you for." She wasn't backing down. Her chest puffed up and down as she also tried to catch her breath from her adrenaline surge. Even after pushing me, I could see the pain in her eyes. I placed my hands beneath me and pushed myself back onto my feet. Straightened my hat - Maverick's hat - and went in for the next round.

"Fuck, Piper, I could care less if you forgive me. I don't want your precious forgiveness. I don't forgive *you* for ruining my future. Nothing will be the same between us because you ruined my life by not giving two shits about me. And I'm sick of being Puppet's shadow. You're a selfish twit."

The back of her hand flew across my cheek. My cheek burned from the violent impact from the palm of her hand.

Like normal siblings, we didn't always get along. Names were shouted. Doors were slammed. A few strands of hair were pulled. But this was the first time we had gotten really physical.

My gut reaction was to forcefully tackle her. My arms circled her waist and laid her flat on her back. We were rolling around on the floor. Panting, cursing, grabbing each other. Trying to find each other's weaknesses. A point of surrender.

During our tumble of limbs, she managed to punch me in the eye and scratch at my cheek. After what I could only estimate was forty seconds of a struggle, I somehow managed to be on top and had the upper hand. I was sitting on her chest. I pinned her arms under my knees and delivered a powerful left hook to her eye.

She screamed in pain. I was panting like a dog, and even though my hand ached from punching her, I wasn't about to admit it. I rolled off her and tried to catch my breath.

"You win, Maddy. I hate you. I hope that's what you wanted to hear." She curled up into a ball and started to sob.

I stood up and straightened my clothes. Wiped the blood from my nose. I won. *Why don't I feel good? Isn't this what I wanted?*

I had one more blow, but I wasn't going to use my fist. "I don't think you hate me yet, Piper, but you will."

She lifted her head slightly in my direction as she was cupping her hand over her left eye.

"How come you never told anyone about the rape?"

A bolt of lightning lit up the sky and provided me with a clearer image of my heartbroken sister laying on the floor. Her eyes revealed fear and pain as she processed the question.

"How do you know about that?" She choked out in between sobs.

"Dear sister, I staged it. I sent Mr. Jarro that morning to the school to violate you. Unfortunately, he didn't know it was you he was fucking, and he broke up with me not long after that. You must not have been a very good lay."

"Oh my God..."

My verbal punch was much more powerful than any sucker punch that could have landed on her face. I don't think Piper would agree with the old saying, *Sticks and stones may break my bones, but words will never harm me.*

When I exited the room, she had returned to a fetal position, sobbing. I had to admit that a small nugget of remorse entered my heart. She'd been my best friend and constant companion for almost all my life. I was part human, but my pride and resentment towards her kept my feet moving.

Before I slammed the door shut, I turned the lock on the door. I told her, "You need a minute to cool off. Maverick can find you when the party's over."

At that exact moment, a monstrous *boom* filled the house. The electricity shorted and the blaring music stopped. But instead of loud rap music, screams filled the walls of the house. Calls to friends in the dark quickly turned frantic. Glass shattered, and I heard an aggressive sizzling noise.

The partygoers were trying to feel their way around in the darkness. The commotion had me rooted to my spot at the top of the staircase. I was unsure of my surroundings, so I didn't dare take a step down the stairs for fear that I'd tumble to my death. Instead, I listened to the frantic chaos below me.

"What was that loud boom?"

"Did a bomb go off?"

"Why did the power go out?"

"What's happening?"

"Do you smell smoke?"

I heard these questions bouncing off the walls and sliding their way up the stairs to me. A few teenagers grabbed their phones from their back pockets and started to light up the rooms, which made me feel for my phone. It wasn't in my hoodie pocket where I remembered putting it last. It must've fallen out during our little wrestling match. I tried to retrace my steps as headache started to creep in.

The birth of the terror had formed just over my left shoulder. Hissing and crackles increased with each passing second. Amber and yellow flames shot out from under the door of the room next to the one that I exited less than a minute ago. The smell of burning wood, burning metal, burning plastic filled my nostrils. An aggressive, hungry fire beast chewed its way through anything that dared to cross its path while spitting out the contents of its destruction as ash. It crawled closer and closer to me as the floor beneath warmed.

Smoke haunted the gaps around the door and sniffed its way ahead of the flames as if clearing a path for the pending destruction. Before I was able to assess my current situation, the sneaky killer smoke invaded my lungs. I started to choke as I collapsed onto the hard, wooden hallway floor.

Out of the darkness, a figure - perhaps a guardian angel - appeared, grabbed me, and carried my obedient, limp body swiftly down the stairs and out the front door. The fresh air filled my lungs, forcing out the acrid fumes. The unknown male who saved my life dumped me on the freshly mowed grass and sprinted back into the mansion as I tried to collect my bearings.

Everything had happened so fast. My head was spinning, and my lungs were burning.

Through my one good eye that hadn't been sucker punched, I noticed that everyone from high school was standing or kneeling on the front lawn. The majority of the crowd was holding each other, tears rolling down their cheeks, screaming and crying. A small group was completely speechless while a few others used their cell phones to call for help. A couple responsible teenagers took control of the situation, ordering people around, asking if everyone escaped, making sure everyone was safe. And a few of us that were close to the flames were still in a bit of shock. Our primary focus was on breathing.

While the buzz from my alcohol and weed consumption was quickly wearing off, my throat was raw from inhaling the smoke. My head pounded in regret. Even though I was unable to participate, I heard the other partygoers' chatter from under the safety of the big oak tree.

"The flames were everywhere."

"Anyone that was near the garage is toast."

"Literally, burnt toast."

"I bet it was lightning. A sharp, quick bolt of lightning. I think it struck the east wing of the house."

"I had no idea that the storm was right on top of us."

"Do you think anyone's dead?"

"Maverick's parents are, for sure, gonna find out about this epic party. He'll be dead come Monday."

"Shit, man! All of our parents are gonna find out. Mother Nature is one evil witch."

Someone was tapping me repeatedly on the shoulder. I recognized her from school. She had a short, stylish bob with diamond studs in her ears as well as one dainty one in her nose. Her kind face was familiar, but I was having a hard time concentrating. I couldn't understand what she was asking me. Her lips moved, but the meaning of her words couldn't be interpreted by my ears.

In the tree's shadow, I noticed another person lurking, intensely staring at me. She was dressed in dark clothing, and her hair was wet and clinging to her face. Under her long, soaked bangs, her dark, squinted eyes were questioning.

I returned my focus to the patient classmate kneeling in front of me. Pity and concern filled her eyes. "Honey, you are safe now." Her finger tapping my shoulder had turned into a gentle upper back pat once my bloodshot eyes searched hers. "Help is on its way. Firetrucks and ambulances, all headed this way. Please tell me your name. Can you tell me your name?"

Like another bolt of lightning struck my head, my thoughts cleared, and I instantly remembered what had just happened moments before this disaster. The moments that led me into the hallway. The moments that included the punch to my right eye. I remembered her.

"Piper?"

Chapter 34

Piper - April 23, 2016

How could we have shared the same womb? How can she not see how much I love her? That I would do anything for her? Why do I still love her after all she's done to me? She used me any chance she could for her own personal gain. And tonight, she seduced Fritz. There were no lines for Madison. She crossed, jumped, and stomped on them all.

And she orchestrated Mr. Jarro raping me. What kind of person did something like that? Especially to her own twin sister. The most terrifying minutes of my life were staged by my own sister just to get back at me. Mr. Jarro raped me?

My heart broke in my chest. I howled in pain. Red, hot tears rolled down my cheeks. *Is this really my life?*

I felt betrayed by both of the people whom I loved the most. Even though Fritz was oblivious that Maddy was pretending to be me, it broke my heart that he couldn't tell the difference. He was hurting and had numbed it with too much alcohol, but I was also devastated.

To purposefully cause me heartache was an all-time low for Maddy. Normally, her scandals gained her personal advancement - at least in her opinion. She cheated on exams to gain a higher grade than she'd have received by trying to answer the questions on her own. She abused drugs and alcohol to ease her conscience for a limited amount of time. Make her forget all the disappointment she caused people around her. However, I wasn't sure how Madison gained anything from tricking Fritz and breaking my heart.

From my fetal position on the floor, I felt the floor shake beneath me. The entire house shifted.

An earthquake in Minnesota?

An enormous, thundering explosion rattled my ears. Seconds later, the house's electricity went out, and I was lying on the floor of a strange house in pure darkness. My ears were ringing, and the floor felt unstable. Instantly, my hands reached for my cell phone.

Crap! I lost it. It wasn't in the front pocket of my hoodie. It must've fallen out during our little tussle on the floor. I patted the carpet near me but didn't find anything.

I quickly stood up and put my hands out in front of me to guide my way to the door. Out of the darkness, I banged my knee on a sharp wooden object - probably a dresser. *Ouch!* My hands felt their way around the table towards what I imagined was the space where the door would be located. About six tentative steps forward, my hands proved my calculations to be correct. They explored their way to the doorknob.

What a relief to feel that metal, round object that would be the key to my escape. However, I was uncertain what I'd find on the other side of the door after hearing the deafening sound. I turned the knob to the right and caught resistance. Then I tried turning to the left. Again nothing. My relief was quickly replaced by fear. The door wouldn't open from the inside. I was trapped.

Following my natural instinct, I pounded on the door and screamed at the top of my lungs hoping that someone on the floor below would hear me. I realized with the power out the music wouldn't be blaring, so the possibility that someone might hear me was better. I pressed my ear to the door and pulled away - the door was warm. I wasn't sure if my ears were playing tricks on me because after the loud bomb-like noise, they were still ringing.

Panic.

What is going on? Think, Piper, think.

Even though the heavy shades were pulled shut, I could detect a very small glow of light from outside. It was midnight, so where was that light coming from?

I took a deep breath and started coughing. It felt as if I was being choked. My lungs hurt, and my breathing became labored. I smelled smoke. *Oh God...*

The warm door, the loss of electricity and loud crash - the house was on fire. And I was trapped inside. The only person who knew where I was was Maddy. I was sure that she ran for help, but I wasn't sure how much time I had.

With my hands stretched out in front of me, I sensed my way to the window on the opposite side of the locked room. After twelve steps, I pulled back the velvet curtains and noticed a crowd of people scattered across Maverick's enormous front lawn. They were my classmates. They were wet, scared, and crying...but safe.

Even though I was standing in darkness, I knew that the smoke had penetrated my space. Like a sneaky murderer, it was crawling under the door, looking to kill me. Its acrid, eye-watering stench filled my nostrils. As it invaded my chest, I was struggling to breath without coughing. I didn't have much time.

As I raised my arms to bang on the window to get someone's attention, I noticed *her* - Maddy sitting on the front lawn under a big tree. She wasn't searching for help like I believed she was. Instead, she appeared safe, unharmed, and completely...self-absorbed. She had abandoned me. Left me in this room to die.

Her head was between her legs as she appeared to be coughing. She raised her head, looked up at the massive house with panic in her eyes. I saw her lips move. She was saying my name.

Chapter 35

Eleanor - April 23, 2016

From forty feet away in the safety of the nights' shadows, I observed her, coughing and a bit lethargic after she had been carried effortlessly by a tall, muscular classmate out of the burning house. He set her down under the nearby shade tree. And sprinted back into the house. The tree managed to keep her and a few others dry, but was it really the best location after a lightning strike? *Whatever.*

With her head between her legs, she was hacking into the grass. She didn't seem injured, so I wasn't sure why he carried her out of the house, except that she continually coughed. She had gone upstairs just before the screaming and flames started. I'd followed the two shadows up the winding staircase. First, I was curious as hell, and secondly, I wanted to protect Piper. I wasn't sure if she had a strong enough backbone to stand up to her own sister.

When I noticed that the front door was a clusterfuck, I ducked out the back of the house towards the pool using my cell phone's flashlight to guide my way. People were screaming, crying, and running all around me. I stood there and stared. No one noticed *my* scared eyes and flowing tears from a few feet away. Even as wet Eleanor, I was invisible - good to know.

Something felt off, but I couldn't pinpoint what it was. Sometimes, I could read the mood of the situation and could predict what was about to happen. I wasn't sure if it was a premonition or something that my childhood invisibility superpower morphed into a heightened sense of my surroundings. But my gut was doing flip-flops, and my heart ached in my chest.

Even more unexpected was that my feet weren't allowing me to move from the shadows to join and console my friend. Something invisible to the naked eye held me back in the shadows beyond my normal anti-social behavior.

She looked like Piper, she acted like Piper, she was dressed in Piper's clothes. But something was off; that was all I could explain. I disappointed myself after my years of observing and note-taking that I couldn't put my finger on exactly what was holding me back in the shadows. Piper was the one who should've escaped. Maddy was messed up and drunk.

Our senior class president, Missy - or was it Melanie or maybe Michelle? I couldn't recall. She was being so utterly responsible and collecting everyone's names to verify accountability. *Smart thinking, Ms. President. So glad you're our fearless leader.*

I watched her collect and jot down names of the classmates around me. Her fingers typed feverishly on her phone. To a few inconsolable teenagers, she gave their shoulders a tender squeeze. She was calm and sympathetic to everyone she encountered. Her eyes landed on me, standing alone in the shadows. She quickly made her way in my direction.

"Hi, there. Were *you* at Maverick's house party?"

It was obvious that she didn't think I belonged. *Thanks for the harsh, unnecessary judgment.* My response was a blank stare.

"What's your name? We want to get a head count in case someone is missing."

"Eleanor. Eleanor Cutter. Cutter, as in someone who cuts with a sharp knife." I was being a smart-ass at an inappropriate time, but I couldn't seem to help myself. I didn't appreciate her tone. "There was a headcount taken before the fire? There was a shit-ton of people at the party. It seems odd to take a headcount at a rager." My response was laced with sarcasm.

Missy, Melissa, or Michelle - whatever her name was - returned my sarcastic comment with a rude glare. "Thanks, Eleanor. I'll be sure to reassure your loved ones' worries about your safety." Quickly, she moved onto the few drier partygoers under the tree. I watched her show sympathy and kindness to each one as they gladly divulged the information that she was seeking.

"Honey, you are safe now." She knelt in front of her face to make sure her words were being heard. "Help is on its way. Firetrucks and ambulances, all headed this way. Please tell me your name. Can you tell me your name?"

I knew what was wrong.

Out of her lying, two-faced mouth, I heard her respond, "Piper."

As firefighters arrived at the scene, water-resistant blankets were distributed to the wet, scared students. I didn't get one. The constant blinking blue and red lights bounced off the soaked streets. The glistening tree leaves reflected the lights. The loud, annoying sirens echoed down the street.

The rest of the night was a loud, wet blur. Emergency personnel talking in my face, checking for injuries or smoke inhalation. Screaming, worried parents arrived, searching for their teenagers among the party crowd. I leaned deeper into the shadows and walked home twelve blocks in the rain.

The wrong twin had died.

Part Two

"Everyone says that forgiveness is a lovely idea
until he has something to forgive."
~CS Lewis

Chapter 36

Pine Hill Star Post

April 23, 2016 - Headline, Front page
High School House Party Ends in Flames

Last night's thunderstorm caused a home to ignite in flames. Firefighters received several 911 calls from 11166 Country Club Boulevard claiming an uncontrollable fire broke out during a house party.

Several teenagers were rushed to the nearby hospital. At the deadline for print publication, no information was known about the severity of injuries or if any casualties occurred.

April 24, 2016 - Headline, Front page
Lightning Strikes Mansion, Leaving Two Teenagers Dead

The house fire on Country Club Boulevard proved to be deadly. Lightning struck the house at approximately 12:30 a.m. during a house party attended by many Pine Hill High School students. Within minutes, the east wing of the home was destroyed and engulfed in flames. Luckily, the lightning strike hit an unoccupied section (the garage) before it quickly spread to the rest of the home.

However, two casualties have been reported: Madison Mae Sterling (18) and Winston Ray Showfeld (17), both of Pine Hill High School. Sterling was a popular senior set to graduate in May. Showfeld was a promising junior, a starting point guard for the high school basketball team.

"A tragic loss like this forces us all to question goodness and justice. In this time, our community must come together to remember Madison and Winston for the light they shared with others - though it shone for far too short a time. We must carry that light." Principal Klawonn added that the school plans on installing a park bench near the front of the school building in remembrance of these two bright and promising students.

Obituaries will be available in the life section of tomorrow's paper.

April 25, 2016 - Headline, Editorial Section
Deadly Lightning Strike – Could It Have Been Prevented?

Following a house fire that was caused by lightning, questions are forming in regards to the two dead teenagers. Where were the owners of the home? Could this tragedy have been prevented? Almost a hundred students survived, so why couldn't Madison Sterling and Winston Showfeld escape the house in time?

No one can predict where and when a lightning strike will occur, so that part of the tragedy couldn't be prevented and isn't being questioned. However, questions are being raised as to why these two students were unable to escape in time. What part of the house were they in when the lightning strike occurred? Did alcohol or drugs hinder their ability to escape?

That question leads to where did the alcohol and drugs come from? Is there an adult responsible for this tragedy, or is it simply a terrible accident?

The homeowner, Christopher Wilson, of Wilson Orthopedic, could not be reached for comment. See the Obituary Section for full obituaries.

April 25, 2016 - Obituaries, Life Section
Madison Mae Sterling (April 22,1998 - April 23, 2016) of Pine Hill, Minnesota tragically lost her life after lightning struck the house where she was celebrating her eighteenth birthday.

Madison was an active member of her high school cheerleading squad as well as the drama team. Madison enjoyed creating YouTube videos with tips on how to apply makeup and accessorize outfits. Her love for mischief and adventure will be missed by everyone who knew her. Madison was scheduled to graduate from Pine Hill High School this spring.

Many loved ones and friends will miss Madison's witty comments and outgoing personality. She is survived by her twin sister, Piper, her parents, Ryan and Elaina Sterling, her maternal grandparents, many aunts, uncles, and cousins.

She was preceded in death by her paternal grandparents, Everett and Vera Lange, and her aunt, Peggy Lange.

The family is holding a prayer visitation on Thursday, April 30, at 7 p.m. at Hudson's Funeral Home. The funeral will be held on Friday, May 1, at 1 p.m. at Trinity Lutheran Church, followed by a family-only burial.

Winston Ray Showfeld (September 5, 1999 - April 23, 2016) of Pine Hill, Minnesota, tragically lost his young life and will be sorely missed by his family and friends.

Winston was born on September 5, 1999, in St. Paul, Minnesota. Winston lived in the same house for his entire life and created many memories in the neighborhood. In his spare time, he was a boy scout and an active volunteer at Holy Spirit Church. When he wasn't shooting hoops, he was watching basketball and cheering for his favorite team, the Minnesota Timberwolves. Winston's love for having fun and *snorting* at anything humorous will be missed.

He is survived by his older sister, Grace, his parents, Tina and Brian Showfeld, his maternal grandparents, many aunts, uncles, and cousins.

He is preceded in death by his paternal grandparents as well as a younger brother, Evan.

The family is holding a prayer visitation on Thursday, April 30 at 7 p.m. at Hudson's Funeral Home. The funeral will be held on Friday, May 1, at 1 p.m. at Holy Spirit Church, followed by a family-only burial.

Chapter 37

Maddy - April 23, 2016

What have I done? Is Piper dead? Maybe someone found her, and no one has told me yet? Oh my god, what is going on?

Yep, a huge fire broke out, and someone had time to check all one hundred rooms for a stray partygoer. Yep, that happened.

Piper is dead! Am I to blame? Am I a murderer? Should I tell someone that I'm really Maddy, and this is a colossal misunderstanding?

This isn't an episode of Three's Company! Jack and Krissy aren't going to take the blame. Plus, it's been twenty hours since you clammed up. You think people will believe you?

I know that! I don't know what to do.

My racing thoughts bounced around inside my head. If someone broke open my brain, it'd be like cracking open a beehive during the middle of a hot, steamy summer day. Angry little bees buzzing around with only one thing on their mind: survival. Honey oozing out of their treasured home that they slaved over. Anger and confusion. The buzzing sounds ricocheted off the walls in my brain. Under my lids, my eyes darted back and forth. Every thought that escaped my mind was a frightened bee searching for answers and someone to attack. Anger, confusion, and escape.

Why didn't I scream and tell someone that she was still in the house? What is wrong with me? She was my sister! I loved her.

Upstairs, all alone and weeping. Crying because I pulled a switcheroo on her boyfriend without her knowledge or consent. Number one rule in a switcheroo - do not perform a switcheroo without the other twin's knowledge. I french-kissed the love of her life because I was bored and wished to cause her unnecessary heartache.

Am I finally ashamed of my actions? Is that why I couldn't speak? Did I let her die? Did I murder my own twin sister? Could I have saved her if I'd said something to someone? Anyone. Dear God, please wake me up from this nightmare!

Guilt and remorse lay like a hundred-pound weight on my chest. I didn't trust myself to speak. The last time I spoke I dug myself a huge, gaping hole. I hadn't corrected my classmate when she repeatedly informed people that my name was Piper - the firefighters, the EMT, the hospital nurses, my parents, the doctor, the journalists... Nope. My lips remained sealed. After eighteen years of yapping about every opinion or thought that grazed my brain, I chose that moment to not utter another word while my sister lay helpless in a locked room, burning to death.

What kind of person am I?

Completely evil. Biggest bitch and worst sister of all time.

True. Oh God, Piper, I'm so sorry.

Doesn't do her a lot of good now. She's dead. She can't hear you.

While this lively, volatile conversation occurred inside my brain, my physical body remained motionless. I was oblivious to the people around me. I was unable to respond to my surroundings. My eyes wouldn't open, and my mouth hadn't said a word since I whispered my sister's name.

Cold but gentle fingertips touched my wrists, checking my pulse. "There it goes again. It just spiked."

I heard several sets of feet pacing the floor of my hospital room. I assumed it was my nervous, worried parents. I heard my mom softly trying to relax me. "Calm down, Piper. Everything is going to be okay." Her voice was nasally, as if her nose was stuffed. Probably from crying.

A monitor started beeping repeatedly. A set of squeaky shoes - like the sound of basketball players' shoes as they run up and down the court - rushed into my room. "What happened?"

"We aren't sure, Dr. Drake. One minute she's calm and then the next she becomes very agitated."

"Let's start her on some anxiety meds. I'll get an order in."

You've obviously screwed up your own life. Why not take this chance for a re-do? Let Maddy die in Maverick's house fire. You deserve this second chance. It isn't your fault that damn Melissa told everyone you were Piper. She's to blame for this ultimate and final switcheroo. Piper isn't and can't be here. But she'd want the best for you. She was so sweet. And wasn't she the best of you?

But I left her there...

Yes, you did. Get over it and move on.

How can I do that?

You're a heartless bitch. Everyone knows it.

I could admit that my life had been tanking before that night. My poor choices caused enormous cracks in my boat, the *Titanic*. My ship was about to sink when ironically a lifeboat - the fire - saved me.

I could do this. I could pull off an epic switcheroo. The last switcheroo. I knew Piper as well as I knew myself. Of course, I'd need to up my game in school. Only a month left. I could do that. Her stellar grades and sparkling reputation would help me sail through the next thirty days.

I'd need to care less about my physical appearance - Piper preferred the natural look. I'd always been a great believer in enhancing beauty - thank you to Grandma Mary Kay - that I was blessed with. No more YouTube videos on how to apply makeup. Not a Piper hobby.

My doting parents were hurting with the loss of a child - their favorite. I couldn't cause them additional pain by admitting that I wasn't Piper. No, for them, I needed to be Piper. They'd be hard to trick, but Piper and I had practiced on them hundreds of times growing up. All of these occurrences lasted for a brief time compared to a switcheroo that would last the rest of my life. I needed to bank on them not wavering in their belief that I was in fact Piper. I needed to be sure to also show that sometimes my words and actions would sound like Maddy because she was my identical twin. Sounding like her and doing things that might remind them of her would be normal.

Yes, I could do that. Plus, in the beginning, grief would overwhelm their common sense. They'd see Maddy everywhere. They'd search for her in crowds of strangers. It was what people did when they were in mourning.

You're giving yourself a lot of credit by assuming they'll mourn you.

Shut up!

Next on the list of who I'd need to convince without a doubt would be her loyal, sweet, boring boyfriend, Fritz.

Wouldn't he be able to sense the difference right away?

Well, he didn't last night. He didn't sense that it was you as he jammed his tongue down your throat.

Shut up! I need to think.

Even though Piper never confided in me, I had been sure that Piper and Fritz were bumping uglies. I could tell whenever Piper was hiding something from me - part of the twin feeling we shared. I was sure I could handle Fritz. I'd been with enough men to not be concerned with adding one more to the list.

But what if Piper was a lay-there-and-take-it kind of lover? Could I manage to be a less than active participant? Or what if they were really in love and it was super passionate and hot? Crap! I wish we would've talked about our sex lives. I had no idea.

Her friends, Carrie and Mya, might prove to be more difficult to convince that I was Piper. They knew her well and didn't like me in the least. The feeling was mutual.

My breathing slowed. Because my body was in a state of shock, I didn't realize it was the anxiety meds that the doctor prescribed, and the nurses had added to my fluid bag. In my opinion, I believed it was because I formulated a plan. A way out. A way to make this the best possible solution for everyone involved.

I heard voices around me. Sometimes, they whispered as not to wake me, I assumed. Sometimes, the voices spat out words in between sobbing. It was hard to concentrate on the actual words being shared so instead I focused on the sound of the constant beeping in the background.

Beep... Beep... Beep...

My eyelids were heavy. They wouldn't cooperate when I tried to focus on a sound or a voice that I recognized. I couldn't lift them. All for the best. I was too tired anyway.

Beep... Beep... Beep...

Hours later, or maybe it was days - I have no idea; the concept of time didn't seem relevant in the state I was in... I smelled bacon. My all-time favorite meat. It filled my nostrils, and they flared open in response. I remembered the house rule that Mom created because of how much we all loved bacon. Each BLT would be limited to five strips of bacon.

Never one to let something slide, I had questioned her reasoning. "Five? Five doesn't seem enough, Mom. An even number is always best. You've always said, 'God doubly blessed me because two is better than one.'" I mimicked her voice a little too high-pitched and whiny, but my point was made.

"Of course, I do believe even numbers are best. Because you make a valid point, Madison, let's limit every Sterling BLT to *four* strips of bacon. Four is an even number."

My mouth dropped open. That was not the result I'd hoped for with my argument. When I looked up from my plate, Mom was grinning from ear to ear.

"Got ya." She rumpled my hair and tossed another piece of bacon on my plate.

Mmmm...bacon.

Who would've thought the smell of bacon would cause my eyelids to lift? Not the hospital staff who was casually delivering a tray with my breakfast food and was surprised to see my one eye open - the other one was swollen shut.

"Well, hi. Good morning. Let me set this down and get your nurse." The young hospital staff member dressed in peach-colored scrubs quickly dropped off the tray and darted out the door. I assumed she'd been a bit surprised to see me awake.

Between my head fog and the pirate eye, I noticed my breakfast consisted of two strips of bacon and two pancakes with a generous plop of butter on top of the stack. A miniature maple syrup bottle stood at attention next to my plate. If only I could get my body to cooperate, because I was starving.

As my medicated mind stalled on its next steps, my ears perked up at the sound of shuffling feet.

"Good morning, beautiful. My name is Nurse Sara. Amy told me you were showing some signs of alertness. Must have been the mouth-watering, miracle-working bacon. It's done it again. I've tried to tell the administration that the kitchen's Monday bacon works miracles - I've seen it with my own two eyes. They don't listen to little old me." As she jabbered away, she shuffled around my bed taking my pulse, checking my pupils, looking in my ears, taking my temperature. Nurse Sara was an amazing multi-tasker. "Maybe a pretty, young thing like you can make some noise. Tell them, 'The bacon woke me up, I swear.' They might believe you."

I nodded.

"I knew it! See, I ain't no fool. All my life I've had this keen sense of knowing things. Before something bad happens, I get this feeling of pain, struggle, or doom in the pit of my stomach. I don't get the positive vibes though." She was standing next to my bed reading the monitors on my screen and calculating the results.

I felt the weight of her words. Those were the first few words I'd heard and understood in the last couple of heavily medicated days. Did she mean that she knew I wasn't Piper? Was she trying to tell me something? Did she want me to confess?

She turned towards me with a look of concern across her face. "Oh, beautiful, don't get all worked up. Your blood pressure is rising. Take a couple of deep breaths with me." She placed her cool-to-the touch stethoscope on my bare chest. "In...out...in...out..."

I followed her commands. I didn't realize how quickly my gut reaction would trigger my physical characteristics that the hospital was monitoring. I'd need to be more careful. More prepared. More unemotional.

After we successfully relaxed my body, she showed me how to elevate my bed so that I could sit up to eat. My mouth began to water.

Chapter 38

Maddy - April 25, 2016

"Doctor, what is wrong with her? We can see she's not physically harmed by the fire, but she won't speak. I don't understand." I could hear my mom talking - the words pouring out of her broken heart. I understood that all I had to do was utter one intelligible word. But I couldn't. My brain wasn't working properly. I was a robot, and my main circuit was fried. Wires were shorted and flopping around loosely. Messages were being received, but appropriate responses were undeliverable. I kept my eyes shut so they thought I wasn't listening to them.

"Mr. and Mrs. Sterling, we need to give Piper some time. She has been through a terrible ordeal. We can only begin to imagine what she witnessed. Physically, we know she suffered smoke inhalation, but mentally, she may be experiencing PTSD, post-traumatic stress disorder. Too soon to diagnose her. However, after surviving such a tragic experience of losing her twin sister, I feel that this is a very natural response." Dr. Drake turned to examine me. My eyes could only flutter open before my eyelids would fall back closed again. "Piper is in there. She needs more time to heal."

I tried to keep my eyes open to take in the doctor as he talked about me as if I wasn't there. He was wearing a lab coat and the words *Abbott Hospital* were stitched on the breast pocket. My eyes couldn't focus long. His image was blurry. But his words did burn in my brain - Maddy was gone. Maddy had died in the fire.

Thankfully, the doctor didn't expect much from me, because I had nothing to give. I didn't want to talk. I didn't want to respond. My sister was gone. I could've saved her, but I let her burn to death instead.

Luckily for me, I was completely exhausted and couldn't stay awake for long periods of time. Unfortunately, every time I woke up, I'd remind myself what happened. Piper was dead - people thought that I was Piper. Maddy was dead. No wonder my head pounded. This was too much, too confusing. Sleep was good.

"You know you could've saved me. The bedroom door was locked. I had absolutely no chance to escape. You left me in that room to die, Maddy. Why didn't you go for help? Why didn't you tell anyone where I was? You murdered your own sister." Her eyes bore into mine. They were fire-red, as if flames themselves were flickering in them. Strands of her blonde hair that had escaped her bun were waving in the breeze. A cloud of smoke started to circle her.

"I'm so sorry, Piper! I never meant for this to happen. I never meant to hurt you. I loved you. I was messed up - the drugs, the alcohol, the depression. I'm so sorry." I was sobbing and reaching for her. Trying to pull her out of the smoke that was surrounding her.

"You're so sorry now that you've taken over my life? You're telling everyone that you're me! You're a piece of work. You ruined your own life so you took over mine! Don't tell me that you're sorry. I don't believe a word that comes out of your mouth. Do you believe your own lies? I know you better than anyone, Maddy. You're not sorry that I'm gone. But you'll be sorry when the lies come back to haunt you. Karma is a bitch, Maddy." When she shook her head, her bun came loose. Heavy smoke engulfed her image, and slowly she disappeared in the gray, killer clouds.

"Piper! Please don't go!"

"I'm not going far, Maddy. I'll be haunting you every minute of *my* life." She jetted within inches of my face and screamed. Smoke rolled out of her mouth.

It wasn't Piper screaming. It was me.

As I bolted awake from my guilt-filled nightmare, I choked on imaginary smoke. My hospital gown was drenched. My hair was matted in sweat to my face. My breath came in short pants. I could smell the smoke in my nostrils - the nightmare was real.

A night-shift nurse raced into my room asking if I was all right. Monitors or my screeching screams must've alerted her from her paperwork because she still gripped a ballpoint pen with her right hand.

I nodded in between my heavy breathing.

"Nightmare?"

I nodded again.

After she disconnected me from my monitors and helped me dress in a dry hospital gown, she changed my wet bedding while I splashed cold water on my pale face in the adjoining bathroom. The smoke smell still tinkled the inside of my nose, and even though logically I knew it wasn't possible, I felt my sister's presence in the goosebumps on my arms. When the nurse left the room, she clicked off the overhead light and ordered me to rest.

Laying there alone again, I cried. Hard-core, ugly crying. I couldn't help it. The nightmare felt so real. Piper's hatred and disappointment broke my heart. And she was right - I killed her. I'd never see my sister again. Guilt and regret tried to break my resolve. Yet I remained silent. Not uttering a word since the fire. It'd been days - I wasn't sure how many - and words couldn't form on my dry, cracked lips. I didn't trust myself to speak.

After a few minutes of sobbing, I wiped my face with my hand and took some deep breaths to control my heartbeat. While my eyes burned from the tears, my head pounded from the lack of oxygen. I felt a headache starting to build, and with the headache also came the arguing voices. My vision grew blurry.

You can and must do this. It was a damn dream provided by your guilty conscience. What did you expect?

But I killed her!

You aren't Mother Nature. You didn't cause the lightning to strike that house. You didn't force smoke into her lungs. You didn't light a match and burn her body.

A sob escaped my throat.

Face it, Maddy. You need to be stronger than this. You have no choice now. You're Piper. Get over it and move forward.

I can't do it.

I don't want to hear it. Your damn choices have once again brought you to an ugly crossroads. Now think, is there anything that differentiates you and Piper besides your personalities? We're talking about physical differences.

Instantly, my swollen, bloodshot eyes flew to the tiny, dime-size birthmark on my right wrist. The only trait that physically differentiated us.

Oh God...

We can handle that.

My left hand - that my malicious voice controlled - forcefully grabbed the nurse's ballpoint pen that she had haphazardly abandoned on my tray table. The pen poked and tore its way into my flesh. I frantically tried to carve the birthmark out of my skin. It wasn't sharp enough. I needed something sharper. I jumped out of bed, ripping the monitor cords from my body and causing an insane amount of beeping to bounce off the sterile walls.

We need something sharper.

There's a plastic knife from dinner in the garbage.

Like a rabid animal, I threw out all the contents from the small bin before locating the white, slightly used butter knife. I carved back and forth over my wrist. It hurt like hell, but I was cutting through the skin and starting to bleed quite a bit. It was going to work. Who knew a cheap, plastic knife could carve up someone's skin? While a small, sly smile grew on my lips, a triumphant, sinister laugh escaped my throat.

Several nurses came sprinting into my room. Screaming and hollering at each other to grab the deadly weapon from me. I held it up in the air and spat out a small giggle. Bright, red blood dripped from the white, plastic knife.

They think this is deadly? Wow. Major over-reactors.

However, my reaction to their textbook procedure in handling a suicidal and self-harming situation were not appropriate and were read as temporarily insane. Seconds later and I wasn't sure exactly how, the three petite women confiscated the weapon and forcefully held my hands behind my back. I was shoved face-first onto my bed. As two nurses held me down, the remaining nurse bandaged my messy wrist.

It felt like I was watching an episode of *COPS* where the perp giggled the whole time at the mess and total misunderstanding of the situation. I experienced a small poke on my upper right arm. I started to feel weak and light-headed, but my giggling continued.

Before I knew what was happening, I'd been returned to my bed, but my arms were strapped down at my sides. Monitor cords and IVs were gently reinstalled. The medication pulsed into my veins from the magical IV. From my reflection in the hospital window, my smile resembled the Joker.

My eyelids drooped.

Chapter 39

Maddy - One Month Later

After my brief stint in the behavioral wing of Abbott Northwestern Hospital, I was released with strict instructions to not be over-stimulated or stressed about catching up on my life. I needed to be patient and take things slow.

My hospital-assigned therapist Dr. Andela advised, "Your new normal will take a bit of getting used to, Piper. You need to recognize that there'll be a big void without your twin sister. It's normal to feel sad and angry. What happened was a very tragic accident, but Maddy would want you to move on and be happy. I don't believe that time heals all wounds, but as time progresses, the heartache does lessen. However, when you're the person that requires healing, time doesn't seem to be a good friend.

"A wonderful way to find healing and acceptance might be discovering something to cherish your sister's memory. It can be participating in something that she enjoyed, creating something to remind you of special memories, or perhaps writing a journal to her. Think about that, and during our next visit, we'll discuss ideas that you've come up with."

"I'm not ready."

Dr. Andela was a skillful therapist - she predicted my response. Sometimes, I thought she might be psychic. "Piper, you're ready. This is the next step." She handed me a cell phone.

It was a new one since Piper's and mine both were lost in the fire. However, being in psychiatric care, I hadn't been allowed a phone. Too distracting and caused more anxiety. So, for a month, I was left alone with only my thoughts. No contact with the outside world, which the old me would've argued about, but the new me was relieved.

"Call me, Piper, any time, day or night. I've taken the liberty of programming my cell number into your new phone."

I awarded her a small, thankful smile. During these four weeks under her watchful eye, I'd learned a lot. Many things that I didn't want to know but was forced to learn. The month away rewarded my body with physical and mental healing. My lungs were clear, and my mind understood that this was my choice and I needed to give it one hundred percent effort. That was the actual lesson that I learned, and I applied it to my situation.

During the long ride home from the hospital, awkward pauses filled the spaces in between Mom's random comments.

"Piper, wait until you see the daffodils that we planted last fall. They're in full bloom. Just beautiful." Her cheeks were forced up by her artificial smile, which made her eyes slightly close. I returned her remark with a blank stare. She looked tired.

We planted daffodils last year? What else have I forgotten? Oh wait... Piper planted the flowers with Mom.

Five minutes later, she filled the silence with another random comment.

"Did you hear Carrie earned a full-ride scholarship to St. Cloud? She plans on majoring in biology." Another cheesy grin was sent in my direction, which I returned with another blank stare. I was getting good at not feeling, not reacting.

I hate Carrie.

Carrie with her short wavy blonde hair that seemed effortless. The way that she walked with ease across the skinny balance beam - she even did the splits on that damn thing. Spread-eagle Carrie with her flawless record and never-ending trail of awards. But she was Piper's good friend... Oh Lord...she was now *my* good friend.

Five minutes later...

"Remember Maddy's probation officer, Lily Armstrong? She reached out after..." Mom couldn't finish her sentence because she'd need to mention my name and my death. "I guess she's getting married to one of her former colleagues from Why, Arizona. They ran into each other after he moved up here, and some sparks happened. Their wedding is next summer."

My PO, Lily. Oh crap, she'll see through this charade if she visits.

Five minutes later...

"I'm making your favorite meal for supper tonight: cheddar meatloaves and garlic mashed potatoes."

Yuck.

I hated red meat, but Piper loved it. Oh... I wasn't sure this switcheroo was such a good idea. A month ago, it seemed like my only option.

When I accepted that everyone thought I was Piper after the fire, outside on the lawn, I never imagined it going this far. Initially, I had been in some state of shock. I was unable to formulate the proper words to indicate that I was actually Maddy, not Piper.

Before I knew what was happening, I was loaded onto an ambulance and rushed to Abbott where I refused or couldn't speak - I wasn't sure which at this point. Our high school class president, Melissa, oversaw my hospital admittance, made the appropriate phone calls on my behalf, and directed my parents to my sterile hospital room. It all had happened so fast. Words were being thrown in my direction, but adequate responses were not returned. Shock, guilt, betrayal blocked my brain from the ability to properly respond.

She was gone. I left her there. It was my fault that she died. How could this have happened? I should've died, not her. She was the good one. I couldn't make a proper decision to save my soul.

Even at the time of her death, I didn't stop anyone from calling me her name. I allowed it - I wanted to hear her name. It helped me to feel her all around me. Maybe if I kept hearing her name, it would come true.

When my parents rushed to my side in the emergency room, I cringed at their touch, coiled at their embraces. Piper was the affectionate one. Piper was the hugger. I was more a fist-bump kind of gal. I didn't deserve the attention. But they didn't notice my limp arms or silent greeting. They were in their own stage of shock and denial. I was sure that they were just thrilled that their favorite daughter survived.

However, they hadn't known one of us was missing yet. The first responders had still been actively looking for survivors in the wreckage. It was a large property. I'd had a few visitors stop by the room to verify my name, but whoever was with me verified it for me each time. I didn't need to utter a word.

During moments of self-pity, I imagined the looks of chagrin and utter shock on my parent's faces when I'd tell them I was Maddy, and not Piper. I didn't think that I could handle it. I was a disappointment to them - Dad had just said those exact words when I'd been caught cheating.

Dark, gray circles lined the outside of my mom's eyes. Redness filled the whites. I could only imagine the number of nights that she had cried herself to sleep with worry. The gray hair speckles in the roots of her hair were because of the stress that I'd caused in her life. I couldn't tell them. If they were this distraught from losing me, I could only imagine how much worse their mourning would be if they knew it was Piper who died in the fire.

We pulled into the driveway of our modest split-foyer home that had been built in the 80s. Dad, who had been his normal quiet self the entire ride home, shut off the engine and then opened the garage door. "Elaina, why don't you head into the house so I can talk to Piper for a few minutes?" Mom looked surprised at Dad's request, but I was sure that she'd ask him later what we discussed.

As Mom's car door shut, Dad turned his body around in the driver's seat so he could face me, sitting in the back behind the passenger seat - which I realized wasn't Piper's usual spot; it was mine. I would have to get better at the little things if this switcheroo was going to succeed.

"Piper, we're so glad that you're home with us. Under the psychologist's direction, we've removed all sharp objects from the house. We realize you were under extreme duress and depression when you tried to take your own life after the fire, but hopefully now after your therapy sessions, you understand that we only did that because we love and want to protect you." He paused for a moment to swallow a huge lump that had formed in his throat. "Please understand that we're mourning like you are. We miss Maddy too, Piper. We'd give anything to change the past and have her back with us." This time when he paused, a small sob escaped.

I'd never seen my dad cry before. He was the head of the house - the strength, our voice of reason, and our solid parent. Even when Mom struggled with her anxiety, Dad never wavered. He had a strong faith that kept us all grounded. Seeing him cry was like realizing for the first time that he was human.

I reached my shaky arm towards him as he was wiping the tears that had crept down his cheeks. My hand rested on his shoulder, and I gave him a small, weak smile. The best I could muster. I had no words that would help. I had no advice to give. I gave his shoulder a little squeeze.

After I choked down a bite of the meatloaf and moved my fork around the potatoes, we started cleaning the kitchen.

"Thanks for dinner, Mom. It was delicious." I tried to sound thankful, but my words felt flat. The medication that the doctors had prescribed for my depression curbed many natural tendencies, like fluctuating my voice, or when I asked a question, there wasn't much of a raise at the end of the sentence. Every little effort exhausted me. Sleeping for twelve hours a day became my new norm. Being awake and doing what was expected of me required an enormous amount of energy.

My therapist, Dr. Andela, had told me, "You need to be patient, Piper. Not only with your own improvement, but also with your friends and loved ones. No one will know what to do or say around you. Everyone deals with grief and tragedy differently. There is no correct path except to deal with your feelings and know that they're normal."

I tried to constantly remind myself that soon I'd get my life back. It would be very different, but normal would return. I needed to focus and take things slow.

Mom's words interrupted me from my daydream. "While you were...away" - she couldn't say *the psych ward* - "you had a lot of friends calling and asking how you were doing. Your doctor recommended that you didn't have any visitors but family until you were stronger. As soon as you were home, she recommended maybe one visitor per day until you started feeling like yourself again."

I only feel like myself when no one is around.

"Dad and I invited Fritz over after lunch tomorrow. He's been worried sick about you. We figured you'd want to see him first."

Fritz! Crap!

Would he be able to tell? He'd be the first one who I needed to convince besides Mom and Dad. They were so caught up in their own grief and misery that they hadn't noticed any differences. Or at least mentioned them to me. I'd need to be on my A-game to fool Fritz, who knew Piper as well as I did. Maybe even better these last few months before the fire. I'd been so out of control and self-absorbed that we had grown apart. I did regret how carelessly I'd treated my family. My twin sister didn't deserve to be the brunt of my snarkiness, and she took it all until that last night, the night of the fire. The night that she died and I seized her life.

But I'd accepted that there was no turning back. I needed to own it. I needed to be her, think like her, and act like her. No one would ever know. I needed to fool everyone and luckily for me, my failed suicide attempt by slashing my wrists had everyone's expectations low. I could work with a low bar - had done that my whole life.

During my month-long stay at the psych unit, I vowed that the only thing I could do was make her proud. Make her dreams come true. Make Piper the best Piper that I could be. However, I'd already decided Fritz was not part of the new Piper's future, *my* future. I had faith in my acting ability, but I didn't want to fake love or passion. I had the evening to formulate a plan. Fritz had to go. He was also a huge threat to my success at pulling off this final twin switcheroo.

"That's fine. But do you care if I go to bed now? I'm exhausted." And I knew that I looked it. Huge, dark circles embraced my eyes. My pale skin completed the ultimate mournful exterior. I hadn't taken more than a few minutes for my appearance for the last month.

"Sure, honey. You head up to bed, and I'll bring you a glass of water for your nightly medication." Mom patted the top of my head like I was a toddler.

I accepted the dismissal and started for the stairs. With each heavy step, my heart ached for her. Memories flooded out of my memory vault: we raced up these stairs, we sat on these carpeted steps sharing secrets and giggles, we stomped up these same stairs after being sent to our rooms.

When I reached the top, my body automatically turned right and pushed open the door to my old room. Everything was as I left it the night of our eighteenth birthday. That night I'd stormed up to my room after another lecture on how they expected more from me. I'd been caught cheating on a final exam. In hindsight and sobriety, I didn't blame my parents. They hadn't known what to do with me. Every choice turned into a bigger mistake than the one before. I was in a major self-destructive phase. No reasoning or strict punishment made any difference. I didn't care. I didn't respect myself enough to want or think that I deserved help. Therapy helped me realize what I was doing to myself.

My covers were frozen into a position of recently having been vacated. The pillow still had a slight indentation of where my head had rested. My unicorn night light illuminated the corner of my room. The pictures taped to the wall above my desk showed a popular party girl giggling and posing for a photographer. Poser. That was what I recognized now in the photos.

At the desk sat a laptop, a collection of pens and pencils in a souvenir mug from a family vacation to San Diego. A black frame displayed a picture of two identical girls. Their hair was in braids, freckles dotted their identical slightly up-turned noses. Each girl was a mirror image of each other...on the outside. That picture had been taken four years ago on our fourteenth birthday. We had slowly been drifting to different activities and interests. That was the first year we didn't agree on party preparations. I dreamed of a big, loud party filled with everyone we knew; on the other hand, Piper wanted to invite two friends over for a more intimate evening. We met in the middle, or at least Mom decided for us. We each invited a couple of classmates over for a slumber party. Piper had invited her two closest friends, Carrie and Mya. They were in all her accelerated classes. They shared her love for following the rules and making their parents proud.

Although my invite list consisted of twelve classmates, Mom trimmed my list to three girls. The three that made the cut all shared my love for adventure and mischief. It was the start of our rebellious tribe: Dee, Kat, and Tania.

The two groups of girls had nothing in common except that we lived in the same area and attended the same school. Even though it would've happened eventually, this birthday was the starting point in the decline in our twin sister bond. The shift had been gradual and smooth, nothing alarming. We both realized how different we'd become.

We shared a bedroom in our three-bedroom home until a month before our sixteenth birthday. I'd requested to move into the spare room. When I'd brought it up over supper, Piper's eyes had immediately widened with surprise. She was devastated that I was ready to put space between us and she wasn't. Because she was so sweet and kind-hearted, I knew she wouldn't try to talk me out of it. She'd let me go even though she didn't want to.

Dad thought it was a great idea. "You two could use your own space. Plus, your growing wardrobe is bursting at the seams in your shared closet."

It was no shock that Mom didn't agree. She wanted us to never grow up. "Are you sure, Madison? Even when you two were babies you slept better in the same crib. You hated to be separated."

"We aren't babies anymore." I hated to be the one to burst her bubble.

"I know that. I'm just saying while it might sound like a good idea, you might miss each other."

"And Piper'll be just across the hall. If I get scared, I'll sneak into her bed in the middle of the night."

Mom turned to Piper. "What do you think, sweetheart?"

We all turned our attention to Piper. She had stopped eating and appeared on the verge of tears, but she managed to choke out, "It's a good idea. We aren't sharing the same embryo anymore. And yes, I'll be across the hall if Madison ever needs me." She looked up and held my gaze as if asking, "And you'll be across the hall if I ever need you, too, right?"

Chapter 40

Maddy - May 2016

Breaking up with Fritz was harder than I thought it would be. Not because I had any true feelings for him. No, I wouldn't have been able to pull off dating him for any amount of time. His charming personality and boyishly handsome good looks didn't captivate me like it did my sister and most of the female population at my school. Fritz wasn't my type. He was the perfect guy to introduce to your parents. He was the ultimate boyfriend material - impeccable manners, deep faith, flawless record at school, not wanted by the law, bright future, star athlete, and undying devotion for people he loved.

But all that bored the hell out of me. I wanted and needed more of a challenge. I didn't want one who already professed his love and admiration for me. I wanted a man who made my heart flutter, knees weak, and challenged me. I wanted a love story that you read about in romance novels. Fritz wasn't my Romeo or my Edward. He might have been Piper's, but I was Piper now, and this man-boy couldn't turn me on even if I provided him with specific instructions to ignite my jackpot.

Kiss here, caress this, and poke two fingers here.

It was hard to break up with Fritz because he didn't want to let the relationship come to an end. And ultimately, Piper was looking down at me with utter disappointment. I'd fucked up my life and now, I was ruining everything she loved and cherished.

After Dad answered the door, Fritz strolled into the living room holding a dozen daisies and wearing a silly-ass grin that resembled fear or a dog with his tail between his legs. He was walking on eggshells. Pitiful and not attractive. Confidence was a turn on; lack of confidence was a complete ball-buster.

Thank goodness, Mom was a master at filling awkward silences. She leaped off the couch and offered to put the gorgeous bouquet of flowers in a vase.

"Aren't they amazing, Piper?" She was raising her eyebrows, trying to prompt a response from me. I was still really good at staying silent, but my therapist had encouraged me to speak.

"Not only is it rude not to respond to someone who's speaking to you, but it'll also help you become engaged with your life and your feelings." Dr. Andela's voice echoed in my brain.

In an old Maddy style, I'd countered with, "What about that saying, if you have nothing nice to say, don't say it?"

Dr. Andela considered my question for a moment. "Of course, that's true. But blunt honesty is different from being cruel. You may not like something, but it's better to be tactful than rude. However, choosing to just stare at me when I ask you a question can be considered disrespectful." She was onto me and my survival skills.

Mom cleared her throat.

"Thank you, Fritz," I managed to say as I remained seated on the couch.

"Have a seat, Fritz. Ryan and I will grab you guys a couple of drinks." Mom was excusing themselves from the room. "Ryan? Can I get your help in the kitchen?"

Dear Lord! Obvious and super awkward.

Fritz slowly made his way over to the couch. Before he sat down, he leaned over and delivered a quick peck on my cheek, like my grandmother did when she didn't want to smudge her lipstick. I hadn't moved to offer anything else.

A flicker of a lightbulb turned on in my foggy brain. I blamed the medicine prescribed by Dr. Andela for my delayed response to an evident situation. Fritz was nervous about talking to me - Piper - because of making out with me - Maddy - at the party. That was the last time I saw him - the last time he saw Piper. Piper had just caught us kissing in the kitchen. She didn't even allow him to apologize or say anything before she dragged me up the stairs to have our own fight.

"You look good, Piper."

I looked like crap, and I knew it. He was afraid of saying the wrong thing so that I might end up back at the Nut Shop - what I called the psych ward of the hospital. Dr. Andela said I shouldn't mask my feelings with humor, but she had still grinned at my reference to her employer.

"I've missed you so much. I hope your parents told you that I called every day. I was so worried about you and the..." Because he was nervous, he was rambling, and the real me was losing interest. My mind started to wander, and I noticed he was checking out every inch of my body. That made *me* a bit nervous. He knew Piper's body like his own, I imagined. And I was sure that he'd heard the rumors about my failed suicide attempt. "How are you...feeling?"

His staring made me uncomfortable - first time for everything. I crossed my arms over my chest. I was wearing another one of Piper's baggy sweatshirts that said, *Life is Good* on it. Because he was staring at my stomach, I looked down to see if I'd spilled some lunch on it.

Dad politely cleared his throat as he re-entered the room with two cokes poured over ice. Mom carried the daisies in a big clear vase. Because there wasn't much conversation taking place, I could hear the carbonation from the pop bubbling in the glass.

"Dad and I are going to sit outside on the patio and enjoy our afternoon coffee. You two have a nice chat. Holler if you need anything."

As soon as they set our drinks and the flowers on the coffee table, they moved onto the patio. Fritz and I were left alone to get reacquainted. Even though he was sitting only about two feet away, my pulse quickened and butterflies bounced around in my stomach. I wasn't interested in prolonging this conversation. I needed to get it over with. Rip it like a Band-Aid.

"Fritz, we need to talk." It was the key phrase before every breakup in books and movies. Fritz's face drained of color - he knew what those five words meant. "I need to focus on healing and moving on. I think it'd be easier if I did that on my own."

"Piper, are you breaking up with me?" I couldn't look at him because I could hear his voice crack. He was about to cry. "You can't do this, Piper. You can't do it alone. We have plans for our future together. "

"Fritz, this is what I want. I don't want to be with you anymore."

"But Piper, I love you! I'd never hold you back. We lift each other up. You just need some time, and I can wait. I get it. You lost your twin sister. It's huge. Your life will never be the same. I understand, but you need me, Piper. We need each other. You can't do this alone. Don't push me away. Not when you need me the most." He grabbed my left hand - the freshly scarred one.

I tried to pull it away. It was still in a minimal bandage. As he looked down at my wrist, he rubbed his thumb gently over it. When he looked up at me, he had fresh tears in his eyes. He looked heartbroken.

"I'm not going to change my mind. It's over, Fritz." I jerked my hand out of his grasp and shot him a look of determination.

"Is it because I kissed your sister?" His eyes searched mine. Trying to find the answer inside them. "I totally thought she was you. You know how she is...was. She always wanted to push us apart. She was jealous of our close relationship. I had no idea that she was playing me. I don't want to speak ill of the dead, but it's true. Maddy tricked me. I love *you*. I thought I was kissing *you*. Is that why you want to break it off?"

I was never jealous of the two of you. In fact, you grossed me out.

This switcheroo was harder than I anticipated.

"Yes, Fritz. It is." I knew that he wouldn't give up easily, so I needed to add an extra harsh punch to secure my decision. "We're finished. You cheated on me with my own sister - my own *dead* sister. Do you think I'll ever get past that night? Every time I look at you, I think about how the last few moments of her life were spent making out with *my* boyfriend."

Dramatically, I stood up, grabbed my coke, and stormed upstairs to my room. Leaving my sister's first love crying and alone in my family's living room.

Chapter 41

Eleanor - May 2016

When my phone lit up with an incoming call from Fritz, I knew it couldn't be good. He'd been invited to Piper's house for the first time after she'd been released from the hospital. After the fire, we became friends – or maybe 'people who talk because of mutual concern of an important person in their life' would be a more accurate description of our relationship. It wasn't like Fritz and I had anything else to discuss besides Piper. We had nothing else in common. I wasn't going to fake a newfound love of baseball to have a shared interest. The only thing we had in common was the fire. Without it, I would've never spoken to Fritz.

Of course, we were worried about Piper for different reasons - he worried about the pregnancy, and I worried if I was wrong about which twin survived.

But life threw us a curveball - okay, I had learned a little bit about baseball due to Fritz's influence but only because he used sports analogies all the time, and I had to ask him what the hell he was talking about. As I was saying, life could throw you a curveball, and you found yourself in an unfamiliar situation. That was where Fritz and I were.

Since April 23, we had talked on the phone almost every day. The conversations either consisted of Piper news, gossip, or worries. He was the one to call me after he heard Piper finally started talking. "Her mom said it wasn't much. Mainly to her therapist, but at least we know she's still *in* there."

Of course, I never told him that she confided some of *their* major secrets to me. I was Piper's sounding board. I knew we weren't truly close. It was a very one-sided friendship. I didn't have much to share. My parents were both dead, and I was living with my grandmother, who never left the house. I was an only child. Obviously, I didn't have much of a social life, so I had been completely content with focusing on Piper's life. I'd been doing that with my note-taking for the last four years.

I envied her and her so-called problems. She was gorgeous and also unaware of that fact. Not only did God create a masterpiece of beauty, but He also constructed another one just like her. I didn't believe in God - I was simply repeating Piper's beliefs in a higher being.

But that was where the similarities ended in my book.

When Madison looked at you, you could almost hear her judgments. Her eyes traveled up and down, cataloging every article of clothing - "white crew-neck T-shirt possibly from Wal-Mart, Old Navy mom jeans, black and white knock-off Vans also from Wal-Mart, self-dye job probably Clairol color 'Average Joe'" - guessing your weight, body fat, and muscle mass - "one hundred and fifty pounds, about five feet eight inches tall, with very little muscle so perhaps thirty percent body fat." It was like she had X-ray vision and could laser right through you. Her stare made you uncomfortable. Yet after checking you out, she'd flash you one of her million-dollar smiles as if signaling she was finished, and you could move on now - dismissed. I hated her. It amazed me how I could be completely enamored with her twin sister and detest every fiber of Madison's being.

Piper's eyes reflected her genuine care and concern. When she asked how you were, her expression revealed that she truly wanted to know. She was approachable, kind, and sweet.

No one ever referred to Madison as sweet, I was sure of it. The football team had nicknamed her 'Praying Mantis' because of her ability to seduce the opposite sex. As soon as a young man was captivated by her every move and word, she'd figuratively eat him and spit him out. Legend had it that in one four-day weekend, she broke four hearts from the starting lineup. The young men didn't even see it coming.

Piper couldn't hurt a thing. As her chemistry lab partner, I had actual proof. She couldn't and wouldn't puncture a dead frog with a needle. Tears poured out of her eyes on dissection day. And as her loyal friend, I covered for her. I didn't want her sensitive heart to change or diminish at any level. Piper was perfect the way she was. Perfect Piper.

"Fritz. What's up? How was she?" Cut to the chase. Fritz was a nice guy, but too talkative and in touch with his feelings for a jock, in my opinion.

I heard a faint sniffle.

"Fritz?"

"She broke up with me."

"She what?" I must've heard him wrong. I knew that they had lifetime plans. I knew Piper loved him with all her heart and soul. Another point in my *It's Madison* bucket What was Madison's endgame? I figured she'd keep him around to make everything easier.

"She broke up with me." He couldn't contain his heartbreak and let out a loud cry. "She said she doesn't love me anymore. She can't stand to look at me. My face stirs up too many painful memories."

"Wow. I can't believe it. I'm so sorry, Fritz. I'm sure she just needs some time to adjust. Let her find her new normal."

He blew his nose and tried to collect himself. "You weren't there. You didn't see her. She was different. Her eyes - they were cold. I could always see her love for me in her eyes, if you know what I mean. But today, her eyes were empty. She didn't seem to care a bit that she ripped my heart in two. She broke up with me and stormed out of the room. I had to let myself out of the house. I don't know what to do. I love her." Loud sobbing resumed.

"I'm sorry, Fritz. I don't know what to say."

He cleared his throat and choked out, "I gotta go... You know, the only other time we broke up was when *you* happened..." Then I heard a click.

When Piper and I had been assigned lab partners, something electric happened. I couldn't explain it, but we both felt the pull - the spark - when we were together. There was a deep connection that we couldn't deny. My heart fluttered when she'd enter the room, and her cheeks would flush when she was near me. Both of us assumed it was because we were sexually attracted to each other and decided to entertain that feeling. After one afternoon alone in my room, we'd realized that that wasn't what we were experiencing. It was a deeper, intense connection. Nothing sexual.

Piper had attempted to put it into words. "Maddy and I also have an unexplainable connection. I'd call it a sensation of what she's feeling. It isn't like I hear her voice in my head, more like an invisible link. It's similar to what I think you and I are experiencing. A magnetic pull towards each other."

After our disappointing kiss experiment, we had been sitting against the wall behind my bed. We'd agreed that the kiss wasn't what we'd imagined or dreamed. In actuality, kissing Piper had sent the opposite feeling in my body.

After I discovered that Ryan Sterling was my real father, the connection that we were experiencing made more sense. But after the fire, the magnetic feeling evaporated. That was the difference I was feeling.

Piper - not the bitch pretending to be her - was gone.

Chapter 42

Maddy - May 2016

When I reflected on the events of our eighteenth birthday, I was ashamed and devastated. I had acted like a spoiled brat, and obviously in hindsight something was mentally imbalanced even at that time. Instead of asking for help, I acted out.

Would I go back and change the events of that evening if I could? Of course.

However, that wasn't possible, so I'd accepted my fate - or my sister's - and had chosen to move forward. Some people would consider it a sinister, evil choice, but they hadn't lived in my shoes. I stayed mute for several weeks only uttering that one name that had a spiral effect on anything that transpired after the fire. My choices were limited.

Mom and Dad had finally returned to work after guarding me like a hawk ever since I was released from the psychiatric wing of the hospital a week ago. Their hovering stemmed from a place of love, but that still didn't make it any easier to stomach. As Piper, I did my best.

The first chance that I was able to escape, I did. I jumped in my car and drove to Ink Envy, a new edgy, hip tattoo parlor in St. Paul. I needed and wanted to do this. I'd thought about it while I lay in that same boring hospital room day after day.

I'd always wanted a tattoo and planned on inking myself as soon as I turned eighteen. But now I had an underlying drive to accomplish it. Plus, the summer heat in Minnesota was bearing down, and I didn't know how much longer I could get away with wearing long sleeves in May.

I was the first customer to arrive at the shop that morning. Scottie, the owner, whom I recognized from the website, was lighting up the open sign as I pulled on the heavy, glass door. Mystical door chimes announced my arrival, and the stale smell of cigarette smoke greeted me.

"Hey, doll, park it in that blue chair, and I'll be right with you." His website bio claimed he had over one hundred 'meaningful' tattoos on his body, along with a few 'unmeaningful' ones.

I climbed into the blue almost-dentist-like chair and looked around the shop. I counted five other chairs. Scottie seemed to be the only artist working at ten in the morning. Must not be a popular time of the day.

During my stay in the Nut Shop, I had created a list of the obstacles in my path to becoming Piper. Fritz was number one, and luckily that had been removed. The birthmark and now fresh scar on my wrist also proved to be a hurdle that I needed to erase. Since plastic surgery was out of the question, a fresh, meaningful tattoo seemed like a logical choice.

Before Scottie made his way over to me, I heard him shut the register and click on some music. "I hope you don't mind some old man music, doll. When the young'uns are here, it's all the loud, noisy shit music. I need some country to start my day off right. Please tell me you've heard of Garth Brooks?"

Scottie was about to touch me with a long, sharp needle. I wasn't about to judge his taste in music. "Did you know he made an album under the name of Chris Gaines, his alter ego?"

His face lit up. "Well, now I'm impressed, which doesn't happen often. Name's Scottie, but my friends call me Scooter. Got your ID on you?"

From my wallet, I pulled out Piper's driver's license and handed it over to him.

"Good. Nice to meet you, Piper. I didn't want to have to turn away a smart, young thing like you. What do you have in mind?"

I showed him the scar that I needed to cover up and a simple drawing I'd doodled while I was in the hospital. It was the initials *PJ* and a jellybean. "The scar is a daily reminder of a very difficult time in my life. I'd like to move past it by covering it with a gentle reminder of someone I love."

"It's your body, your choice. But since you're young, let me give a small piece of advice that I give to anyone before they permanently write someone else's name on their body. Permanently inking a name on a part of your body that's visible to everyone might not be the best idea at your age. You're young, doll. Love changes and sometimes fades. I'd hate to see you back here after you -" he looked at my drawing to see it again "- and PJ broke up."

"I appreciate that, but she's dead. I'm hoping with your artistic skills that I won't ever forget her. Keep her close and remind me to move forward."

Scottie nodded in understanding. He gently took the piece of paper with the hospital logo on top and set it down on his movable, four-wheel cart.

The scar was the last bit of evidence of Maddy. I was no longer her. I was Piper, and I needed the reminder that I could be better. I *would* be better. I wouldn't take anything for granted. This tattoo was a symbol of renewal. Starting over. A fresh beginning. Carve out the old me.

Chapter 43

Eleanor - May 27, 2016

Back and forth. Back and forth. I paced my room from one side to the other. I didn't want Grams to witness my anger. She'd worry about me - she always worried. Instead of watching *Wheel of Fortune* like we did every night after dinner, I excused myself after I cleaned up the kitchen. I claimed that I needed to study. Grams had no idea what happened on the second floor of our home.

Back and forth. Pacing or patterns helped me concentrate. And release some stress. My elevated anxiety level had been caused by Madison Sterling.

No one questioned a word that came out of her mouth. Truly, how could I be the only one who knew? How could her parents not see it? Did she break up with Fritz because she was afraid that he'd figure it out? There was no doubt in my mind that she was not Piper.

I needed a solution. I needed to come up with a plan. Somehow expose her for who she really was. Force her to tell the truth. Guilt her into doing the right thing.

That's it. Guilt.

Unless Madison was more of a bitch than I realized, she'd feel some level of guilt about claiming to be her dead sister and taking over her life. It just didn't seem possible that there wouldn't be an ounce of remorse within her. I just needed to tap into it.

Back and forth. With each step, I was moving closer to a solution.

To claim I was mildly obsessed with my two gorgeous, identical classmates would be an understatement. Being a straight-shooter, I knew where I stood in life. What I lacked in beauty, I strived to make up with brains.

Madison and Piper - on the outside, mirror images, two matching smiles, four sparkling blue eyes, wavy blonde hair, petite, upturned noses and flawless figures. You either adored them or hated them.

Honestly, my fascination with the two sisters started during our freshman year of high school. While I was normally an attentive pupil, if either sister was in my class, I took notes about them rather than what was being taught by the teachers. How many times she smiled, if she opened her book, when she flicked her hair over her shoulder. Rather than paying attention to the teacher's lecture, I concentrated on them.

The other fascinating truth about Piper and Madison was the fact that inside they were nothing alike. From their confidence to studiousness, from their athletic ability to the other's clumsiness, from their good nature to the other's cunning. Madison and Piper were night and day.

Madison ran in the popular crowd - jocks, cheerleaders, the wealthy. Every party invitation landed in her lap. She oozed confidence. While Piper's attractiveness had been subtle and natural, Madison used chemicals and coats of paint to accent her virtues. Madison's long blonde hair was sprinkled with lots of artificial, white-blonde highlights. Her makeup was flawless and highlighted her cheekbones, full lips, and big blue eyes. Her style had been ripped right out of a fancy website detailing what to wear.

On the other hand, Piper was the girl-next-door, everyone's friend. She was a natural beauty that didn't spend hours on her appearance. Because she tended to trip over her own two feet, Piper spent time with books and activities that didn't involve balls, running, or jumping. Even though Piper was gorgeous, intelligent, and successful, she was approachable. Her celebrity comparison would be Princess Diana, the People's Princess. Royalty.

And I served the princess. I was her devoted subject. I filled spiral notebooks of notes and notes of her daily activities, her likes and dislikes, anything funny or thought-provoking she said. I wrote it all down.

Again, I was only *mildly* obsessed.

Chapter 44

Maddy - May 27, 2016

I'd always been good at lying. Before the fire, I considered it a skill, a talent. But living a complete lie was a different, bigger ballgame than the little white lies here and there that I was naturally good at.

Yes, I walked the dog.

Of course, I never said those awful things about you.

I didn't see him shoplift the TV. Sorry.

Previously, my lies were like regular season baseball practices. Wear the practice gear, talk smack with your teammates, spit some seeds, hit the ball but don't run. However, living as Piper was like playing first string in the championship game of the World Series without any formal practice. Suit up, baller. No room for error or misjudgment. If I missed that mile-high pop-fly in centerfield, I might as well pack my baseball bat and balls. Grab my glove. My life would be over.

Waking up every day pretending to be someone else was exhausting. I had to constantly stop myself from saying something Maddy-like. It was difficult to keep my thoughts and words PG. Of course, sometimes I couldn't help myself and out of my mouth came Maddy. Mom and I had been watching a taped *The Bachelor* episode and before I knew it, I'd screamed at the TV.

"Are you kidding me right now? You chose *her*? She's a backstabbing bitch!"

"Piper!" Mom must've been as shocked as me at the words that came out of my mouth. After a second to absorb my words and her own reaction, she looked sternly at me. Then, she giggled. "Okay, very true, but let's not use that word when your mother is around."

"Sorry, Mom. Have no idea where that vile language came from."

Watching *The Bachelor* had always been Mom and Piper's popcorn-for-supper Monday night routine. I was usually somewhere, doing something with someone. Maddy's life was too important for a quiet night at home. Even now I couldn't remember what was so important that I chose to be out every night of the week.

A week after I was released from the hospital, Mom had gently knocked on Piper's bedroom door. "Piper? Your therapist, Mrs. Andela, said it was important to get back to normal. And since it's a Monday night, I thought we'd watch *The Bachelor* like we used to. I DVR-ed the ones you missed. I already made the popcorn just like you like it - extra butter. What do you say, Puppet? Wanna join me?"

She was really trying to be strong. Losing Maddy - me - had taken its toll on my parents. She looked older as she was hovering in the doorway. I needed to be the best actress that I could be. I went down and relaxed that night with Mom, and enjoyed watching *The Bachelor*. Who knew a bunch of Barbies fighting for the attention of one hottie would prove to be so entertaining.

Each passing day that I kept this lie was a one-pound pile of dirt shoveled on top of this huge choice - Piper's grave - that I made to become my sister. To take over her life. Each day, even though I had my doubts and wanted to confess, I pressed on. I didn't think anyone would feel sorry for me if they knew, but it was hard.

I missed her, too. But I couldn't tell anyone. Night after night, I soaked my bed pillows with tears for the sister who was my rock, my one true supporter. She always believed in me, even when I didn't believe in myself. She was an angel. Because I had her to thank for this second chance, I needed to be the best Piper I could be.

One of the most difficult parts of this switcheroo - besides missing her - was Piper's wardrobe and lack of care for her appearance. I was aware how vain that sounded, but it was true. I was shallow, but I missed my fitted and designer clothes. One morning before breakfast, I tiptoed across the hall to my old bedroom - that was kept as a shrine to me - and stole my favorite pair of PopSugar jeans that were ripped in the knees. They fit me like a glove and were so comfortable. Piper's Old Navy high waisted mom jeans didn't cut it for me.

Unfortunately, Mom noticed I was wearing them right away when I strolled into the kitchen. She abruptly stopped whisking the eggs.

"Good morning, honey. How did you sleep?" She quickly looked over her shoulder. "Are those Maddy's old jeans?"

I looked down at my legs and then back up at her pained expression.

"Umm... yeah." My mouth paused to let my brain catch up - a new skill as Piper that I picked up. "These were Maddy's favorite pair. Makes me feel closer to her. I thought I'd try them out. She was always telling me how I needed to be more fashionable, and they were just collecting dust. And I'm thinking she was right - I should've splurged on my own pair a long time ago." I was rambling like the old me used to do.

A sad smile formed on Mom's thin lips. "Okay. That makes sense. She had great taste in clothes." Mom quickly turned back to the scrambled eggs as she started to choke up.

"I'll take them off if you want me to, Mom. I never meant to upset you."

"No...no...it's not that at all. Take whatever of hers that you want. I just miss her, is all."

"Me too, Mom." I smiled sadly at her and stared into my steaming mug of hot coffee.

Very odd and surreal to know that my parents held my funeral while I was strapped to a hospital bed after my failed suicide attempt. I hadn't been trying to kill myself. I just wanted that damn birthmark gone - the scar that people might recognize as from Maddy's body.

After that whole plastic knife ordeal, I deserved a little psycho ward treatment. I'd felt a bit rabid when I was scratching off my skin. I couldn't seem to stop myself once I got started. I saw it working and needed to finish.

I was afraid to ask too many questions about my own funeral - it felt morbid. But I did look up my obituary online. It was very kind and generous. To be honest, it sounded fake and perhaps copy and pasted from someone else's. But then again, I'd never read an obit that didn't reflect the dead person in a positive, affectionate light. Although just once, I'd like to read one that was honest...

Kelvin James Coffin (January 27, 1972 - June 8, 2016) Uncle Kelvin, age 44, liked his whiskey neat and never met a blond that he wouldn't tap. Always a crude joke on the tip of his tongue. Uncle Kelvin was a womanizing racist. His monthly *Playboy* magazine subscription was addressed to 'Ben Dover.' We are glad that he is gone.

That would be a gas. Everyone would read and remember Kelvin's obituary.

I realized the real Piper Jean Sterling, my sister, would never have an obit written for her, but I'd die twice. Strange to realize.

Surprisingly, a single, hot tear escaped my eyes and ran down my cheek. To myself, I said a silent prayer: *I'm so sorry, Piper. I never planned this. It just happened. I loved you.* I knew if anyone would be able to forgive me, she would. She probably received her angel wings without hesitation. God probably told her that she earned them long ago for putting up with me for eighteen years.

I wondered if I'd even go to Heaven. *Where does a sinner like me go? Someone who lies and takes over someone else's life to get a fresh start - where do those people go?*

Chapter 45

Eleanor - June 1, 2016

It was lame. A bit amateur, but I needed something easy. I decided to write her a cryptic note telling her I knew her secret. I'd seen it in the movies. It was harmless and not scary.

I wanted to be effective and to the point. I wanted to provoke some panic that someone else knowing who she was wouldn't be good.

With her on an approved break from school, I needed to be creative in its delivery. I knew that her mom was collecting her homework weekly from the school. But there wasn't much homework to complete because school was ending soon.

I convinced myself that I was doing this because Piper deserved to be rightfully mourned and laid to rest as herself. Plus, it was morally wrong. And the other major reason why I'd do this was because I hated Madison Sterling. It was amazing to me that they were twins since their hearts were polar opposites.

I'd just convinced Principal Klawonn to reveal Madison's true nature - caught her cheating - and now, supposedly, she was dead! *Seriously, Universe, you're killing me!*

Reverting to old-fashioned avenues, I drafted a handwritten note. Decided not to be too dramatic and use newspaper clippings with the words I wanted to use. I ripped a simple piece of notebook paper out of my tablet. With a black pen, I wrote in big block letters:

I KNOW YOUR SECRET.

That seemed like enough. Short and simple. No threats or acts of violence yet.

I folded the paper into quarters and slipped it into her calculus textbook that was waiting in the office for her mom to retrieve. Piper could take a month off from calculus and still pass at the top of her class. But Madison didn't know this fact, so she was probably requesting all homework and books to cover her bases.

Chapter 46

Maddy - June 1, 2016

"Piper, honey, I'm worried about you. You can't stay cooped up in the house all day. It's not healthy. You need to join the world again. Netflix can't entertain you forever. Why don't you call a friend? Meet for coffee or go for a walk? Shopping? I'll even give you some money to buy a new top." Mom - who made Scrooge look generous - was desperate since she was offering me money to leave the house.

I didn't have the energy to argue with her. Tell her that I was fine. I didn't need anyone else and didn't want to go anywhere. I was scared. I knew I needed to leave the house. I just wasn't sure if my acting ability was strong enough. When my parents left for work, I'd watch old family movies to watch Piper and mimic her actions. My heart ached when I'd see her smile or giggle on the screen, but I had to remind myself that I was watching her for research.

As the master at our shadow game, I reminded myself that it was no longer a game - this was my new life. I stayed mute for a few days in the hospital to calculate my next move, and I'd chosen my words very carefully since then.

Entering the outside world was the obvious next step. But it wasn't a step that I could fail or attempt without being fully prepared.

I must've paused too long before answering Mom, who wasn't good with silence in conversations anyway. "How about a new outfit for graduation? You have your famous valedictorian speech to present. You need to look fabulous for that." When I still didn't manage to respond, Mom shut the refrigerator door and set the coffee creamer on the kitchen table next to the two mugs of steaming hot coffee.

I could only imagine what my facial reaction was. Deer in headlights, I assumed.

"Piper, honey, did you forget about your speech?" Again, I was unable to spit out a response in the small breaks that she allowed. "I'm sure considering all that has happened, the school would understand if you declined this honor."

The valedictorian speech...how could I forget?

Piper had been beyond thrilled with her achievement. She worked so hard all four years of high school to earn exemplary grades. Furthermore, my parents had beamed with pride when Principal Klawonn made the announcement.

Piper had taken notes of ideas that she wanted to include in her speech. She wrote on napkins while we were out for a family dinner. She dictated notes into her phone on our way to school. When I copied her Spanish homework while she was in the shower, I found her ideas - surrounded by little daisies - jotted down in her notebook.

Include everyone - athletics, scholars, the average Joe?

Music, slideshow during speech.

Add humor.

Piper - always the considerate, generous, kind twin. She wanted to write a memorable, touching speech that left everyone feeling warm and fuzzy inside. She'd always felt pressure to succeed, but even more than that, she was a massive people pleaser.

Oh, Piper, it must've been exhausting being you. I need to make some changes.

But crap! I needed to find that speech. Graduation was in one week.

I climbed the stairs to her bedroom. It still felt odd to turn left and not right into my room. But like Dr. Andela informed me, time made things easier. Racing up the stairs didn't involve sad memories of Piper every time. Sometimes, I'd even smile at a memory.

As I grabbed her laptop from her desk, I plopped down on her bed.

Password? It had six spaces.

I tried our birthdate.

042298

Password Error. Try again.

Fritz*

Password Error. Try again.

Puppet

The laptop came to life. Her background image was an old photo of the two of us standing on the back deck after we'd adopted Baxter. He had been the size of a shoe. We'd begged and begged for a dog. Under Piper's direction, we'd created a slideshow presentation of our promises and dreams for our new furry family member. In our compromise, we allowed Dad to name him after his favorite Will Ferrell movie, *Anchorman*. Baxter became the center of our world.

On her home screen, she had the most popular icons that she used as well as a document called, "V Speech."

Piper, thank you for being predictable.

Chapter 47

Eleanor - June 8, 2016

This whole situation was entirely out of control. I had left the cryptic note in Madison's - actually Piper's - book, and nothing ever came of it. I wasn't sure what I thought would happen. Maybe a news bulletin: "Twin burns in fire while surviving sister takes over her life" or maybe an overhead school announcement claiming, "Thank you to whomever scribbled the anonymous note in the Sterling twin's homework. Your four words pushed Madison Sterling into confessing that she killed her sister, took over her life, and fooled us all. Only you, the anonymous tipster, could see the painful truth."

This wasn't a Lifetime movie. I needed to up my game. Guilt might still prove to be helpful; however, I needed force behind my punch. Perhaps I needed to tell her *what* I knew. Who knew, maybe Madison hadn't even seen the note taped to her assignment. Maybe she thought it didn't pertain to her. Maybe she thought it was Piper's. But the most likely scenario was that she didn't even open her calculus textbook.

The real Piper wouldn't miss turning in an assignment after her month-long absence. She would've seen it as a chance to increase her grade point average, prove that she deserved all the glory and rightfully earned her sparkling reputation. She'd feel terrible about the fuss everyone was making in her absence.

But Madison...she was a different story. My bet was that she hadn't even cracked open any homework since the fire. She was probably sleeping until noon and watching soap operas all afternoon. She would milk the attention and grab every handout she was given.

Even though I was only friends with Piper, I knew what made Madison Sterling tick. For years, I'd watched her charm her way through life. What Madison wanted, Madison received. The same could be said for her angelic sister Piper, but Piper worked for her achievements, while Madison stole, begged, and tricked her way to her goals. These two mirror-images of each other didn't bleed the same red blood. *Interesting thought.* I'd love to see what color Madison's was.

I quickly ran a brush through my hair. I pulled my shirt over my head – a pale pink sweatshirt that Piper had previously complimented. She'd claimed it was a beautiful color that accentuated my skin tone.

"Sounds cheesy, I know, but my grandma taught Maddy and I how to enhance the 'gifts God blessed us with.'" She'd plopped down in a chair across from me in the school library.

"I don't believe in God." She had been accustomed to my blunt comments. Because of our difference in opinion, we had many lively conversations. It strengthened our friendship and respect for one another.

After she sat down across from me, our eyes met. Her eyes reflected sadness - not pity for my lack of belief. "Ellie, I know you don't. I wish that I could make you understand that God loves you. But that's for a different conversation. It's honestly just a saying, but I can eliminate His name and simply refer to it as gifts." She quickly pulled out her advanced biology textbook and searched everywhere in her backpack for a pencil.

I handed her one. "Here, I have extras. Plus, I know you prefer this brand."

Again, our eyes met as she accepted the mechanical pencil that I offered. "Thanks, Ellie. You're so observant." Her cheeks flashed a deep shade of pink. It was faint, but I noticed.

She was the only one who I allowed to call me "Ellie." It was the nickname my mother had called me when I was little. I wasn't sure why or when it stopped. But Ellie had always been a nickname that reminded me of better days, when I was young and my mom was happy. When Piper called me Ellie, it made me feel special again. Nicknames were given to people you were fond of. She never asked me if it was okay, but she didn't need permission.

Remembering that study date with Piper made me feel even more determined to confront Madison. I couldn't let her get away with this charade another day. I wasn't sure how I would push her to admit her false identity or who I wanted her to admit to besides me. I only tried once to visit her in the hospital. I wanted to see for myself that

Piper was alive like the news claimed. I wanted to be wrong about what I witnessed. I was a big enough person to admit maybe it was Piper who had been carried out of the burning house. I had been under the influence of alcohol that night.

However, on the day that I chose to make an appearance as a concerned, caring friend, she had been transferred to the fourth floor for psychological evaluations. No visitors were allowed.

During that month, I used one of the superpowers that I had mastered throughout my life - patience. The hunter must stalk its prey. Sitting in the shadows watching her. Sizing up the potential for threat. Calculating the margin for error. Then, when the time was right - pounce.

My cell phone indicated that I'd received a new text message. I didn't have many friends, so I was curious to see who messaged me.

My heart skipped a beat.

Hey. how r u? The text indicated that it was from Piper. But I knew better.

It was time to pounce.

Chapter 48

Maddy - June 8, 2016

Mom wanted me out of the house, back to normal, reaching out to a friend. But getting back in touch with a friend meant one of Piper's friends, and I didn't like any of them. Plus, Mom was friendly with all their moms as well. I was sure there would be some side conversations to make sure my name - Maddy - wasn't brought up during my little outing. Didn't need to bring up anything that might trigger a relapse.

My new phone contained Piper's contacts restored on it. As I scrolled down the list of potential candidates for my pathetic attempt at getting a life back, I read the name, Eleanor Cutter. Eleanor hadn't visited to say hey. Furthermore, during one of the last switcheroos that Piper and I pulled, Eleanor confessed a secret to me, thinking I was Piper. She thought that we were half-sisters. After that afternoon, Piper had mentioned that Eleanor had acted strangely towards her, and she asked me what had happened that afternoon in class. I'd convinced Piper that it was nothing.

"Puppet, she's a strange one - that Eleanor. We hardly communicated. She parked her weird, smelly ass next to me while I took a little cat nap."

"Be nice, Maddy."

I texted her a simple, *Hey. how r u?* It was a Sunday afternoon. Not too many options for exciting activities. What I did know about Eleanor was that she wasn't popular, social, or friendly. Chances were that she wasn't doing anything.

I chose to reach out to Eleanor after I weighed my odds with Piper's friends. Carrie had been my sister's constant companion since junior high. I would bet Carrie could see through my desperate act. Mya would have been the easier of the two - a bit more gullible and willing to trust. But her whiny sing-song voice would make every fiber of my being itch.

When Eleanor's name was in Piper's contacts as I was scrolling through, I figured that she might be easy to pull the wool over her eyes - another one of my mom's coined sayings. The Eleanor that I knew was a full-on nerd with a bad haircut and a depressing wardrobe consisting of gray or black. She didn't seem to have any friends besides Piper. Everyone noticed her sitting alone in the cafeteria during lunch, writing things down in her notebook. She'd often roll her eyes or mutter to herself as she was jotting something down. An odd duck.

Furthermore, I recalled that odd conversation during Piper's advanced biology class. Eleanor had claimed that we were sisters, and that my dad was her biological dad. This chick was one crazy-ass bitch. I was sure that our coffee date would be the most interesting, hence the reason I chose her.

The little dots that indicated she was replying to my message popped up.

Ok. You?

Bored. You wanna hang?

Throw it out there. Get it over with. Mom was right. I was ready to leave the house.

Now?

Yeah. Zook's Coffee Bar on Main in 20?

Before I left, I threw on an old baseball sweatshirt that I assumed Piper inherited from Fritz. I tied my hair up in a messy bun and slid on a pair of clean jeans. I couldn't believe I was going out in public looking like this. I took more care of my appearance when I was sick with the flu or had a major head cold. But whatever.

I needed to accept this. I made my choice. No turning back. I was Piper. She was me. No more Maddy.

As I pulled open the front door to leave the house, I discovered Mr. Jarro - Daniel - in mid-knock with his fist in the air about to hit our front door. He was just as stunned that the door opened as I was to discover him standing on my front step. Wide-eyed and stumbling for words, we stared at each other.

What is he doing here?

"Hello, Piper." I'd never witnessed him acting so awkwardly. His eyes couldn't settle on anything. They were darting from every object in his line of vision. During our affair, he had been very confident and even arrogant, not at all the nervous, hesitant man fidgeting in front of me. He cleared his throat. "Ahh...I wanted to stop by and express my condolences to you and your parents regarding...Madison. I'm so sorry." After looking down at his feet, his eyes finally moved upward and met mine.

I'd always been skeptical of things I couldn't see. My faith wasn't as strong as Piper's. My upbringing taught me that all things were possible through God, but I had a difficult time believing He was looking out for me, still loving me after all the trouble I participated in. I hadn't seen God, so how did I know he was there? Furthermore, I was skeptical of Piper's and my twin telepathy. If I hadn't actually witnessed it or felt it, I would've never believed it.

The same could be said for the connection between Daniel and me. Standing six feet away from him, sparks ignited. When our eyes connected, a bolt of static electric shock registered. It felt like when you walked in slippers in the wintertime and then you touched someone and shocked them. His eyes popped up as he met my gaze. He felt it as well.

Oh, shit!

In all honesty, it was reassuring that the spark between us was mutual and not just me. However, I was Piper and needed to stomp out this little flame before my cover was blown. My loins didn't get a vote on this one - its voting days were over.

"Mr. Jarro, right?"

I hope he doesn't notice that I didn't roll my R.

Piper hadn't been enrolled in any of his classes, so I wasn't sure if she would've known his name. She'd finished her language credits her junior year, before Mr. Jarro joined Pine Hill High School. Being the accelerated student, Piper was able to roll her Rs like a true honor student. I, on the other hand, couldn't roll any letter, unless I was drunk...then I rolled all my letters. Therefore, I pronounced his name like the English language taught me to. "Thank you. That's very kind of you to think of our family." I pretended to be tentative and shy by casting my eyes downward. That was when I noticed that he was holding a casserole dish in his hand.

"Ummm...please give this to your parents as a token *pequeño* of my condolences." He thrust forward the casserole dish in my direction. Careful not to touch his hands, I accepted it. Didn't need to feel the static electric shock to know it was there. I heard him sniff the air as I leaned forward. He had a heightened sense of smell like a beagle.

"I'll tell them. Thank you." I quickly retreated into the security of our house. My heart was beating double-time.

Chapter 49

Eleanor - June 8, 2016

I still could hardly believe Madison had invited me for coffee. Of course, my morbid curiosity was thoroughly excited for this encounter. On my drive to the new coffee shop, my stomach did backflip after backflip. I'd be early, but that would help me relax and be prepared. I'd pick the perfect seat and settle in before she arrived. My blood pressure was through the roof.

Fake wasn't a word that blessed my vocabulary. My face normally reflected my exact feelings. In order for me to make it through the coffee date, I needed to keep my mouth shut, bottle up my feelings, and keep my expressions to a minimum. I was praying for a miracle.

The next twenty minutes or so were extremely important to my end goal - getting Madison to confess that she'd taken over Piper's life. I wasn't sure what would happen after that, but I was willing to bet it wouldn't be favorable to her.

When she strolled into the coffee shop, it was obvious that she was indeed Madison by the arrogant air surrounding her. Her walk had a purpose, a confidence that Piper never possessed. Piper was tentative and soft-footed. Madison's walk claimed, "I'm a big deal. Notice me."

One of Piper's old baggy sweatshirts hung on her curvy frame - trying to appear casual and at ease. She had it pulled off to one side so that part of her shoulder peeked out. She wore a pair of designer jeans - rips in the right spots as well as worn out for comfort. On her feet, she'd slipped on a pair of Nike tennis shoes. Her attire screamed, "Something is off." Her blonde hair was strapped into a knot on the top of her head but purposefully placed and finger-curled strands elegantly framed her face. It said, "I'm trying too hard."

I planned on letting her lead the conversation. My patience would pay off as I listened to her dig herself further into a hole filled with lies and deception. I'd use her words against her. I'd make her pay for being alive. Maybe she didn't kill Piper, but by taking over every aspect of her life, she was killing her memory. She had *betrayed* her memory and stolen everything that Piper stood for - truth and kindness.

Everyone was grieving and immortalizing Madison. Speaking of her as if she was a saint, a true example of a life taken too soon. No one mentioned how awful she was to anyone she thought was beneath her or how she had been suspended from school for cheating on her eighteenth birthday. No one brought up how she'd bullied one classmate so harshly that he attempted suicide by overdosing on his mother's sleeping pills. His suicide note had said, *Is this better, Madison Sterling?*

Instead of being able to rightfully mourn my friend and pay her the respect that she earned, I was losing sleep over how to pressure Madison into confessing who she really was. Instead of preparing for a graduation party, I was journaling conversations that we'd had.

Madison was to blame for my relationship with Piper coming to an abrupt halt. The sisterhood that didn't have time to develop. She was here when Piper should've been.

I didn't stand as she approached the table. I wasn't a hugger. Plus, I wasn't about to wrap my arms around that bitch. Instead, I greeted her with, "I took the liberty of ordering your favorite."

Looking at her from across the table, I felt the difference. My heart could sense that she wasn't Piper. No goosebumps automatically rose on my arms. My arm hair didn't tingle at the sight of her. Hatred boiled in my veins.

No, none of those revelations would make a difference to anyone - her parents, the police - no one, but me...and her. They solidified what I felt from the first moment outside on Maverick's lawn. It made me feel validated, but in a small way. I'd hoped and prayed that I was wrong. Because if I was wrong, Piper would still be alive.

My eyes bore into her. I had a resting bitch face caused by my growing disgust at human nature. Madison couldn't read my expressions of validation. She just thought that I was a bitch and wanted to test out her new act on me. She underestimated me - the Universe Corrector.

I was addicted to the feeling of vengeance. I understood how surgeons developed a God complex. You completed something that no one else managed to. You achieved the unspeakable. You learned things that only the patients themselves knew. When the expectations were low or nonexistent, any achievement felt like an enormous accomplishment.

"Wow. Thanks, Eleanor. Very kind of you." Her tone of voice was flat, dull. She slid down into the chair across from me and dropped her purse onto the floor next to her. Wrapping her hands around the cup, she lifted it to her lips. "Mmm...caramel macchiato. Just what I needed. Thanks for meeting me. I really needed to get out of the house."

"Sorry about Madison." Obvious pleasantries out of the way. I wasn't interested in *acknowledging* the elephant in the room - I wanted to stab it.

"Yeah. Thanks." She tentatively sipped her coffee. She noticed me checking out her apparel. "These are Maddy's old jeans. I thought she was completely nuts to pay so much money for them, but crap, they're comfortable. Plus, they make me feel closer to her. Weird, right?" She mumbled on and on about why she was wearing Madison's jeans, her jewelry. She was creating excuses, hoping that I'd believe them. She aimed her big puppy dog eyes at me, begging me to believe her and affirm that it was normal - every sister who lost a sister would rifle through the dead one's closet looking for treasures. *Not!*

I gave her a slight nod - mainly to acknowledge that I heard her. I sipped my black coffee. A caffeine buzz was sure to overtake my body. I was counting on it. I needed to be alert and observant to take her down.

Chapter 50

Maddy - June 8, 2016

As I walked into the coffee shop, I heard the bells announcing my arrival. My eyes scanned the cozy, coffee-scented sitting room for mousy, frown-faced Eleanor. There to the left of the barista station sat Eleanor perched in a stiff, metal chair. Waiting. Watching. Judging.

Even though at school I never acknowledged her, I knew she sat alone in the farthest, darkest corner of the cafeteria. She thought she was better than us, because she chose not to participate in our insignificant high school life. She thought it was all her choice. But I saw her, and I pretended she was invisible just like she wanted. She wasn't worth my time and energy. She wanted to be a viewer, a person who watched rather than participate. Fine by me. I enjoyed having an audience.

Again, here at Zook's, she lingered on the edge of her chair yearning to be entertained. But I needed to remind myself why I was here. I was here to perform. Like the four years of high school, she was my audience, but this time was different - I needed to persuade her, not just entertain.

A small, sweet smile formed on my makeup-less face as I strolled towards her. On the small bistro table sat two disposable cups of coffee. She knew Piper's order - I didn't even know it. She was already proving to me that this was going to be a tougher conversation than I anticipated.

But I was up for the challenge. Hell, I was living a challenge.

Across the small table, no more than eight feet away, she was perched in her chair all smug, sizing me up. It looked like she wanted to chew me up and spit me out. I thanked her for the coffee, and of course, she immediately mentioned me - Madison. *Awkward.*

I wasn't sure what the two of us would talk about, but I was hoping this coffee date would last more than - I glanced at my Apple watch - four minutes. My coffee hadn't even cooled down yet.

This damn nerd was putting me in defense mode right away. In a very casual Eleanor-way, she said she was sorry about *my* death, but her tone of voice was what mattered. There was no emotion laced with her words. It was as if she was commenting on the spring weather. Simple pleasantry.

With her arms folded across her chest, Eleanor licked the excess coffee from her thin upper lip. I shivered as goosebumps rose up and down my arms.

Piper, how did you stand her? Her presence alone *irritates the hell out of me.*

I couldn't believe that my sister wasted her time with someone that completely lacked a personality. Eleanor reminded me of a big, heavy rock - one that I wanted to pick up and toss into a deep lake.

"So, Eleanor, what are your plans for the summer? Mine have obviously changed. Not sure what I'm doing tomorrow, let alone for an entire summer." I paused to give her a chance to answer.

I hated awkward pauses – like my mom, I realized. Sitting in the silence waiting for her to spit out any words felt like eternity. I knew that Piper would've had the patience for this odd wallflower, so I mirrored what I imagined my sister would've done. Piper wouldn't need to fake genuine concern.

Just playing the shadow game, Piper. Not much fun without you.

Maybe Eleanor didn't hear my question. Perhaps she was partially deaf or hard of hearing. Come to think of it, I really didn't know her that well. Could that be the reason she chose dark, distant corners of a room? Did the loud echoes in the room hurt her ears? Like a bat who hung itself to the ceiling?

Maybe she's a creepy, blood-sucking vampire?

I glanced around the small cafe for any type of distraction while I waited for Miss No-Personality to answer easy small talk.

"Summer plans..." She formed her words in slow motion, like I was hanging on her every word - which I was, but I wouldn't admit that to her. "My summer plans are to discover the truth, right a few wrongs, maybe solve a great mystery."

Did she always speak in boring riddles? What the hell did I get myself into?

"Sounds super exciting." In my head, I heard those words with a sarcastic tone, but I managed to squeeze out those three words with enthusiasm. "More exciting than anything that I've got going on." Even though I'd adopted Piper as the new me - or was it the new me as Piper? - I still hadn't controlled my natural chatter. "Most people our age are trying new things or getting ready to head off to college. You're a rare one, Eleanor. All interested in history." I kept my comments vague, so I didn't dig myself a hole.

Deep breath. Inhale. Exhale. Take a sip of coffee.

"Do you care to join me in my truth-seeking adventure?" Her left eyebrow rose, causing wrinkles to form on her forehead. And I wondered if I saw a small smirk form on her thin lips.

Something was going on.

Am I on one of those hidden camera shows? What Would You Do *or* Candid Camera, *maybe?* This was literally the oddest conversation I'd ever had.

Chapter 51

Eleanor - June 8, 2016

I'd had enough of the game and small talk, and I realized that it'd only been about ten minutes. Ten minutes too long with this evil, backstabbing woman. I couldn't do it anymore. I couldn't sit across from her while she pretended to be *her*. She wasn't wholesome like Piper. She didn't deserve to pretend to be her for one more second. For Piper, I had to reveal the truth. For Piper's memory and my love for her, I'd make this bitch pay.

She asked me about my summer plans. Seriously? How dorky was that? Of course, I had plans. My plans consisted of destroying hers. I just didn't know how yet.

"Do you want to join me in my truth-seeking adventure?" I watched her take me in. Consider my question. She asked an odd question, so I gave an odd, vague answer. Her eyes searched my face for a clue as to what I was referring to.

"Sure. I'm up for anything." She continued to keep control of her positive, upbeat persona. It was fading, but the wall was still there. She was a strong adversary.

It was the beginning of June. In the Midwest, that meant the humidity was rising and people were getting uncomfortable in their own clothes. And across from me in a cafe, sipping her hot coffee sat a blonde-haired beauty wearing a long-sleeved Nike sweatshirt and a pair of jeans. The only people who wore long sleeves in the summer were people who worked in construction or people who had been recently sunburned or someone who was trying to hide something.

At the end of her shirt sleeve, she kept spinning her bracelet. Nervous habit.

I noticed a tattoo on her wrist as her long sleeve creeped up her arm when she took a sip of her coffee. "Nice ink." Only a psychopath would tattoo her own name on her wrist.

"Uhh...thanks." She tugged down her sleeve to cover up the exposed portion. "Wanted something to remember her by. She literally was my right arm."

"Nice gold bracelet." I nodded to her wrist. "I heard that's the wrist you slashed." I'd never been one for small talk. I didn't understand why people didn't just say what they were thinking. It made it easier. Plus, I doubted the whole suicide attempt. Madison would never kill herself. There had to be another reason that she took a knife to her wrist.

Wrinkles formed on her forehead as her eyes searched mine. "Umm...yeah. I regret that, obviously. But this will always remind me of her and how important she was to me."

"Your own initials and a peanut shape will remind you of Madison?" I wasn't buying it, and I didn't intend on letting it go. I had helped Piper pick out Madison's birthday present - a shiny, golden bracelet personalized with the word *Queen*. If *Madison* had died in that fire, that bracelet would have burned with her.

Chapter 52

Maddy - June 8, 2016

Wow. I wished Father Time wasn't such a mean bastard. He worked side-by-side with Karma. I pictured them as Bonnie and Clyde, a 1930's infamous couple who robbed and murdered their way across the United States. Arm in arm causing drama and heartache wherever they went. Karma enjoyed making people pay for their mistakes - she was patient and had an incredible memory. Karma and Father Time loved to throw unexpected hurdles in everyday life when their victim least expected it. I envisioned the two of them - Karma with fire-red hair and piercing green eyes and Father Time as a stout man with a thick, long, gray beard - throwing back a couple of beers and eating peanuts and discarding the shells on the floor as they watched the scene from my life play out on a big screen TV at the bar. The jukebox repeatedly played Miranda Lambert's song "Kerosene." Father Time extended his hand out to Karma for a dance.

Light 'em up and watch them burn, teach them what they need to learn. Ha!

As Father Time led Karma in a simple two-step, he tipped her back and her contagious, loud cackle echoed throughout the bar. They were oblivious to the trouble they were causing for me.

While I'd been savoring the best cup of coffee ever with the most tedious company, Karma was enjoying her game of cat and mouse – Eleanor and me – respectively. The chances of survival for the mouse decreased as another cat entered the room. *How is a mouse - me - supposed to survive two hungry cats - Eleanor and Fritz?*

Thanks, Father Time.

Fritz walked into Zook's as he was texting on his phone. When the door closed behind him, he ended his message and robotically placed his cell phone in the back pocket of his shorts. He looked up at his surroundings. As soon as his eyes came into focus, he noticed Eleanor and I seated to the right of the counter where the barista took the coffee orders. We were directly in the line of vision of any incoming customers. I wondered if Eleanor had planned that. She normally preferred a dark, isolated corner.

The volume of conversations seemed to drop a couple of octaves as Fritz's awkward entrance gained attention. It was a small town, and they intended on eavesdropping. The rumor mill that entertained the facts and fiction of our famous breakup creeped into the far corners of the streets of Pine Hill.

"You've got to be kidding me." His words came out in a hard, sinister tone. "I forgave you. I trusted you, and I was right. It's *her*, isn't it? So, is *she* gonna help you with it?"

"Fritz...hi." I had no idea what he was talking about, but he was visibly upset. His jawline had tightened as he clenched his teeth, and his cheeks flushed in anger. He appeared to be holding his breath and was about to burst.

Before he was able to spit out another word, he turned around and headed for the door.

"Excuse me, Eleanor, but I should really go talk to him."

As I sped-walked my way out of Zook's, I reminded myself to allow Fritz to do the talking. I had no idea what he was talking about, and I needed to let him fill in the blanks.

My eyes scanned the parking lot and found him kicking his truck tires. The old me - Maddy - would've rolled my eyes at the sight of a grown man throwing a little tantrum, but the new and improved me as Piper rushed towards him.

"Fritz! Fritz, wait a minute!" I yelled. He heard me as he was climbing into the cab of his truck. "Please, Fritz, wait a minute. We should talk."

"Why? Why should I talk to you?"

"I'm sorry, Fritz, for everything."

"You're sorry for breaking my heart?"

I'd made it to the open door of his beat-up, red Ford pickup. My fingers were curled around the inside of the door, holding it open so he wouldn't drive away. He was seated with his hands on the steering wheel, keys dangling in the ignition.

Softly, I answered him, "Yes, I never intended to break your heart." Even though Fritz did nothing for me below the waist, he had meant a great deal to Piper. And I'd abruptly broken up with him with no explanation. I owed him a little patience.

"Well, you did, Piper, after everything that we've been through and will continue to work through." When he turned towards me, he had fresh tears pooling in his eyes. "We need to try to work this out, Piper. We have a future to think about."

"Fritz, I can't right now. I never meant to hurt you. But I just can't." I definitely didn't want to lead him on. I had only followed him to his pickup to see if I could understand what his comment meant inside the coffee shop.

I was also finished with Eleanor. She was even worse company than Fritz.

"I've been there for you, Piper. I'm the one who has been by your side. I forgave you for cheating on me. How are you going to do this alone? Does she know?" With each statement, his anger grew. "Is she my replacement? I thought you said you were just friends, and that was a mistake. Are you lying to me or yourself?"

I was a lone deer standing in the middle of the road on a dark night, eyes wide open, shocked and too stunned to move as a pair of headlights blinded my eyes and headed straight for me.

Move. Say something.

What the hell is he talking about? Piper cheated on him? With who? What? Where? When? What does he think Eleanor knows? And he thinks Piper is interested in Eleanor? What the hell is happening? Too many questions! I'd paused too long trying to decide what to say.

"No response? You have nothing to say? Well, I do. Get your hands off my door. I'm leaving." He yanked the door shut just after I'd woken up from my state of shock and removed them. I stepped back a few feet as his tires squealed out of the parking lot.

Instead of answers, I collected more questions.

What the hell, Piper? Did I even know you? Your life seems as messy as mine.

What a fiasco of a simple coffee date. I'd only wanted to practice my Piper personality on Eleanor. I hadn't planned on the snarky conversation with nerdy Eleanor or Fritz's appearance at the coffee shop.

Again, I realized how much difference a matter of seconds could make in a person's life. First the fire that killed Piper. My regretful comment of saying her name had taken one second. And now, Fritz's very public accusation of an affair. All in a matter of a few seconds.

After Fritz tore out of the parking lot, I was left with my mouth wide open in wonder, my heart in disarray, and my anxiety level high. Following him had only led to more questions than answers. I shook my head in complete bewilderment. The old me would be on the prowl for some mood-alternating drugs; however, the stint in the hospital gave me sobriety, and I didn't want to mess with it.

Piper, who were you?

As I was rummaging through my purse for my car keys, I heard a sarcastic voice say, "Don't you wonder what he was talking about?"

I looked up at the voice I thought I'd deserted in the coffee shop. She was stomping towards me in her big army boots. She was confident, arrogant. I was trapped even though we were standing in a wide-open space. She knew that I needed answers, and I could tell my little act as Piper hadn't fooled her.

"Excuse me. I'm not sure what you're talking about. It was a private conversation between me and Fritz." I wasn't about to give up. I had my whole life on the line. Some nosy nerd wasn't about to ruin everything. My blood pressure rose to a new level.

"Yeah, real private conversation in a public parking lot for the whole town to overhear. You aren't at all interested in knowing why Fritz thinks that we're lovers?"

I wanted to slap the smirk off her face. The fact that she was dangling information over my head made my skin crawl. I wasn't about to let her have the upper hand.

"Eleanor, it's obvious you've been in love with me for months now. If you could be less obvious about your feelings, things wouldn't be so awkward, and rumors about us wouldn't be created."

"You? You think I'm in love with *you*? You're mistaken. I had strong affections once, but those feelings were misguided. Plus, the woman I had feelings for is gone now."

She was baiting me. She was the fisherman, and I was the prize-winning catch. She dangled the bait in front of me as if I was dumb and greedy enough to take a bite. If only I truly was Piper and I could have been patient and untouched by her rudeness. But instead, this bitch pushed my buttons, and I was irritated beyond words.

I wasn't going to bite until she released more fishing line. I was annoyed but stubborn.

"I've had feelings for you. True. But they definitely aren't of love. Your mere existence makes my head pound, and every fiber of my being crawl. I hate you, Madison."

Chapter 53

Eleanor - June 8, 2016

She blinked and then blinked again. She perhaps predicted my words, yet she wasn't sure how to respond. I respected that. Normally, when I righted the universe, I didn't receive instant feedback. When I keyed that rich bitch's red sports car, I didn't visibly witness her reaction, although I was sure that she was livid. When I convinced Principal Klawonn to catch Madison cheating on her final exam, I didn't get to see her expression when she figured out that the jig was up. But my heart knew. In my heart, I imagined the reactions, and those visions filled me with pleasure.

Watching Madison process that I addressed her by her given name filled my heart with pure satisfaction. Watching her squirm was gratifying, watching her hesitate in uncertainty. This feeling of control was addictive - probably similar to the pleasure that a murderer experienced when he watched the life drain from his helpless victim.

Yes, I was guilty of poisoning my father, but I didn't consider myself a killer. When you assisted the universe by eliminating the rotten, you didn't find fault in your actions even if it was murder. Rocky deserved to suffer - he was a miserable excuse for a human. He hated his life, his wife, and the girl who he thought was his daughter. Truly, he had no reason to live except to cause misery to others. Furthermore, he was too much of a coward to kill himself. I had to help.

Watching the light abandon his eyes hadn't been a euphoric event. Slowly poisoning someone over the course of several months didn't yield immediate results. Sure, he started complaining about his indigestion, blaming me or Mother for feeding him unsanitary food.

"A dog couldn't properly digest the shit you cook."

The sharp words hadn't cut like they used to. Maybe it was because I had been patiently enjoying these last pieces of his abuse knowing that it'd be over soon. Or maybe it was because I needed these last few slams to really leave a punch and make it all the more reason that he should die.

Hearing someone cut me down didn't hurt my feelings, didn't make me bend over and take it in the ass. Hearing negative words created a drive to succeed. After telling Madison that I hated her, my body ignited a fire of desire, not a sexual desire. It was a hunger - a need to be fulfilled. Until fulfillment, I would be preoccupied with desire.

Chapter 54

Maddy - June 8, 2016

"Whatever you think you know, Eleanor, you don't. I should've ended this excuse of a friendship a long time ago. I'm sorry that you're such a loser and feel you need to make up lies so people will pay attention to you, but I've had enough."

I was aware of the fact that Piper would've never uttered those words, but Piper was different now. She possessed a backbone and was trying hard to find her place in life. She wanted to take advantage of this second chance. The new Piper had better things to do.

Eleanor hovered twenty feet away. Goosebumps traveled up and down my arms. I was her prey. I felt like a fuzzy, helpless rabbit about to be pounced on by a hungry, aggressive coyote. I was frozen in fear of the unknown and being eaten alive.

How did I think I could've ever won her over? Why did I test my Piperness with her?

When I caught her eye, I vigorously shook my head. I couldn't wait to get home and distract myself from the chaos of this failed attempt to get back to normal. Thank goodness that the *Bachelor* was on tonight. Mom would prepare the snacks and would snuggle up next to me on the couch. I needed a night of mindless drama. I turned around to walk away.

"Oh, but I do think we should talk...Madison." If I hadn't been trying so hard to forget who I truly was, I might not have caught her using my birth name again. Frozen like a statue, I waited to hear more. "I think you can find five more minutes for me. Can't you, Madison?"

She was baiting me, getting my attention. It worked.

I slowly turned around to face her. She'd moved closer as she followed me to my car. Six dramatic steps brought me closer to her, close enough to smell her nervousness. Glad to know that I wasn't the only one. Feeling that I no longer needed to hide or pretend, I stared at her...Maddy-style. My stomach may have been doing back flips, but I needed to appear confident.

She read my focus change as agreeing to her terms. "Good. I thought that might grab your attention. I've never enjoyed beating around the bush."

I continued to stare at her. I wondered what her angle was. What did she want? She hadn't gone to the authorities with her knowledge, so that either meant she wasn't one hundred percent sure, or she preferred to watch me sweat. I was betting that it was the latter. She didn't seem like the kind who cared or worried about the police. She handled her issues her way. Case in point.

"I'm sure that you're wondering how I know or what I know or even how long I've known. I'll tell you all that later. I *ensured* my knowledge will be disclosed at a later date, so I'm not worried. Karma is on my side." I had no idea what she was talking about, but it was clear that she watched too many crime TV shows. "For right now, I wanted to gauge your reaction. I'm not sure how this will play out yet, but it feels satisfying to watch you squirm."

My eyes narrowed as I sized her up. Amazing how fast the old me surfaced. I thought I'd buried most of Maddy - bottled my true self. Eleanor thought that she possessed the upper hand. I wasn't about to lose a battle that I hadn't even fought yet. She underestimated me.

"Madison, you can't fool me. Piper was the good, wholesome one. You're trash in comparison. I can't believe that you thought you could get away with taking over her life. You're so clouded by your own self-righteousness, your own self-love, and your own pride that you can't see that you aren't worthy of being Piper. Even on Earth, she was more of an angel than you'll ever be."

Her harsh words – that reflected everything that I questioned about myself – were true, but there was no way in Hell I'd give her any satisfaction that it bothered me. "Eleanor, you're pitiful. Always begging for acceptance and love, but never receiving any. My sister spent time with you because she felt *sorry* for you. You have no friends, no family. You were her charity case."

"That's where you're wrong, Madison. So very wrong. She didn't get a chance to tell you before you murdered her, but we are sisters. The three of us." She was hoping for a bigger reaction from me, but I stuffed it down. This wasn't new knowledge like she intended it to be. She didn't realize that when she had revealed her discovery, Piper and I had been pulling a switcheroo. "Your loving father is my biological father. He impregnated my mother around the same time he knocked up your mother as well. I have family, Madison. It's *you*."

As she spat out those words, her left eyebrow rose, just like my dad could do. His eyebrow would move up whenever he was interrogating me... like Eleanor was doing. The similarity was uncanny. If she was in fact my half-sister, I hoped to Hell that she didn't possess my evil, vindictive nature.

"We will never be family. The title of family needs to be earned. A simple blood test and a drunken sperm donor doesn't make us family."

Chapter 55

Eleanor - June 8, 2016

The idea that Madison Sterling was lecturing me on the definition of family infuriated me. Through my clenched teeth, I managed to explain, "It is obvious what your definition of family is, Madison. Family are the people who you take for granted and believe should bend over and let you walk all over them. Your sister did that for you every day of her life, and as a matter of fact is still doing it for you now as you stole the life she worked so hard for."

I watched her squirm a little. "You don't deserve the family you have, Madison. I plan on making sure everyone realizes the true Madison that Piper helped you hide.

"Speaking of a growing family, Piper was pregnant a couple of months ago. In fact, she should be showing by now." Extending my hand out in front of me, I took a tentative step towards her to rub her supposedly growing waistline. She stepped back to avoid my petting. "How are you gonna manage that, dear Madison?"

"You're lying." Her face had lost its coloring. She had no idea, and it bothered her. That was what I was counting on.

"Unfortunately for you, Madison, I'm not. But it's an interesting fact that Piper didn't share her news with her twin sister. Must not have trusted you with the delicateness of her situation. You've never been good at small meaningful gestures like loyalty, honesty, or kindness, have you?"

Watching Miss High and Mighty sweat honestly made my day. With one sentence, I was able to rip apart her dream of starting over as Piper. Ever since I'd known her, Madison embodied confidence and arrogance. No one ended a relationship with her. Men or women.

Her friends never left her side, always loyal and dependable for an added snicker or sassy comment. To be honest, I thought they were scared of her. Turning your back on Madison Sterling was sure to end with a very sharp knife.

No one stood up to Madison. She was vicious and people feared her. For years, I had too. I didn't venture out of the shadows because she'd notice me and send out a tongue-lasher in my direction. For obvious reasons, I'd avoided being the center of anyone's attention, especially Madison's focus.

"Who else knows?" Her eyes were still wide-eyed like googly eyes used for craft projects.

"How the hell should I know?" I loved this entire conversation. The universe had finally heard my pleas - more like shouts, ranting, or explosions of anger. "I wasn't your sister's keeper. I was her *friend*. Like true family, I made time for her, listened to her when she needed someone." My eyes shot down to the personalized bracelet encircling her wrist. "I even helped her shop for your birthday gift."

Chapter 56

Maddy - June 8, 2016

Holy fuck! Pardon my language, but shit! You were pregnant, Piper? Did Fritz know? Is that why he was acting so strangely?

I hated with my whole being that Eleanor had known this delicate fact about Piper and that she knew that *I* didn't know. She'd been sitting on this knowledge for months. Why hadn't she said anything until now? I had to think fast. This simple get-out-of-the-house coffee date had turned into a complete and utter disaster.

Why would she wait to reveal this fact? Unless she wasn't sure. She wasn't one hundred percent positive that I wasn't Piper. Unfortunately, now she had no doubt. But still that meant she hadn't gone to the authorities or spread the information any further. She'd mentioned insurance, but I wasn't sure what she was talking about. She was a thinker, a patient thinker.

I needed to be sure that she'd kept quiet. "Who else knows?" Not that she owed me the truth, but it didn't hurt to ask.

"How the hell should I know? I wasn't your sister's keeper. I was her *friend*." My sister had confided in this piece of crap because I'd pulled away. While I was out making poor choices and living my life, Piper found out that she was pregnant. I was sure that she had been scared to death. Although Piper was known as the sweet, gentle, caring sister, she didn't like her plans altered.

Perfect Piper planned purposefully.

I was sure that she was completely rattled and beyond consolation when she discovered that her meticulously planned future was scarred. Poor Piper. My mind wandered off on memories of the lists she'd make. She had written a list for our family vacation: *see a Virginia sunset, find a flawless seashell, let the ocean carry away your worries.*

I remembered asking her about that last task on her list. "How will you know it's done, and you can check it off?"

"I'll know, Maddy. I'll feel it on my shoulders. The weight being carried away."

"What weight? What worries do you have at thirteen years old? Chill out, Puppet." She giggled at me. It was a family joke that she was the worrier, and I was the free spirit.

Because she was an A student, she created all kinds of lists to get projects complete, papers finished. "Create outline, research point one..."

Eleanor had finished her rambling and was waiting for my response - I had none. I needed to get home and think. This was a big deal. A huge, heavy metal wrench in my plan.

I needed to think.

I spun around on my heel and walked towards my car. Eleanor had not breathed a word. Her only response was a squint - if looks could kill. But she knew, and I had chosen the wrong friend to mess with.

When I reached my beat-up, white Ford Focus, I yanked the door open. I climbed in and turned on the ignition. The radio station was coincidentally playing "White Liar" by Miranda Lambert.

"Hey, white liar, truth comes out a little at a time. And it spreads like a fire."
Inhale... exhale...

As I exited the Zook's parking lot and used my blinker to signal my intention of a right turn, I noticed in my rearview mirror that Eleanor was idling behind me in her car.

Is she following me?

I didn't want to head home for fear this crazy bitch had more to say. I didn't need my parents overhearing what accusations she'd spew from her mouth. I needed to shake her.

After my planned right turn, I cranked my steering wheel to the left onto a gravel road that wound its way up a hill to an overlook that many teenagers enjoyed with a cold beer and an easy date. It was notorious for a little trouble and bumping of uglies. I wondered after I made this turn if Eleanor even knew where this road led. She wasn't popular, and I'd never seen her up here. Most likely she had no idea where I was driving to.

Her beat-up Buick was right on my bumper - so close that through my rearview mirror I could observe her intense facial expression. Her wrinkles were back on her forehead, and her eyebrows weighed heavily above her eyes. She was pissed, and I guessed she didn't like how our conversation ended. *That makes two of us.*

Because the road was gravel and I wasn't a seasoned gravel-road driver, my speed topped out at forty-five miles per hour. I was driving down the middle of the road, swerving from side to side simply to piss her off and keep her behind me. No matter what I did, she stayed glued to my tail.

Chapter 57

Eleanor - June 8, 2016

My mom had left no trace, no explanation of why Ryan Sterling was forking over his hard-earned money. If it wasn't for the bank statement of *CHILD SUPPORT*, I would've figured that she was blackmailing. Most likely scenario considering my mother.

But there was no reason that the bank would code the deposit description as such if it wasn't true. Did they require a DNA test to prove that statement?

Whatever happened and why remained a secret of the past. Honestly, I didn't hold any hope for a real relationship with Mr. Sterling. For my whole life, I'd lived in the same town, attended the same high school as his daughters, and never once did he attempt to contact me. Obviously, he wasn't interested in getting to know his illegitimate daughter, and I wasn't about to beg for his love and acceptance. The adults - excluding Grams - in my life had all disappointed me. I had no interest in seeking out another relationship that was destined for failure.

Having a true friendship with Piper had filled the need for a close relationship. Grams and Piper were all I had. Quality versus quantity.

Piper deserved retribution. Madison deserved punishment for falsifying her identity hijacking her twin sister's life. Nope, not on my watch.

As soon as she turned on her heel and strutted away from me after our altercation in the parking lot, fury boiled inside me. A beast of vengeance flourished in my soul. No more waiting. No more calculating my next move. Action was demanded.

I jumped into my old car and tailgated her down the road. At first, I assumed that she was headed for home, but then she took a sharp turn onto a gravel road. That was when I discovered she was trying to lose me. She didn't want me to follow her home.

Is she slow? Mentally challenged? I knew where she lived. I knew her name and what school she attended. How would losing me in Pine Hill change what happened? Change what I knew to be the truth?

She must be flustered. She was scared and didn't know what to do. This was perfect timing. She was weak and vulnerable. I just needed to record her admission with my cell phone. If I could get her to pull over, I was sure that her short temper wouldn't be able to contain itself. She was bursting with guilt.

To apply pressure and make her uncomfortable, I followed her too closely. I planned on making her sweat before I forced her to stop her car. When this coffee date started less than an hour ago, I hadn't been sure how everything would play out. This wasn't something that you could plan.

She kept swerving from side to side, not allowing me to pass. Super irritating.

I cranked the steering wheel to the left and then sharply back to the right. I was sure the Buick LeSabre - who I nicknamed Lance - had never had so much action in its whole life. My tan four-door sedan wasn't meant for street races and high-speed chases. LeSabres were dependable family cars that putzed down Main Street on a Sunday afternoon looking for a local ice cream parlor. Maybe I imagined that because that was its previous life when it was Grams' car.

But as a hand-me-down car, Lance was like a forty-year-old trying to fit in at a college frat party. Chugging keg beer and chain-smoking Marlboro Lights, all added up to a major headache that would last the whole weekend. I prayed that my trusty, old Lance survived that long.

We continued to car-battle up the gravel road for another mile.

I couldn't help myself from screaming at her in my car. "I'm gonna freakin' punch you, Madison! You deserve everything coming to you. Piper was good. You are not! I hate you!" As my anger mounted, so did the pressure that my foot applied on the gas pedal.

Accidentally, I tapped her bumper. She either slowed down a bit or my foot applied more pressure than I was ready for. I saw her shocked facial expression in her rearview mirror. She was enraged.

Score one for me.

Although I was sure that it didn't look like a Hollywood movie car chase, it was gut-wrenching and stressful. My forearms were stiff as my knuckles clenched the steering wheel trying to maneuver sharp turns on a gravel road. As we escalated up the winding hill, I tried my best to anticipate her next move. Our game worked for another half-mile before I was able to get on the side of her car. It caught her off guard, and as I pulled up beside her on the bumpy, dusty road, our gazes met. Both slanted, intense and filled with rage. Neither of us were about to back down.

Madison quickly jerked her car towards mine as if she was about to sideswipe me. I overcorrected and ended up losing traction and skidding towards the ditch.

But on a hill, the ditch wasn't like a normal road ditch with a channel for drainage. The hill's ditch was more of a steady decline into a jungle of trees. While the nose of my car headed straight for the edge of the road, the steering wheel did nothing to deter my destination. My LeSabre had given up, no fight left to defend me. I was trapped in my suicidal car.

As my car tipped over the edge, I felt gravity pulling us down. Even though my seat belt restrained my body, gravity yanked and tried to free me by crushing my ribs. We tumbled nose over ass down the hill. As my car hit the ground, we flipped again. This deadly cause and effect broke many body parts. I screamed in fear and pain. As Lance moaned and hissed, screams escaped my mouth where my jaw had once secured my teeth.

Like a roller coaster at the county fair, the bumpy, terrifying ride stopped just as I'd thought I couldn't survive another second. Bile struggled to stay in my throat.

Lance landed upside-down in a tall evergreen at the bottom of the hill. Everything hurt, and my LeSabre was steaming and creaking in relief.

I wasn't screaming anymore. I didn't know when I stopped. Even though seconds before I felt complete bodily pain, strangely I only felt peace. It was an out-of-body experience.

As I was suspended by my seatbelt in the air, my breaths were becoming labored and my eyes heavy. I reached for my phone, which had somehow landed on the roof just above my head.

But that slight movement caused Lance to readjust his position in the tree, and without warning, we crashed one last time onto the hard, unforgiving ground.

Chapter 58

Maddy - June 8, 2016

When I finally pulled up onto our driveway and turned off the car, I realized that I was shaking from head to toe. I pulled the keys out of the ignition, and my right hand was so unsteady that the keys rattled. As I leaned back in the driver's seat, I pressed my eyelids shut.

Pull it together, Maddy. Pull yourself together. Breathe.

But the vivid memory of the last twenty minutes burned in my mind. The pounding in my head was leading towards a massive headache. My trembling fingers massaged my throbbing temples.

I couldn't believe that I'd forced Eleanor's car off the road. I'd purposely caused someone to die. Our cars leaned into the turns of the road. The dust that our cars were creating surrounded us like a heavy dark fog. Under the dust cloud, Eleanor and I were enclosed in a battle that no one else could witness. I couldn't see her. It wasn't my fault.

When I had jerked my car towards her, it was a natural reaction to defend myself. I didn't know that she'd lose complete control of her car. I hadn't meant to run her off the road. I was angry. I wanted her to stop. *Stop following me. Stop calling me Madison.*

After I had witnessed the rear end of her car fall over the side of the cliff, I slammed on my brakes, and instinctively, I jumped out of my car and ran to the side of the road and looked below. Her car had been lying upside-down, broken, dented, and lifeless at the bottom of the ravine. Smoke had been bubbling out from under the hood. The engine had seemed to be grunting from the long fall.

Shit. Damn nosy bitch. Now, look at what you've done.

Because the anger was so intense, my nostrils flared, and my breathing was labored. Before I could second-guess my decision, I'd tossed my treasured bracelet at her car. If she noticed the minuscule details, I was sure other people would recognize it as well. I'd wanted to keep the bracelet as a reminder of how thoughtful and generous Piper was. But Eleanor ruined it, and I couldn't keep it anymore.

Inhale. Exhale.

What the hell am I going to do now?

Inhale. Exhale.

The voices were back...the arguing voices from the hospital. Dr. Andela had diagnosed me as having a panic attack, and those voices were my guilt arguing with my conscience. "It's completely normal, Piper. You experienced a trauma. While your body will heal much faster, you have to give your mind a more flexible margin to heal."

I tried to remember her wise words. But the voices were loud and frightening.

Chapter 59

Maddy - June 8, 2016

I managed to calm myself down after the deadly altercation with Eleanor with a valium. Dr. Andela's methods and advice were proving quite useful, plus the anxiety medication quieted the voices.

Breathe in.

Breathe out.

Imagine that you're on a sandy beach surrounded by calm, blue waters. The waves gently slide into the shore creating a repetitious serene sonance. The sand feels warm and soft under your feet. A light breeze blows your hair away from your face. As you close your eyes, the sun sends its Vitamin D to warm your skin.

Breathe in.

Breathe out.

It was Monday night and four hours after my coffee date. Mom and I were sprawled out on the couch watching another episode of *The Bachelor* when the doorbell rang.

Mom aimed a questioning look in my direction. "Are you expecting anyone?"

As I shook my head, I pushed the pause button on the remote. Neither of us wanted to miss the rose ceremony. We both had our favorite bachelorette. To make the show even more enjoyable, Mom and I had made a bet - whoever correctly picked the winning girl didn't have to wash, dry, or put away the dishes tomorrow night after supper. The stakes were high.

The old Maddy recognized how mundane my life had become since taking over Piper's life. Never in a million years before the fire would I, for one, look forward to quality time on the couch with my mom, or two, make a lame bet about who'd do the dishes. But I still hated cleaning dishes.

Obviously, the old Maddy would've rolled her eyes at the dullness of this evening, poked fun at Piper for being such a Momma's girl, and never would've considered joining the two of them for a night on the couch. Nope, I had better things to do, weed to smoke, laws to break, fun to be had.

I rolled my eyes at the old me for thinking that I was so badass and tough. I had been wasting my life by hanging with the people I chose to hang with and by choosing to partake in illegal activities. What was I trying to prove? In hindsight, I could see what a mess I was, how much help I needed. Maddy was a lost cause. Thank goodness for this second chance. I wasn't about to waste it. I planned on being the best Piper ever.

Since the only muscle that I moved was to push the pause button on the remote, Mom tossed off the throw blanket that she had covering her legs and strolled over to the front door. From the living room couch, I had the perfect view.

I crossed my fingers that whoever was knocking at the door wouldn't be long. Maybe someone was just dropping off a delivery at the front step. Perfect. Then we could get back to the one-dimensional drama on the screen.

The next few seconds moved in slow motion, as if the fast forward button on my life had been pressed and was stuck. Each frame was like a cartoon strip, starting and stopping without a smooth transition. As Mom cracked open the heavy front door, I caught a glimpse of two uniformed, female police officers standing at attention. Their lips gave away no emotion, no cheek bones were elevated. Their facial expressions were grim and serious.

How'd they figure it out so quickly?

My mom's hand flew to her chest, and she softly muttered, "Oh, God. Is it Ryan?"

The breath caught in my throat for a different reason than Mom's.

The shorter officer who was the first to reveal a kind smile spoke. "Sorry to startle you, Mrs. Sterling. We aren't here regarding your husband. I'm Detective Jorgensen, and this is Officer Schwans." Officer Schwans nodded in acknowledgement, but her shifty eyes were landing everywhere in our house. As her eyes searched her immediate surroundings, she was cataloging notes in her mind. I didn't trust her. "We have some unfortunate news about your daughter, Madison."

When I heard the cop declare that they were visiting because of Maddy, I was instantly relieved. They hadn't found Eleanor yet, or at least, they hadn't tied me to her accident.

My mom's hand remained on her chest, protecting her heart. Neither of us had any idea where this conversation was going. What news could they have about Piper unless they somehow figured out she wasn't me?

"Mrs. Sterling, Madison's remains were recovered from the fire. We wanted to let you know that your daughter was pregnant at the time of her death."

Mom didn't have any time to adjust to the image of the police officer standing on her front step, let alone the news that the officer delivered.

"I'm sorry to deliver this very delicate news to you, Mrs. Sterling. I wanted to inform you before the press got a hold of the information."

"Why would the press be interested in Maddy's pregnancy?" My mom didn't understand how gossip and entertainment news worked.

People were more interested in racy gossip than politics, weather, or history. People wanted to hear about the poor decisions, the fights and arguments, the adultery and murders. That was the news that captivated an audience. That was the junk that neighbors were discussing out on the sidewalks as they retrieved their mail. This was exactly the type of news that was headline worthy. "Bright, innocent teenager at the top of her class dead and pregnant with the baby of a surviving star baseball player."

Of course, I was able to admit that I enjoyed juicy gossip about someone I knew. The good thing about gossip or juicy local news about an unwed pregnant dead teenager was that it wouldn't last long. If only that was *all* the news the news discovered.

Crap! Shit! Damn it!

The pregnant girl who died in the fire was supposed to be me! People were going to think that *I* was pregnant. Not Piper, the studious one with the baseball boyfriend. It was supposedly my body that they found. How many guys were going to wonder if they were the father of my dead baby? The headline would read, "Slutty teen perishes in fire while pregnant. Several local teens and one local teacher wonder if they were the father."

Oh, crap!

"Unfortunately, Mrs. Sterling, we can't control what news is published."

"Are you sure it was Maddy's body?"

Detective Jorgensen nodded. "We were able to retrieve this from her body." The officer pulled out a silver - but tarnished - necklace. The small silver disc looped onto the chain had been etched into a baseball with the number sixteen on it.

Oh, crap!

The police officers had no idea why Mom's expression reflected pure bewilderment. I could only imagine the confusing thoughts racing through her mind. It didn't add up. Two plus two didn't equal five. Why would Madison wear a necklace that was obviously Piper's? The two officers had no idea what a huge piece of evidence they were handing over to my mom.

Instinctively, she held out her hand to accept it, but she was utterly speechless and shell-shocked. She'd been through so much already. I had no idea what to do now. My guilt and fear rooted me to the couch. I feared bringing attention to myself and feared what she would ask me.

Officer Schwan cleared her throat. "Furthermore, we also recovered Maddy's phone from the property. It wasn't near her body, which we found odd since most teenagers never venture anywhere without their phones. It was found near the pool. We retrieved this picture from her camera roll. Do you know who it is, Mrs. Sterling?"

The officer held out the printed picture for Mom to accept. She glanced back at me as if asking for approval. It felt like we were playing a card game, and depending on what she flipped over, I'd win or lose. Mom slowly picked up the picture and flipped it over. It wasn't the Ace of Hearts or the King of Spades. Mom gasped at the image before her.

Oh, crap!

Chapter 60

Maddy - June 8, 2016

"Mom, I need to tell you something."

After exposing their bombshell of information, the police officers had closed the front door, and I followed Mom into the kitchen where she dropped down onto a wooden kitchen chair. The energy and life had evaporated from her body. She was like a wet noodle.

"Right now?" As her back hunched forward, Mom leaned onto the table for support. "After what Officer Jorgensen just told us? Can't we wait to let this news settle first? She was pregnant. Did you know?"

"No, I didn't know. Hell, I never even knew she had sex... I mean, I knew, but she never told me about the pregnancy." I forgot for a moment that it was me who was dead and pregnant. Of course, the whole house knew that I had sex numerous times, which made me embarrassed and ashamed now. "But yes, Mom, I need to tell you now. Now is actually perfect."

I took a couple deep breaths and sat down in the chair across from Mom, who was wiping away her tears. It was amazing how many tears a body could produce. After the last couple of months, they should've all dried up.

I needed to keep this short and simple. "Mom, I'm not Piper. I'm Maddy."

The words hung in the air. I knew before I confessed that she was already distracted, so my words would take a bit to process. I couldn't take my eyes off her. I wanted to and needed to observe her honest reaction. Gripping a tissue in each hand, she wiped her nose and dabbed at her eyes since they were both still dripping.

The old me waited for the look of disappointment, as hellion Maddy was used to receiving. I was the child who yearned for attention and accepted negative feedback. I was a pro at getting that.

But the new and improved me - the one who'd been given a second chance by becoming someone else - ached for acceptance and forgiveness. I needed to hear that she loved me no matter who I was - Maddy or Piper. She accepted me as I was - a better version of Maddy, but a slightly defected version of Piper.

What felt like thirty minutes was thirty seconds. My patience had come unglued.

"Mom?" I prompted.

"I heard you, Maddy. I heard you." She had called me by my birth name, and her tone wasn't harsh. Her words came out like a whisper. As she finished blowing her nose and drying her eyes, her eyelids slowly opened. I saw her bloodshot, tired eyes looking back at me - seeing me. No disappointment filled her expression - I only read sadness and exhaustion.

Tears - real, natural, not actress-inspired tears - poured out of my eyes as my confession burst out of my mouth. "I'm so sorry, Mom. I never meant for it to go this far. It just happened, and then suddenly there was no turning back. I was Piper, and Maddy was buried. I'm so sorry." I dropped my head down onto the kitchen table and draped my arms over my head as if shielding myself from what would happen next.

"Honey, it's okay." She rose from her chair and dropped down on her knees at my side. Her hands were petting the back of my head as she tried to console me.

I didn't deserve her kind, motherly touch. I'd ruined and jumbled up her memories of Piper by pretending to be her. Her good daughter was gone, and I remained. I didn't deserve her love, but I was extremely appreciative of it.

"Honey, look at me." She was coaxing me out of my pity tantrum. Again, I was afraid of what emotion her eyes would reveal. I'd tried so hard to be a good Piper, and I wanted to protect my parents from unnecessary pain. I wasn't ready for it to end.

Reluctantly, I raised my head and wiped my tear-soaked face with the sleeve of my shirt. When my eyes found hers, I recognized that the look of love hadn't changed. She accepted my words, but her eyebrows showed some concern.

However, I wasn't at all prepared for what she would say next.

"Maddy, honey, we knew."

Knew what? Her words made no sense.

"Your father and I had our suspicions. We knew you two like the back of our own hands. We recognized the differences, Maddy, but we also understood that if anyone else knew, you might face jail time for false impersonation. We couldn't lose another daughter. Plus, it was as if we had the best of both of our daughters."

"Dad knows too?"

"Yes, Maddy, we figured it out. But understand that we loved you both so much. We wish you hadn't chosen to lie about this, but we decided, rather than focus on why and what could've been, to react to what did happen and learn to deal with what we could control - our reactions. You can lead a horse to water, but you can't make him drink. We saw how hard you were trying." Mom reached for my hand as a gesture of forgiveness and understanding. While her fingertips were cold, her smile was warm but tentative.

"Maddy, no one knows. No one else can know. You've made this decision, and you must live with it. Be the best that you can be. Piper would want you to, Maddy. It was a tragic accident that all of us wish we could've prevented, but again, we need to realize that we can't control the past but learn to work with what we have."

Chapter 61

Maddy - June 8, 2016

After confessing to Mom who I really was, relief poured out of my senses. Tension lifted from my shoulders while tears exited my eyes. The tightness in my chest eased with each passing breath. No more pretending to be someone I wasn't around my parents. Unknown to me, they'd figured it out weeks ago. Mom explained that they both started noticing little things that didn't add up to much until they shared their stories.

"Dad noticed that you stopped eating beef when it was part of the meal, but you chowed down on the chicken recipes. And bacon, you've always loved bacon. Your food preferences were his first eyebrow raise. I perceived something was off when I washed a load of laundry that you had no underwear in your dirty hamper. Being the nosy mom that I am, I searched your underwear drawer, and it was filled with thongs. Piper's favorite Victoria's Secret underwear was shoved in the back of the drawer. I understood wanting to wear Maddy's fashionable jeans, but not her underwear." She wrinkled her nose a bit, trying to encourage me to smile.

If I thought wearing Piper's mom jeans was bad, nothing prepared me for the granny panties that she preferred. I couldn't do it. After the first couple days in the psych ward, my parents had brought me some of my own clothes to wear. They were Piper's clothes, but I was beyond ready to rid myself of the hospital gowns, so I welcomed the wardrobe change. On that first day wearing Piper's clothes, I had chosen a pair of PINK sweatpants that I'd gifted her for Christmas last year, a Pine Hills baseball sweatshirt, and the hugest pair of undies that I'd ever seen. They were bigger than my crop tops. Every time I moved, a wedgie secured itself in my butt cheeks. I would've been better off wearing nothing than that gargantuan article of clothing that my sister called underwear.

I recalled a conversation that we had during a back-to-school shopping trip to the mall. As we were checking out, Piper was appalled at the price of my undergarments. "Twelve dollars for a piece of material that literally lays between your butt cheeks. How can you even stand to wear those? I have five times the amount of fabric and only pay fourteen for something that actually does its job." She handed the sales clerk her debit card. The minimum wage employee was grinning at our sister bickering session.

"Puppet, please enlighten me. What is the purpose of a thong or your granny panties? I'm sure you even know who invented them." I lifted up a pair of her white, plain-Jane underwear.

"Very funny, Maddy. They're supposed to cover and protect your privates. Not floss the crack between your butt cheeks."

When I finally returned home from the hospital, the first thing I retrieved from my old room was my thongs. Sorry, Piper, but there were some things that I couldn't accept.

Thongs were delicate for obvious reasons, so I washed them by hand. Years before when I'd switched to wearing them, Mom had questioned me as well. She noticed that none of my underwear was ending up in the wash.

Another big giveaway was the fact that I wore my - Maddy's - shoes and not Piper's. We were a half size different, and I attempted to wear a few pairs of her backless shoes. Besides the birthmark that I was able to cover up, I couldn't shrink my feet - the only other thing that physically set us apart.

The rest of the hints were minuscule - in the family car, I initially walked to the left side of the car rather than the right. I used phrases like, "This dessert is GOAT," or "That driver threw you some nasty shade, Mom," or "Feeling a little hangry. What's for supper?" My personality oozed even when I was trying my hardest to suppress it. There were some things that you couldn't change even if you really wanted to try.

When Mom squeezed my hand, her voice squeaked when she said, "But Maddy, what the police showed me isn't good. Even if we - you, me, and your dad - know that this is the best possible outcome after a terrible tragedy, it is also breaking the law. And the police...their questions about their discoveries aren't good."

"What are you talking about, Mom? We can play off the baseball necklace. So what if Fritz gave it to Piper? Maybe it fell off or maybe Maddy stole it?"

"I'm not talking about the necklace, Maddy. Officer Schwans showed me a picture from your phone."

"What picture? And where did they find my phone anyway? I thought the phones burned in the fire."

"They just said that they found it on the Wilson property, so I don't know where it was recovered. But the picture is you, Maddy...naked in bed with a man..."

She was pausing to assume I would fill in the blank.

Oh, shit! Daniel!

Chapter 62

Maddy - Graduation, June 11

Near the back of the stage, the faculty perched themselves in metal folding chairs to hand out the diplomas and award a surprise scholarship. I noticed that Mr. Jarro's seat was empty. He had been assigned the seat next to the French teacher. I wondered if he was using the bathroom or was home ill. I wasn't sure, and it didn't matter one bit.

Principal Klawonn was wrapping up her speech. "...has been an honor and a privilege watching you all progress and succeed. Our next speaker has earned the honor of being the Class of 2016 valedictorian. Please help me welcome Piper Sterling to the stage."

Polite clapping filled the football stadium. Butterflies flew haphazardly in the pit of my stomach. Nervous energy coursed through my body, not because I was about to be the center of attention but because these people wanted to hear me speak. As Maddy, being the center of attention was my bag. But never in my history was it because my audience wanted to hear what I had to say. Previously, it was for my talent of chugging a keyed beer can, or for my flexibility of doing the splits and kissing my knee, or for tying a cherry stem with my tongue. Party tricks were the reason for my performances. No one asked or believed I could formulate intelligible phrases.

As I approached the stage, I silently coached myself using Dr. Andela's advice. *Believe in yourself. Take a deep breath. Calm your extremities. Relax every muscle from the tips of your toes to the ends of your fingers.*

After climbing eight stairs, I was the focal point. All eyes landed on me. I scanned the crowd. In the first ten rows, my 2016 classmates were seated in black nun-like gowns and square hats on their heads. A symbolic yellow tassel dangled on the right of each of their caps.

The scene that I witnessed reminded me of a conversation that Piper and I had after watching *Breaking Dawn*.

"Why did anyone think that wearing a huge drape with shoulder pads would be sexy?"

Piper had rolled her eyes at my comment as Jessica was making her epic valedictorian speech.

"Maddy, not everything is about sex."

"We're sixteen, Piper. Everything is about sex."

"The graduation cap and gowns tradition dates back to the medieval European universities, but in 1321, university faculty ruled that no excessive, fancy clothing would be allowed, so these matching gowns were required."

It was my turn to roll my eyes at her. "Irrelevant. And I don't care, Piper, I don't want a history lesson. History lessons are *not* sexy. I was just making a comment because I hated Edward being all covered up. He's yummy."

"Well, did you know that the square cardboard hat has an unknown origin? No one knows if the square shape was chosen because it looked like a book or if it was the quad shape of the Oxford University campus since they were one of the first universities to require formal apparel."

"Again, I don't care! The dorky hat has no significant purpose except to make us look like buffoons wearing the first shape that we learned in elementary school."

I looked at my fellow buffoons wearing squares on their heads. Even though I still thought it was a silly tradition, their smiling faces filled my heart with pride. Behind my classmates sat hundreds and hundreds of family members and friends enjoying the beautiful Midwest afternoon. Because the school was bursting at the seams, the graduation ceremony was held on the football field rather than the gymnasium. Sunglasses and sun hats littered the scene. On the folding chairs and in the bleachers, every seat was occupied. It was a packed house.

Thankfully, I'd discovered Piper's speech on her laptop. It sounded exactly like something she would say. I needed to honor her by reading it, but I added a small token of me to the ending. She had indicated in her notes that the approved pictures and music for the slideshow had already been turned in to the principal's office. All that was left was the crucial delivery.

I heard my high heels clicking on the stage floor. My heart was beating at an escalated pace. Before I reached the podium and was able to adjust the microphone, I heard soft instrumental music playing in the background.

Nice touch, Piper.

After clearing my throat and taking one deep, cleansing breath, I looked down at my notecards and began.

"Dear classmates, Pine Hill High School faculty, and hundreds of family and friends, thank you for joining us today to mark the end of our high school education at Pine Hill. Thank you for your essential role in our journey into adulthood. We couldn't have done it without your support." I noticed a few people in the crowd pointing to the screen behind me. Curiously, I paused for a moment and followed their line of vision. The master of ceremonies had started a slideshow of pictures that I assume Piper had referred to in her notes. Pictures of our class in random situations filled the big screen.

"The last four years have been epic and filled with many accomplishments. We have learned how to build a robot to assist with our daily chores."

I heard a clip of a video showing two students working on a homemade robot. The robot had been programmed to mop the floor. My delivery was right on the money.

Damn, Piper. Nice job.

"We have our phenomenal coaching staff to thank for many sporting highs and lows. No matter if we brought home victory or defeat, you were there to teach us how to deal with the result. Not only did we learn the rules of a sport, but also many life lessons."

The smiles in the crowd proved that Piper had accomplished her goal of including everyone in her speech. The audience was impressed.

The slideshow showed pictures of our boys basketball team winning the state championship. As sweat rolled down their faces, the team lifted each other up as their images were frozen in time. The next slide showed our football team losing a playoff game in the last quarter, and then our gymnastics team posing with a trophy larger than the smallest team member.

"Without you, we wouldn't have learned that x plus y does equal z?"

I earned a few chuckles from that comment since I delivered it laced with sarcasm. We saw pictures of our math and chess teams doing what they did best - problem solving.

"Your resolve and determination earned this class an average GPA of 3.3 – the highest cumulative GPA in our school's history."

Everyone clapped their hands, and I allowed an extra-long pause before everyone quieted down. It was an amazing accomplishment. I wondered since I was dead if my GPA had been removed from the total so that the score was higher. I was confident that my numbers would've brought down the average.

"We have you to thank for never giving up and expecting only the best from us."

Random pictures of the students in class working on projects, raising their hands, at their lockers, hanging out on the bleachers.

"Families, your unconditional love and unwavering support have been the backbone of our success. You're the tires on our car, wings on our jet plane, and the legs on our table. Without you, we'd be stationary, wingless, and sitting on the floor."

Piper's simple, elementary sense of humor won the admiration of every audience member. I held them in the palm of my hand. It felt satisfying to earn positive attention versus attention for my negative actions. First time for everything.

"Friends and classmates, we share this well-deserved victory together. We challenged each other while managing to cheer each other on. What a journey it's been. I'm proud of how well we've all turned out. I'm looking at future lawmakers..."

Missy, our class president, appeared smiling on the slideshow. She was an essential leader on our school's debate team. Everyone was sure she'd pursue a law degree like both of her parents had.

"...possibly some law*breakers*..."

A picture of me - as Maddy - and Dee, Tania, and Maverick filled the screen as we were caught in the teacher's lounge drinking pop and eating the food donated for teacher conferences. It earned many giggles and snickers from the audience.

"Among us will be future doctors, dentists, teachers, counselors, athletes, and CEOs. The future is ours. Let no one hold us back."

It was time to get serious and stop getting me and my audience distracted by glancing at the slideshow. For the conclusion, I needed their undivided attention to pack a memorable punch. I was proud of the closing statement that I'd written myself.

"Class of 2016, we've experienced heartache this past year that made us realize we aren't invincible. We need to cherish each blessed moment. Be thankful and learn from mistakes. Classmates and friends, please lift your caps and celebrate with me. 'May we get what we want, what we need, and never what we deserve.'"

As I closed my eyes for a brief moment to bask in pride, I plastered one of my biggest, proudest smiles on my face. I'd done it.

Where is the applause that my last line deserved? Why is no one clapping?

When I opened my eyes, no square hats were raised and ready to be tossed in the air. No applause followed my conclusion. No smiles. I'd lost the crowd's attention somehow.

Their eyes were glued to the slideshow behind me. People were pointing at the pictures, covering their mouths with their hands and shaking their heads in disbelief. Wrinkles creased their foreheads.

Before I had a chance to turn around and see what demanded everyone's attention, I noticed my parents standing on the opposite side of the field. Dad wasn't smiling, and tears ran down Mom's face. Next to them stood the two police officers that had previously visited our house, delivering the news that Piper had been pregnant when she died. To the right of one of the cops, I recognized Daniel - Mr. Jarro - standing with Fritz.

What an odd combination of people to be standing together.

I hadn't noticed that Mom and Dad hadn't been in their designated spots with the rest of the families or that Fritz hadn't been seated among the graduates. I'd been too focused on delivering my speech to worry about anyone else. My brain swelled with questions.

Why is Daniel standing with his hands behind his back next to my parents? When he dropped off the casserole the other day, did he notice that 'Piper' didn't roll her Rs? Had he discovered that it was Piper - not me - that fulfilled his sexual fantasy in the library? That I'd tricked him into meeting Piper in the library that morning?

He had confessed to me his desire to overpower an unsuspecting female. I had agreed to fulfill his fantasy. I suggested before school in the library because I knew Piper volunteered every first Wednesday of the month. She had bragged about it over dinner at the beginning of the school year. My parents had been thrilled with the significance of the gesture. The news had made me vomit in my mouth.

I had assumed she wasn't a virgin, and perhaps she'd be turned on. I didn't know or care at the time. Dad had confronted me about the weed in our shared bathroom, and this scenario had seemed like a good idea. A little payback for her snitching on me.

Fritz looks completely heartbroken, like he lost his best friend. Had Fritz figured out that his dream girl was forever gone?

Mom isn't crying happy, proud tears. Dad looks defeated as his shoulders sagged. Had my parents succumbed to confessing the knowledge of which daughter was still alive? Had they turned me in?

I turned to examine the slideshow. It was a picture of me and Piper sitting outside on the front lawn of the school. We were both smiling and posing for the camera. The editor of this photo had circled my wrist birthmark and typed my name at the top of my head and typed Piper's name above hers. As I watched and tried to process the contents of the slide, another image replaced it.

She is not Piper. Piper Sterling died in the fire. Madison, true to her malicious behavior, has tricked us all.

And the picture of my tattoo - *PJ* with a jellybean - that I had shared on a private snapchat story appeared.

The birthmark may be covered, but now is time to UNCOVER the true twin.

Automatically, I glanced down at my wrist. Part of the birthmark was still there - it colored in the jelly bean, giving it a pinkish hue. But in the picture, the editor had been able to enhance the coloring to define the cloud-shaped birthmark. My mouth dropped open.

Who did this? The slideshow had been submitted before Piper died. Someone tech-savvy hacked in and added these pictures and accusations.

The music abruptly stopped, and a voice from beyond the grave filled the speakers. "This is my insurance."

Oh, shit. It was Eleanor.

I understood why my parents were standing with the police officers, Daniel, and Fritz. People must've started to piece the puzzle together.

If I run, where will I go? What is the punishment for what I did? Besides eternal shame and ridicule?

I looked down at my last notecard. How ironic.

May we get what we want,

what we need, and never what we deserve.

Chapter 63

Pine Hill Star Post

June 11, 2016 - Headline, Front page

Twin Sister Impersonates Dead Sister

Local teen arrested for false impersonation of her deceased twin sister. Nearly two months after Madison Mae Sterling was considered a fatality in a tragic house fire, she was found alive and living under her twin sister's name. On the eve of April 22, Madison and Piper Jean Sterling, identical twin sisters who were seniors at Pine Hill High School, both attended a house party at the home of Christopher Wilson. Unexpectedly, a powerful lightning bolt struck the Wilson estate, and immediately, the house was engulfed in flames.

"It sounded like a bomb went off, and then the lights went out, the music quit, and everyone was screaming," Pine Hill High School senior, Cindy Noel, explained. "It was chaos. No one knew what happened."

During the chaos, most of the partygoers safely escaped outside while they waited for emergency personnel to arrive.

"I remember carrying a pretty blonde girl down the stairs. She mumbled something, but I was in too much of a hurry to get out of the house to concentrate on what she was saying. It sounded like 'Puppet.'" Justin Lake managed to help several of his classmates escape the deadly fire. He is being hailed as a local hero.

Based on this new information, we understand that it was Madison who was saved from the burning home, not her sister Piper.

"This miscommunication is rare. During my police career, it has never happened before." Police Chief Jay Huss was extremely apologetic about the huge mix-up. Unfortunately for Madison Sterling, Police Chief Huss isn't at fault for this crime and will not receive a hefty fine and possible jail time like the young woman most likely will.

Months after her sister's tragic death, Madison delivered her sister's valedictorian speech where law enforcement was patiently waiting. At the conclusion of her graduation speech, cuffs were locked around her wrists, and her cap and gown were collected by the school administration. Her classmates watched the drama unfold.

Principal Klawonn of Pine Hill High School shared her disappointment. "This is a lamentable event, and to say I'm disappointed would be an understatement. There were no warning signs prior to this discovery. The staff and I will continue to support the students of our community that were affected by this unspeakable tragedy."

At the time of this publication, Madison Sterling was being finger-printed and held until her bail hearing on Monday morning.

June 12, 2016 - Headline, Editorial page

Twin Charged with False Impersonation, Questioned in Classmate's Death

Madison Mae Sterling, who was arrested yesterday for false impersonation of her dead sister, is being questioned in the death of a fellow classmate. Eleanor Cutter had been reported missing by her grandmother, Donna Cutter, three days before graduation after not returning home.

Miss Cutter's body was found trapped in her car at the bottom of a ravine off Redneck Boulevard. Details supplied in the police report and from Donna Cutter indicate that there had been another car on the road at the time of the accident. "My Eleanor was a loner and would've never ventured on that road herself. The whole town knows nothing but trouble occurs on Redneck Boulevard."

The Cutter family is an infamous family from the Pine Hill area. Years ago, Donna Cutter was charged with not providing reasonable assistance to her husband as he suffered a heart attack in the next room. All charges were eventually dismissed. Her son and Eleanor's father, Rocky Cutter, was also well-known to the Pine Hill area for his disorderly conduct violations before his death. Rocky's wife, Mary, had been arrested on numerous occasions for indecent exposure. Earlier this year after being chased by police for failing to stop at a red light, Mary Cutter died in a head-on collision. However, the eighteen-year-old victim, Eleanor, had no priors.

Police Chief Huss was unable to be reached for comment.

June 16, 2016 - Headline, Editorial page
New Dramatic Details Regarding Pine Hill's Infamous Twin

Madison Mae Sterling, who was arrested last week for false impersonation of her dead sister, has also been charged with manslaughter. Miss Sterling seems to have a web of deceit surrounding her.

Police Chief Huss explained at today's press conference, "Not only will Madison Sterling be charged with false impersonation but also manslaughter. She has admitted to running Eleanor Cutter's car off the road and into a ravine in order to silence Eleanor, who had discovered her true identity. Further investigation into Madison Sterling's life has revealed a sexual affair with a teacher at Pine Hill High School, Daniel Jarro. Mr. Jarro has fully cooperated with our police investigation but will be charged accordingly."

Through his lawyer, Fritz Leslie, Piper's boyfriend, released this statement: "Two days before graduation, I cooperated with the police and answered their questions. Before that afternoon, I had no idea that Maddy had taken over Piper's life. They showed me pictures of a necklace that was found on her body - the same necklace I'd given Piper for her eighteenth birthday only hours before the fire. I also identified Piper and Maddy's phones that were recovered from the Wilson home as well as some pictures that had been stored on the phones. I had no idea about Madison's relationship with Mr. Jarro. The events that have transpired recently have been quite a shock. We hope the public will understand my family's need for privacy during this painful time."

Inside sources tell Pine Hill Star Post that the family is devastated by the news of the pregnancy. The Leslie family denied prior knowledge and even questioned the paternity of the unborn baby.

June 16, 2016 - Obituaries, Life Section
CORRECTION

Piper Jean Sterling (April 22, 1998 - April 23, 2016) of Pine Hill, Minnesota, tragically lost her life in a fire on the eve of her eighteenth birthday.

In her short life, Piper learned a lot about the importance of giving back. Piper had a caring, generous nature that melted even the roughest visitors at the homeless shelter where she volunteered every weekend. Not only did Piper have high expectations for herself, but she also held the students who visited the tutor lab where she worked accountable for their own success. Piper possessed a gift for making people feel valuable.

When she was only thirteen, Piper founded the school's backpack program, Backpacks for Children. Children in need received a backpack filled with donated food for their weekends. Before the circumstances surrounding her death was uncovered, a large, anonymous donation was made in Piper's honor. The donation simply read, "Piper was an angel here on Earth." Backpacks for Children will continue in her honor for years to come.

Piper is survived by her twin sister, Madison, her parents, Elaina and Ryan Sterling, and her paternal grandparents, Mary Kay and Carter Sterling.

The family is holding a private ceremony in remembrance of Piper. Due to the turmoil surrounding her death, no supplemental funeral will be held. Her parents requested in lieu of flowers, donations in Piper's memory are made to the Helping Hands Homeless Shelter.

Chapter 64

Eleanor

*P*ostmarked: June 5, 2016

Central California Women's Faculty
Inmate Ava Tarrell (5952162506)
23370 Road 22
Chowchilla CA 93610

Dear Mrs. Tarrell,

How's federal prison? I hope you're being treated well.

You don't know me, but I'm a massive fan of yours. I watched your story on Dateline, the episode that revealed the details of your husband's murder. I learned so much from that episode – those sixty minutes. I'd been fantasizing about eliminating my father for a long time. The night that Dateline aired that episode, the stars aligned. Thallium was the perfect poison.

You were sentenced to life without parole because the court proved that it was a premeditated murder. Laws would be different if they were created by people who broke a few. The laws would be more flexible and most importantly realistic. I mean, you didn't kill him simply to watch the light drain from his eyes. You did it because you had no other choice.

You and I didn't end a life for our own sick pleasure. We were victims and did what needed to be done for our own survival. Kill or be killed.

The simple fact that my father was a raging alcoholic, a complete asshole, and an abusive prick truly aided my plan. He deserved his one-way ticket to Hell. No one was sad about his death. That may have been why your plan didn't work in your situation. Authorities are less likely to look into a suspicious death if the man was a poor excuse for a human. I don't know much about your husband, Mr. Tarrell. The Dateline show focused primarily on your guilt.

I don't mean to rub it in your face that the thallium worked for me and not for you. That wasn't the purpose of my letter. I simply wanted to thank you. You were my inspiration.

After you murder one person, you would think that it's like sex, and it wouldn't be as big of a thrill the next time. But it was. I hadn't meant to kill her. She was in the wrong place at the wrong time. It was supposed to be her twin sister that died.

I followed them upstairs to listen to their argument, and when Piper came out, the fire started. The lights went out. I heard Maddy still inside the room, and she tried to open the door, but I was right there. And with Piper safely removed, I decided to stop Maddy from escaping once again.

Unfortunately, I killed the wrong twin that night. Instead of ending Madison's life, I killed my friend. I feel remorse, of course, I do. I'm not a monster. I've gotten away with murdering two people now. It's rather amazing.

I must admit that the drama that Madison created by impersonating Piper was entertaining. I had no idea that that was going to happen.

Graduation day is around the corner, and I plan on exposing the true twin during the ceremony. It'll be very dramatic. I can't wait to see Madison's face when I inform everyone at Pine Hill that she's Maddy, not Piper.

Maybe it's better that she's punished for her crimes versus simply dying. What do you think, Mrs. Tarrell? Are you glad you're serving time for your husband's murder? Or would you have preferred death?

Sincerely,

Eleanor

Cheddar Meatloaf Recipe

by Emersyn Park

Meatloaves: Beat egg and milk then stir in cheese, oatmeal, onion and salt. Add beef and mix well. Shaped into 6-8 little egg-shaped loaves using your hands. Put in a greased 9x9 baking pan.

    1 egg
    ¾ cup of milk
    1 cup of shredded cheddar cheese
    ½ cup of oatmeal
    ¼ cup of minced onion
    1 tsp salt
    1 lb of lean ground beef (not browned)

Topping: Combine topping ingredients. Spoon over loaves. Bake uncovered at 375 for one hour.

½ cup of brown sugar

1 tsp mustard

⅔ cup of ketchup

"I'm not a great cook, I just have fabulous recipes!" ~Emersyn Park

Reviews and Feedback

Thank you!

First of all, thank you for purchasing this book, **Puppet's Shadow**. You could've picked any number of books to read, but you picked mine and for that I am extremely grateful.

If you enjoyed this book, I'd love to hear from you and hope that you can take a minute to post your review on Amazon, Barnes and Noble or Good Reads. Your feedback and support will help me to improve my writing craft and make my next book even better.

Thank you!

Emersyn Park

Debut novel: *"He Loves Me, She Loves Me Not"* released in August 2021

Acknowledgments

What started out as a hobby to cure COVID boredom has turned into a rewarding obsession. The entire writing process tingles my extremities with excitement. I love creating a unique story that I hope entertains readers. Although writing can be a lonely process, I've grown quite fond of my imagination. We spend lots of hours together laughing at our dorky sense of humor. But unfortunately, my imagination doesn't check all the boxes that I require in a friendship or partnership. I need cozy snuggles, uncontrollable giggles (which I always accompany with some snorts) and loyal companionship. That is why every book includes an acknowledgement page. Somewhere, we can thank the *real* people in our lives.

My man checks these boxes for me. Even though he hasn't read a page of either novel, he is my number one fan. He claims he knows everything that happens between my pages by listening to my constant chatter about the characters, twists and feedback. He is my sounding board, the one who I bounce ideas off of and rely on to pick up the slack around the house. Thank you, honey, for doing the dishes that *one* time!

My beta readers - PJ, Gena, Fitzy, Ashley and Caramie - you guys were my guinea pigs. The first ones I let into the crack of my brain. I appreciate all your feedback, edits and insight. You volunteer your time and attention to a project that means the world to me!

Next up is my editor, Clara Abigail. I appreciate your suggestions, questions and knit-picking. It makes you the reason you are so good at your job.

Since this was my second novel, I was able to collect a group of reviewers to back me on my project. As my first ARC (Advanced Reader Copy) team, you guys have been fabulous to work with. My little group of cheerleaders! Not only do you spend hours reading my book, but you support, promote and talk about it along the way. I love receiving your feedback. You give up hours of your time for an indie author like me who appreciates your love for reading.

A big shout-out goes to my buddy in Michigan. (You know who you are.) Girl, you're a problem solver with the biggest, most generous heart. You and your family have been a true blessing. I found you in the gram and feel blessed to call you my friend.

And without my witches - my friend group - I wouldn't have so many interesting characters to build off of. My weird sense of humor enjoys filtering in your names and our inside jokes throughout my books. I appreciate and value your friendship. You are my sisters by choice, my family.

Of course, I need to thank my boys. You are so patient and understanding when Mom needs my alone time. Giving me the space to complete my stories is a very precious gift.

And last but definitely not least, my readers. I had no idea that so many people would enjoy the stories that I create. My imagination and I thank you for buying my book and recommending it to your friends. If you pass along my book to a friend, ask them to leave a review as a payback for the free book.

I hope to entertain you again soon!

Cheers,
Emersyn Park

www.ingramcontent.com/pod-product-compliance
Ingram Content Group UK Ltd.
Pitfield, Milton Keynes, MK11 3LW, UK
UKHW041209180426
11947UKWH00025B/1955